MEET SEDUCTIVE JULIA

The story of Julia Chamoun, a young Lebanese woman, and her men. After a failed first marriage, she is engaged to Jean Claude, a Swiss banker, and accidentally runs into an old flame whom she had met during a yearend trip to Morocco. A seething love affair ensues and she is torn between her love for the two men who both want to marry her. The banker offers her a stable future, but she is rather doubtful about a future with the younger Luis. Julia's exhausting double life goes on for a few months until an unexpected event complicates her dilemma and, in desperation she turns to her first husband, whom she happens to meet on a trip up the Nile.

The story starts in Egypt and takes twists and turns through Morocco, Europe, and the United States. It is a tale of love, passion, and forgiveness

OF JULIA AND MEN

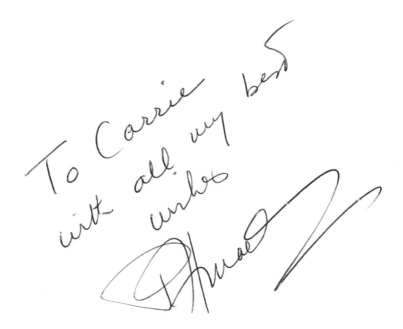

Peggy Hinaekian

Etching on the cover by Peggy Hinaekian - "Girl on a Flying Carpet"
Etchings may be purchased through the author's website
www.peggyhinaekian.artspan.com
hinaekian@hotmail.com

Rev. date: 03/31/2016

To order additional copies of this book, contact:
Xlibris
1-888-795-4274
www.Xlibris.com
Orders@Xlibris.com
716993

CONTENTS

To my husband
who has tried to understand me since he met
me during the summer of 1963.

Daydream

CHAPTER 1

Julia

Julia did not think she was an ordinary person and she was not interested in having an ordinary life. Ever since she was a child she had daydreamed. She daydreamed of an exciting future—of an extraordinary future life. It would be a life full of love, passion and a fabulous career. Her goals were twofold. One was to have an exciting career and the other to share her life with an interesting, passionate man and have children. She yearned for a romantic fairy tale life. This was going to be very difficult to attain in the Egypt of the 1950's.

"Come and help me in the kitchen instead of just sitting there and looking out the window," shouted her mother from across the hallway. Julia was deep in her thoughts and did not want to budge. The apartment they lived in in the heart of Cairo was very large and Julia often secluded herself in one of the rooms and read. She read romance books and daydreamed.

"Come on now, get moving," called out her mother again.

"Coming," Julia shouted back and reluctantly got up from her chair to join her mother in the kitchen. Their kitchen was very old fashioned. It was not a welcoming place. It was dark and bleak and had only one small window perched on top of the sink and it overlooked a narrow passageway between the building next door. Her mother did not seem to mind it but Julia hated it. She hated all kinds of housework, cleaning, cooking, washing dishes, washing clothes or whatever. Not that she did much of that with the young servant roaming around the house all day helping her mother. They were not wealthy by all means but servants came very cheap in Egypt. Only the very poor could not afford one. Her mother was a very good cook and was in charge of the cooking and wanted Julia and her sister to take an interest in it. Her sister somewhat did. She was more of a homebody. Her brother was excluded from that task. The rule in the Middle East at the time—not that it has changed since—was that men worked outside the home and women inside.

"How are you going to keep house and cook for a husband and family if you don't learn?" her mother kept asking her. There was no possible answer to that question. Julia's mind was far away from mundane chores. First of all, she thought she was too young to think that far ahead. She was only fifteen at the time. Secondly, she intended to make oodles of money and marry money and work outside the home—therefore the house would be taken care of by the hired help. Thirdly, she was not going to remain in Egypt, she had plans to somehow go to the States. That's where things were happening in the books she read and in the movies she saw.

Julia was born in Cairo of mixed ethnicity. Her mother was Greek, born in Egypt and her father was Lebanese whose family had come from a remote village in Lebanon to build a better life in Egypt. Her mother's family was in textiles and her father's was in tobacco. Julia had grown up in an unconventional family atmosphere. Both her parents had been very liberal, unlike those of ethnic minorities in the Middle East. She grew up reading American magazines and watching American and European movies. There was no movie rating in Egypt and she and her siblings often went to the movies with their parents and watched all sorts of films on romance and crime. Romance was not that explicit then, nor was crime so bloody. Her big dream of a fairy tale life had been kindled at a very young age by watching these films. Her quest was to leave Egypt, go to the U.S. and have a glamorous life with a flourishing career as a fashion designer in New York, marry an intelligent, handsome, passionate, wealthy and out of the ordinary man, have intelligent children and lead an extraordinary life of love, passion, sex and everything else. She knew she was asking a lot but she had made up her mind to pursue and achieve these goals one way or the other.

"I am not going to stay here, get married, have children and be a housewife," she told her mother. "I am going to the States. I want a career in fashion designing."

"And how are you going to do that? There is no way to get out of Egypt, you know that, you need an exit visa for a specific reason. You cannot go as a tourist, you can't go to college in the U.S.—we don't have the money. Your life is here my dear. You're quite pretty, you'll find a nice man."

Julia was indeed a very pretty girl of average height, very slim (unlike her contemporaries in the Middle East who, she thought, were overweight and over developed by 15), with long, reddish hair, inherited from her great grandmother on her mother's side who had been Irish. She was very proud of her hair and took great care of it. She had lively brown eyes and pouting lips, a great smile and a vibrant personality. She was also an avid reader and she had read somewhere that if you wanted something badly enough you would end up getting it. So she daydreamed and hoped that things would somehow happen. She also believed in God and she prayed. Her mother had taught her to say a prayer every night before going to bed. After praying for success in her father's job, health to all family members including the family cat, she also prayed about her future.

She had always had very modern ideas about boyfriend girlfriend relationships. This was frowned upon by the society in Cairo where she lived. Marriage was arranged by the families and most women stayed at home and took care of the husband, the house and the children. Careers for women never entered the picture. There were no careers for women anyway. The only openings, for girls with no family fortune, were that of a secretary or a shop girl. After graduating from high school, girls of well to do families, as young as 17, waited for the right suitor to come along, preferably an older man from a wealthy family, who would be a good provider. However, if the parents of the girl were not rich, a girl was obliged to seek a husband from a middle class family, one who would hopefully have a promising future. Some young people did manage to have boyfriends and girlfriends but it was all clandestine, not in the open.

Julia refused vehemently to follow that custom. She had her own ideas. She decided that she would choose her own husband. She did not think there was much of a choice in her circle of friends though. She was boy crazy but did not particularly fall for any of the boys she hung out with. They were all mama's boys as far as she was concerned. She had read the book and seen the movie "Gone with the Wind" and she adored Rhett Butler. She was in love with Rhett, not with Clark Gable. That was the type of man she yearned for.

"Don't accept any suggestions from friends and family to introduce me to a prospective suitor," she told her mother.

The very first time that a man had been brought to the house by well-meaning friends to be introduced to her, she did not come out of her room. And people talked about what a bizarre young girl she was. From then on her mother never accepted any more propositions. "My daughter is different" she would say "she wants to make her own choice."

"But you people don't have any money," her aunt told her mom, "how on earth is she going to make her own choice?"

Julia and her siblings went out in groups of girls and boys and no one was anyone's special boyfriend or girlfriend. They went to the movies, to the Gezireh Sporting Club (an exclusive sports and social club with a swimming pool, tennis courts), to basketball games, to the Pyramids, to the zoo, etc. They were always in a group.

One day a new boy joined their group. His name was David and he was the son of a wealthy family who had just moved to Cairo from the Sudan. They had a lot in common. They were both artistic and they both disliked the traditional mentality of life in Egypt. They were rebels. They adored dancing and went to night clubs (teenagers could do that in Egypt) and drank alcohol (teenagers could do that too in Egypt) but never got drunk. They would stay all night with one drink and dance to the latest Italian band in town. Julia and David fell in love and, after a year of dating clandestinely, David wanted to marry her.

They were smooching in the car one evening after coming back from a movie and, while David was kissing her passionately and groping her boobs, he said "Julia, I love you so much, will you marry me?"

Julia was not surprised. She also loved David and she had thought of the possibility of marriage to him. He was her first boyfriend, the only boy she had ever kissed, but what about her dream career? How was that going to work out in this picture?

"Yes, David, I would love to marry you but I thought you were supposed to go to college in the States."

"I'm going to give up that project. I have quite a good prospect of a job here. I'm going to ask my father to put me in charge of one of his photo shops. I can make very good money and we would be able to afford to live very comfortably here. What do you say?"

"I don't know what to say. Of course I'd like to marry you but I also want a career. I thought maybe we could go to the States together. I have no chance of doing anything here except be a housewife and have kids."

David thought about that idea and came up with a plan.

"Okay, let's plan on going to the States together after getting married. We'll think of a way to work it out."

Julia was extremely happy about that prospect. First, they had to figure out a way to break the news to their respective parents. They knew they were going to get opposition, especially from David's parents. So when David told his parents that he had given up the idea of going to college and that he wanted to get married, his parents flipped.

"You're too young to get married. Who is this girl anyway? What do her parents do? Don't be stupid, don't give up on a good future."

He told them about Julia. "I love her and I will not give her up." He then went on to tell them of their plans. Besides the fact that his parents thought he was too young to get married, they objected to the fact that Julia was a "working girl" — meaning her parents had no money, therefore she had to work outside the home. It was kind of a shameful stigma. She had a very good job though. She was confidential secretary to the president of a British bank but that did not matter. To them she was a working girl. David hated his parents for their old fashioned ideas and he stuck to his guns.

Julia's parents on the other hand were glad that their daughter had found a man she loved and wanted to settle down. The idea of their going to the States also appealed to them because they knew that Julia would not be happy just being a housewife in Cairo.

After failing to dissuade their son not to commit this folly and jeopardize his chances of furthering his education by an early marriage, David's parents finally relented and accepted their son's decision. Admittedly, Julia and David were very young to take this step. She was 19 and he was 21—too young for a man in the Middle East to get married. It was okay for a girl to get married in her teens but a husband had to be at least 25 years old. In retrospect, she thought this was pure folly for her to get married at 19. She had not yet had any life experiences, not that she could get any in Cairo anyway. But they were in love so she embarked in this project with enthusiasm, especially since they had plans to move to the U.S. where she would start a new life with the man she loved and have her dream career. In Egypt, married women did not pursue a career. They had children and took care of home and family. Not Julia, she had other projects up her sleeve. She was adamant, she was going to have a career as a fashion designer and it was going to be in New York.

David also had modern ideas and readily agreed that his future wife pursue a career.

Julia knew that life in the U.S. would not be easy to start with, but that's where her future lay and she was prepared to make some sacrifices, but not all the sacrifices.

"I am not going to be the only one doing the cooking and the cleaning once we move to the U.S." she told David.

"Don't worry about that, sweetheart, I will help you," said David. In Egypt, they had servants who catered to their every need. She did not know the first thing about housekeeping or cooking or ironing clothes for that matter. Ironing was done by experienced ironers. It was inconceivable to wear a shirt or a dress that had any signs of wrinkles. Everything had to look freshly pressed. David was head over heels in love with her and agreed to everything she asked for and even took lessons from the local ironer to be able to iron his own shirts in the U.S. There was no such thing as drip dry in Egypt. Everything was of the highest quality cotton and cotton needed expert ironing.

They made great plans but, about a couple of weeks before the wedding, after her dress was made and all the preparations were going on full speed ahead, Julia started having doubts whether marriage to David would really work. They loved each other madly but they were quarrelling about stupid things all the time—mostly about sex. As it was almost unheard of in Egypt to have sex before marriage, they did not go all the way. They kissed and petted but David needed sexual release. Julia thought he was a sex addict as he dry humped her or wanted her to masturbate him whenever they saw each other, which was almost every day. She later found out that most young men are highly sexed up and needed release. Julia hated the act of masturbating him. There was no pleasure in it for her. It was a mechanical act with no romance involved. It also disgusted her. Consequently her love for him somewhat diminished. *Is this what sex is about?* She asked herself.

Her mother warned her, "I am surprised you are marrying this guy, you are always bickering. It will not get better once you're married you know. This is as good as it gets."

"It's okay mom, we can manage and there's always divorce, you know."

"You are not yet married and you're already talking of divorce, are you out of your mind girl?"

"No, I'm just saying that if it does not work out there's always a solution." Julia was very pragmatic about this. She brushed away her negative thoughts and decided to go through with it because deep down she did love David. She told herself that what she was feeling was only a temporary setback. She was very optimistic that once the marriage was consummated, the romance would get rekindled. They would start a new life in the States and everything would fall into place. She would work hard to get her fairy tale life. The first part of her goal had been attained. She had found her man. There remained the second part—an exciting career.

They had a sumptuous wedding in Cairo. The church was full to the brim with family, friends and acquaintances who wanted to see this Romeo and Juliet of Cairo finally make it to the altar after so much opposition from the groom's parents. They honeymooned in Alexandria. There had been heavy petting before the wedding night but, when the marriage was finally consummated, Julia was greatly disappointed because she did not have an orgasm. She had been very much looking forward to this. She had thought that the actual sex act would fix all their problems and she would indulge in marital bliss. Alas, she had very few orgasms during her short married life. David was not an experienced lover. How could he be? His sexual experience had been with street prostitutes—in and out. This was how most young men in Egypt got sexual release. They would pile up in a car, pick up a prostitute in the street and have turns with her in the back seat. David had told her about this practice and it had upset her that he was touching other women. He did wear a condom of course.

"I don't want you to have sex with prostitutes," she told him. "Or, if you do, don't touch them, just go in and come out after your climax." The reason she did not want him to touch a prostitute is because these women all had very Rubenesque figures with large hips and big boobs while she was very slim and had a small bosom. She did not want David to do any comparisons. That's when he had had the bright idea that he would refrain from going to prostitutes if she masturbated him. She should never have agreed to that absurd trade off.

Their married life began in Egypt and then they landed as immigrants in New York. She managed to have a thriving career in fashion designing in Manhattan through sheer determination and he became a very successful photographer. For most of the time they had fun but they still quarreled a lot. Her parents and siblings arrived in the States shortly after she had settled down with David.

After a few years into the marriage, Julia realized that it was not working the way she wanted it to. Passion was lacking in the relationship. Her mother had been right. Things were not getting better. She was heartbroken and decided to break loose and regain her freedom. She did not know how to broach the subject though. She craved to go to Europe and have adventures. She was too curious and could not envision going through life without having had sex with any other man except her husband.

In Egypt she could not even have had other boyfriends, let alone a lover. After having had a boyfriend a girl was branded and men were reluctant to marry one who had already had a boyfriend. Men would consider her to be tainted, touched by another man. They all wanted a virgin of course. Technically all girls were virgins. Some did everything with their boyfriends, except the act of penetration. If, God forbid, there was any penetration and if the couple parted, then the girl would get sewn up to pretend to her next suitor that she was a virgin.

Her friend Mariella was a case in point. She and her boyfriend had gone all the way as they were sure they were going to get married. A few months later they had grown apart and had decided to separate. Mariella came to Julia crying her eyes out.

"Arty and I have separated and I don't know what to do because I'm not a virgin anymore. No one will want to marry me now. What am I going to do? My life is ruined. I have no future."

"You have to tell your mother," Julia advised her. Luckily Mariella's mother had sympathized with her daughter, after severely reprimanding her of course, had kept it a secret from the father and it was arranged that she gets sewn up. A year later she got married to a guy who never suspected that she was not a virgin since there were tell-tale signs of blood on the sheet on their wedding night.

Julia's mother had warned her to be careful when she was dating David. She related to her the story of her uncle who had left his fiancée high and dry when he had found out that she was not a virgin although he had loved her very much. Consequently, he had had a nervous breakdown and later had married a girl he did not really love but she was "pure". It was such a hypocritical society and Julia wanted no part of it.

Julia and David had a hectic life in Manhattan. They worked very hard. Something was missing as far as Julia was concerned though, and that thing was passion and they were still bickering.

One day, after a stupid fight, Julia suddenly blurted out, "this is not working David, I really can't live with you any longer—you are always criticizing me and picking up fights for stupid reasons. You've become a control freak. We are not really happy together. I think it would be better if we separated." She did not want to utter the word divorce yet.

David was stunned at her outburst. "You really mean that?"

"Yes, it will be better for both of us. We can't go on like this."

"Don't you want to sit down and talk about it?"

"Not really, there is nothing more to say really, I've made up my mind; for God's sake David we have been fighting even before we got married," Julia retorted. She was fed up of being chained down and was very eager to investigate other pastures. Her dream of having a perfect life with a perfect husband had been shattered. There must be something better out there, she thought, so she set her mind on Europe. She wanted to meet European men. She loved her career but it was not everything for her. She had to find the right man to marry. Marriage and children meant a lot to her. She could not envisage a life without the right partner. She was not envious of the single career women around her who had arid and barren lives without a man or children. Her criteria for a suitable man were very demanding though.

David was too proud to argue so he picked up his belongings—the car, his stereo and his clothes—and moved out of the apartment the very next day. Julia found a lawyer and they eventually divorced and she moved to Geneva, Switzerland to be as far away as possible from the unhappy experience. She was ready to start on her European adventure. She had no alimony and had only $ 500 in her bank account. If she could not find a job in Geneva, then she had decided on Plan B—go to California and start a new life there.

There was a guy in Los Angeles, an old friend of theirs from their group in Cairo, who was smitten by her. When he heard that the couple was divorced, he flew out to the East coast to see her. They dated a few times.

"Why are you going to Europe, come to California and let's get married," he told her.

"I can't jump from one marriage into another so soon. I like you a lot and consider you a good friend but I don't love you Steve. It wouldn't be fair to you." She refused his proposal. She would go to California, if Europe did not work out, but not to marry Steve.

She loved Geneva from the moment she arrived. It was a small, picturesque, very clean, very well organized (Swiss style) international town and it housed the European Headquarters of the United Nations as well as organizations affiliated to the U.N. The town had a magnificent lake which was called Lake Geneva by the locals but in fact its real name was Lac Leman. People had a very pleasant life in this town where the lunch hour was considered sacred and most shops were closed at midday for a two hour period. In summer it was not uncommon for people to go swimming in the lake during their lunch break. After the frenetic pace of Manhattan, this was ideal for Julia. Imagine going swimming during the lunch break. In New York she only had a half hour for lunch in a dingy hamburger joint on Seventh Avenue. The only drawback was that supermarkets closed on Saturday afternoon to reopen on Monday afternoon. One had to make plans to buy groceries on Saturday to last all weekend.

Julia's life as a free woman began in Geneva. Finally she had sexual freedom. This was the 60's and women's lib was in full swing. She was on the pill and there were no constraints; she could go out with anyone she felt like. She was determined to have a ball with her new found freedom.

"It is very difficult to find a job and an apartment in Geneva," she was told by people she met. "As for men, forget ever being able to get one, because women outnumber men by 5 to 1," a friend of her mother's told her. "Girls are so easy, men can get them for a cup of coffee."

Julia always liked a challenge and she proved everyone wrong. As there was no fashion designing going on in Switzerland at that time, she got a job at the United Nations by lying through her teeth about her office work experience. She did not divulge the fact that her experience was in fashion design. She would not have been hired. She had had one office experience and that had been in Cairo. She invented a c.v. which luckily was not checked out and she got the job. She found an apartment by sheer luck and had men galore pursuing her. She very much enjoyed life in this small yet sophisticated town. The living was easy, the money was good and vacation time unbelievable—six weeks a year besides getting time off work during Easter week, Christmas week, etc.

"Caroline, you have to leave New York and come and join me in Geneva," she told her sister on the phone. "We'll have more fun here than over there and we don't have to work that hard. The money is also very good and it is very easy to meet men." They were both men crazy.

Her sister arrived soon after and also found a job with one of the organizations and they lived together and shared one car. They could not yet afford two cars. She did not particularly like working in an office after having had a creative job in the U.S., but all that time off from mundane office work was very attractive and it allowed her to further her career as an artist (painter). Her principal goal in life never changed though. She wanted to meet the right man who would whisk her off to have a successful, passionate marriage and have children. *Does a passionate marriage really exist? Or does passion fly out the window after marriage?*

She did meet a lot of men but never fell in love with any of them and, much to her dismay, none of them seemed to be of real husband material. Some of the men she met were married, from out of town, on business in Geneva. They all said they were separated, of course, to get into her pants, but she did not believe them and therefore did not take them seriously. She was wined and dined and went on weekends to major European cities as well as skiing in winter either in Switzerland or nearby France. She had not yet met The One but in the meantime she was having fun at least. She had quite an array of boyfriends and sometimes they even overlapped. More than once it happened that she had a lunch date with one guy and a dinner date with another. She was always on the lookout for an attractive marriageable man—a highly intelligent man who would love her unconditionally, care for her, envelop her—a passionate man who would carry her to ecstatic heights—a man who would dominate her sexually but not otherwise. She pursued that goal relentlessly. A career was also very important and she had it now. She was an artist instead of a fashion designer.

During her second week in Geneva, after she had found a job and an apartment, she met Carter, an American scientist, at the Movenpick restaurant, which was the most popular hangout to meet people, right smack in the middle of town. Carter was 38 years old and he was in Geneva on a year's contract with a scientific firm. He was not handsome by all means but was extremely intelligent, had a great sense of humor and he made her laugh. They went out on dates to good restaurants, to the movies, to parties and of course they ended up in bed. He fell in love with her. She liked him a lot but was not in love with him. His sexual performance left much to be desired. He was not passionate. He was tepid. But she was attracted to his mind and liked being with him. Close to the end of his contract and a few of months into the relationship, Julia realized that she was late having her period. This had never happened before and she was very concerned. This was no time to get pregnant. She had to tell Carter.

"Carter, I think I'm pregnant," she blurted out during a dinner date.

"Are you sure?" He looked very concerned and took her hands in his across from the table, looking at her very tenderly.

"Yes, almost sure, I have never missed a period before, ever—it has always been very punctual and I do feel very swollen. I'm very scared. I'll have to see a doctor to confirm it."

"So, it's not such a big deal, I have not come out and told you Julia but you must have guessed by now that I do love you very much. You are the first girl that I have really loved. We'll get married and go back to New York at the end of my contract. We'll look for a bigger apartment and everything will be okay. We'll get help for the baby and you can get back into fashion designing."

Julia looked at him dumbfounded. Marry Carter? She knew that he loved her but had not expected a proposal. He had been a bachelor for a very long time and she knew he cherished his freedom. She thought he would have suggested that she have an abortion. There were no problems with getting abortions in Switzerland within three months of pregnancy. It was a simple matter arranged by the consent of two doctors. There was no government interference whatsoever. She did enjoy Carter's company but that did not mean she wanted to get married to him. There was no way Julia was going to go back to New York so soon after arriving in Switzerland and certainly not for Carter. She was in a dilemma and she told him she was not ready to get remarried. He was very disappointed at her decision.

"What are you going to do then?" he asked not letting go of her hands.

"I don't know what to do. I hate to think about abortion but I may resort to that. I don't fancy being an unmarried mother or having the baby and giving it up for adoption."

Carter was a good man and it was comforting to know that he wanted to marry her but her heart was not in it. It would not work out because she did not love him. A few of her friends back in Cairo had made loveless marriages and resigned themselves to be dutiful wives but Julia did not want that. Also, she did not want to get married just because she was pregnant. She was adamant about this. An agonizing week went by contemplating all kinds of possibilities but in the end she did have her period so the matter was settled. It was such a relief to her that she did not have to get an abortion. They continued seeing each other until his contract was over and he was ready to return to New York.

"My proposal still stands," he said when she took him to the airport, "just give me a call anytime." They hugged and kissed and Julia felt rather sad that he was leaving. She had gotten very fond of him.

They did remain in contact throughout the years. He came to Geneva every summer and asked her "How is your love life, are you still free? Can we resume where we left off?"

Her answer was always the same, "No Carter, I have another boyfriend now, and we cannot possibly resume where we left off."

Carter was a kind man, a very intelligent man and a very dependable one but that was not enough. He had not given her any sexual thrills and there seemed to be no earthly reason to go back to someone who did not excite her senses.

A couple of weeks after Carter's departure, Julia met a German, high-ranking international civil servant, quite a bit older than her, at a U.N. conference. She liked him at first but then he became obsessed by her and was very possessive. He wanted to see her every evening as he had nothing else to do. Well, she had plenty to do as she wanted to also hangout with her girlfriends. When she told him she was breaking up with him, he tried to kidnap her one day. "You are mine and I want to keep you but you don't know what you want," he told her. Of course she knew what she wanted. She just did not want him and was scared of him. She broke off with him and never saw him again.

Julia had met Monica, an Italian girl, during a trip to Majorca who invited her to go and stay with her in Portofino where she had a summer house. At one of Monica's parties, Julia met an Italian lawyer from Milan. He was with a girlfriend and Julia was quite attracted to him but she did not pay much attention to him even though he neglected his girlfriend and tried to monopolize her during the evening.

"Dario," that was his name, "is leaving his girlfriend and wants to be with you," said Monica to her later in the evening when everyone was ready to go home. Julia was quite surprised and could not believe her ears.

"I don't want to be the cause of breaking up their relationship," she told Monica.

"You're not breaking it. She is a good friend of mine and I know that it is at the breaking point anyway."

Julia then took up a long distant relationship with Dario. He was a great guy, worldly, sophisticated, athletic, romantic and debonair as only Italians can be. Sex was also quite good with him. The first time he went down on her, he remarked, "I wish you did not cut your pubic hair so short. I like a full bush." She laughed. This was a new one to her. No man had remarked on that part of her anatomy before. He came to visit her almost every weekend and she had a lot of fun with him. She also learnt Italian pretty fast. They did quite a bit of travelling together, going skiing in the Italian Alps, going on short trips to the Italian coast and visiting quaint small towns. She loved Italy and Italian food. After a few months into the relationship he asked her to marry him and move to Italy. She loved being with him but she did not love him enough to get married, leave Geneva, and move to Italy. *What was wrong with her? Why was she not falling in love? Here was a guy with almost all the criteria. Why was she hesitating?*

"Oh, Dario" she said "I do like you a lot (she could not tell him that she did not love him) but I am not ready to get married and move to Italy. I have my life here in Geneva. I just can't leave it and transplant myself."

"Why not? You do speak Italian now and you'll be quite at home. I earn a very good living—you will not have to work and you can paint all day. Milan is not that far away from Geneva. You'll be able to visit your family anytime you wish. Doesn't this appeal to you?"

"Yes, Dario, it does appeal to me but somehow I don't think I'm ready to leave Geneva quite yet. I don't want to be dependent on a man for my living."

He was extremely disappointed and he kept calling her and writing to her hoping she might eventually change her mind. They continued seeing each other intermittently but she did not budge from her decision and, after a while, he gave up.

An array of boyfriends followed after that. They were just short insignificant relationships or flings, rather.

There was the handsome Turk who was in Geneva for a U.N. internship program. He was very cute and a good lover but she could not envisage life with a man who was not of the same religion as hers. She knew the relationship was going to be short-lived because he had to return to Turkey anyway. It was just a summer romance and a lot of fun. No future in it at all. She was not heartbroken.

There was the Iranian PhD student in Philosophy at Geneva University who dressed impeccably, was very suave and knew how to court a woman. He sent her 24 red roses on her birthday. His philosophical discussions were a bit too long for her and she got bored after a while.

Then there was a Danish young man who fell hopelessly in love with her and wanted to whisk her away to Denmark after the termination of his U.N. contract.

One guy she really fell for was a very good looking Scottish guy. His name was Sean. He looked like Sean Connery. She met him in a hotel in Spain where she was vacationing one summer with her sister. He was there on a business conference. He was stationed in Geneva and "kind of" separated from his wife although they still lived together in London with the children.

"I have not had sex with my wife for the last couple of years. She is just not interested. We live together like brother and sister," he told her. "I won't leave her however because I adore my children and I cannot live away from them." *So with whom was he having sex with?* She did not ask. It was obvious that he was sex starved because he could perform twice a night almost every time he was with her. After a few months into the relationships he laid down his position quite frankly to her.

"I adore you Julia, but I cannot figure out how to plan our future together. If I divorce my wife and marry you, I would lose my children. I would be living in Geneva while my wife would be moving up to Scotland to be near her family and I would rarely see them. You see, I am very attached to my children. I am in a quandary. I cannot figure out a viable solution."

Julia was quite enamored of him; he was handsome, intelligent, caring, amusing, had a good job and was very passionate and good in bed. He was quite the husband material she was looking for. Just as she thought she had found the man she wanted, there was this huge drawback—a wife he did not love and children he loved. She was heartbroken but she decided that she could not continue seeing Sean. He was too indecisive and she did not want to pressure him. She did not want a man who would have guilt feelings of having abandoned his children because of her. He would resent her eventually. The relationship ended when he moved back to London. He kept on writing love letters to her for months and would occasionally come to Geneva on business. She saw him and had sex with him a few times but it was not the same as before. It became kind of casual and her heart was no longer in it. They finally drifted apart.

Shortly after that episode, she met the Spanish Minister of Culture at a U.N. Conference on Literacy. They had a lot in common and were attracted to each other big time. He happened to also be an artist but there was again a huge drawback. He was married—unhappily he told her. *What was the matter with those guys? Why were they all unhappily married? Or were they lying?* He pursued her relentlessly and wanted her to be his mistress travelling with him on state business throughout Europe but staying in the sidelines, of course. He could not flaunt her presence. She went on a couple of trips with him but then felt uncomfortable with the whole idea and got bored tagging along with someone with no prospect of a future. He was not going to divorce his wife although he did not love her. "It would create too much of a scandal in the circles I move in," he told her.

"Bibi," (that was his nickname) she told him "I can't go on like this being your mistress. I want more out of life and unfortunately you can't give it to me." She might have married him if he were available because she came very close to loving him and he came very close to being The One. It was not meant to be, however. They eventually parted amicably and did not have any future contact with each other.

After Bibi, there were a few short lived romances of no consequence. They were just boyfriends to while away the time with. Passing fancies. Nothing to get excited about.

Some men lasted a few weeks, some a few months but none fitted the bill because they were not husband material—there was always something lacking. They all fell in love with her but the feeling was not reciprocated. That was the big problem. She realized that she was looking for the "impossible to find" man. Her criteria were too demanding. He had to be of husband material, intelligent, worldly, knowledgeable, amusing, attractive, dependable and passionately in love with her and she of him. And of course he had to be wealthy—she had expensive taste in clothes—and oh, most importantly, he should not bore her. She could not suffer bores. *But doesn't marriage become boring after a while?*

A French girlfriend of hers in New York had once told her. "There are men you marry and men you have fun with. Don't ever confuse the two. Be very clear-headed about your choice." Julia was a hopeless romantic at heart. She could not make a cold blooded choice. She needed to love a man passionately and be loved passionately in return. She did not want a marriage of convenience just because the man would make a good husband. Some of her old friends in Egypt had done just that and were happy but they did not have Julia's cravings and dreams. They were docile, dutiful and obedient housewives.

Her auntie, way back in Egypt, had come up with the statement, "You are too outspoken. Curb your tongue my dear—men don't like outrageously opinionated women and you'll never find a husband if you continue this way. Act demurely and after the wedding you can change little by little." She brushed her auntie's advice aside. She was not going to think one way and act another way. She found plenty of men who wanted to get married to her, *so there goes your statement auntie dear.*

Her girlfriends in Geneva were all envious of her and asked her "What is your secret, how come you get all these men swarming around you like bees?"

Her answer was simple. "I don't pursue them. I am not needy. Men do not like needy women. They like the chase and I let them chase me. Men like to feel they have conquered a woman. And, I never encroach on their freedom. I don't talk a lot about myself, instead I listen to them. Also, I am not sexually aggressive." She was quite passive in bed and liked being "taken". She had found out that her boyfriends liked her that way. She did not have to put on a show or try to arouse them. She was very sensual and liked being made love to.

There had been the case of one man, her divorce lawyer in New York who, she must admit, had had a lot of charisma. He had a powerful presence which she admired. During her separation period with her husband, her lawyer had warned her, "You cannot go out with any man except me in case your husband hires a detective and finds out you are seeing other men. Your request for alimony would then go down the drain." *What alimony? She was not expecting any.*

She had been rather attracted to him and went out on so called "business dates" a couple of times. Eventually they had ended up in bed. He had made one big mistake though. After sleeping with her the first time, he had solemnly declared "next time you will take me in your mouth." He never did have the opportunity though because she had refused to see him after that and fired him as her lawyer. *How dare he come out with a vulgar statement like that? Who did he think he was dealing with? A penis-crazy woman?* In any case his penis was too big and wide and he had hurt her. For days after that first encounter in bed she had trouble sitting down. That was the end of this one-nighter. She had later found out that he was married but he had kept that important fact a secret while "courting" her.

A friend of hers in New York had once told her that she never kissed her casual boyfriends but gave them blow jobs instead. "It is less intimate," she had said. *How can it be less intimate? Is there anything more intimate than the sexual organ? Stupid girl.* She had never let her borrow her lipstick ever again. Even the thought had repulsed her.

So Julia's life in Geneva went on full swing, going out on dates, having boyfriends and searching for the right man. Her artistic career was thriving. She had managed to give quite a few exhibitions in Switzerland and in other countries in Europe as well. All In all, she was quite happy but would have been happier if she achieved her ultimate goal of finding a suitable partner. And she finally found one.

Le Baiser (the Kiss)

CHAPTER 2

Bernard

After having had a series of unfruitful, unsatisfactory affairs, Julia met Bernard at the United Nations, where they both worked.

Actually it was Francois, a French guy, who pushed her to go after Bernard. She met Francois while having lunch at the Movenpick restaurant. They shared the same table. People did share tables in this restaurant. It was a great place to meet people. They got to talking and she went out with him a few times. His attractive Greek wife had just divorced him and he was rather lonesome. He showed her a photo of his wife which he still kept in his wallet. He was very good company but not the least bit sexy. Every time he saw her, he said "I've got this crazy desire to kiss you," but he never did, obviously sensing that it would not be welcome. Luckily, he did not try to kiss her because she found him dry looking and would have recoiled from his touch and the friendship would have gone down the drain. She liked him and enjoyed having conversations with him, but she did not find him attractive at all. He was not her type. They did become very good friends though. He lent her his car, helped her around her apartment and took her out to dinners and gave her brotherly advice.

One day, while having dinner, he told her that there was a man named Bernard de Bergeron, a wealthy Frenchman of aristocratic descent—not one of these bankrupt ones—working in the same department as herself at the UN and asked whether she knew him. She told him that she had not met him yet.

"Well," Francois told her, "he is a very good catch, you might want to make his acquaintance." She found Francois' directness quite endearing; he had become quite the confidant. He had accepted the fact that she was not interested in him, and he was trying to set her up with an eligible bachelor. He was a true friend. From her past experience, it had almost been impossible to have a sincere man friend. Men were after one thing only, except gays, of course, but she had not met any.

At a cocktail party, given by the department where she worked, she found herself standing next to Bernard and he started a conversation. She could tell that he was very intrigued by her and she coyly flirted with him. She set out to entice. She wanted all men to fall for her, whether she liked them or not. Unfortunately, he was not her type physically. She did not have a "coup de foudre" like she had had with Sean. He was tall and had a good physique—that was fine—but he was fair skinned, had very light blond hair and lifeless pale blue eyes. He looked remote. She liked men to look either macho or sensual. Bernard was neither but he was very interesting, very knowledgeable, well educated, sophisticated and worldly, had excellent manners and spoke beautiful French. He exuded class. He was ten years older than her. That was the right age for her.

Bernard got very interested in this very feminine, youthful, yet sophisticated Middle Eastern girl with the almond-shaped eyes. He was quite the womanizer and suggested to drive her home after the cocktail party. When she told him that she lived on Rue des Delices (street of delights), "What an appropriate street name for such a delightful young woman," he said grinning sheepishly and patting her hand in the car.

They started dating and he taught her a lot about French literature, antiques, and classical music. She always liked men who knew more than her. He enjoyed the good things in life. It was obvious to everyone at work that he was very much infatuated by her, but somehow her colleagues could tell she was not that much into him. Her heart did not flutter at the sight of him. She liked him a lot though and enjoyed his company very much. They did a lot of things together. They went to dinners, movies, art galleries, and antique shows. They also went on weekends to Paris where he had an apartment on a very fashionable street, next to the House of Dior (where he bought her a couple of outfits, because he wanted her to be dressed to kill). In winter they went skiing in the French and Swiss Alps. What she liked most was that he had a wry sense of humor and was very considerate and kind. He was not a snob. She admired his mind and he stimulated her intellectually with his knowledge. Little by little he grew on her and she decided she had found the husband material. Bernard was the man she was going to marry. He met all her criteria except in the passion department. He was good in bed but did not arouse her to orgasmic heights. He was sexual, but not sensual.

Julia always dreamt of a man who would dominate her sexually but the only ones who had done that, had not worked out. She craved to love someone and be swept off her feet and live happily ever after. She had wanted that since she was fifteen years old. She thought at the time that she had loved her husband, but they were both very young and inexperienced. David had actually come close to being that someone, but she had not been satisfied because she had wanted to have had more experiences to be able to choose the right one. *How can one take a lifelong decision when no choice was offered?* Now, however, she had all the experience she needed; she had six years of experience and Bernard came closest to her quest of finding The One. She realized she could not have everything and decided to do without the passion. She reassessed the situation and changed her criteria.

She did love Bernard in a way, and she often wondered whether she was capable of ever *really* loving a man. One loved one's children, parents, siblings and pets but a man was another matter. She had been infatuated by some men, lusted after a few but not really loved them. No marriageable candidate had shown up during the past six years so she decided to go into a second marriage with her head and not her heart. She realized that she could not expect everything from any one man. Bernard pursued her relentlessly and, after a few months, he started talking about marriage.

"What do you say to the idea of getting married?" he asked her while having dinner in a chic Parisian restaurant. It came out of the blue and Julia was surprised at the unromantic, matter of fact way he was asking her.

"That wouldn't be such a bad idea," she said in an offhand manner.

"We'll go and do the formalities at the Mairie (town hall) in Geneva next week then."

"Okay."

"You know you're the first woman I have ever asked to get married to."

"I'm honored," she said with sarcasm.

He laughed and resumed eating his dinner.

She had been disappointed so many times by the men she had met and here was Bernard, a dependable, stable, and a good person who amused her in many ways and with whom she was never bored. *Forget love, passion, and heartbreak. What was love anyway?* For her, love for a man meant lusting after a man for a short period of time because all good things fizzle out over time somehow and the physical attraction dwindles also. Companionship was more important and, therefore, she decided that she loved Bernard well enough to want to marry him. They made plans.

She knew that marriage to Bernard would not preclude the fact that she might have a few short passionate love affairs now and again as some women do. She was almost sure, however, that Bernard would be faithful to her. He was not the cheating type. He was too prim and proper to do that. She, on the other hand, had quite liberal ideas about marriage and cheating. How can one expect to have sex only with one's husband during the span of a lifetime? She had always needed passion in her life, whether with men, hobbies or careers. And most of all, she was too curious to be satisfied with only one man for the rest of her life. Finding a compatible life partner was difficult enough, but deciding to have sex with him only was the most asinine thing one could ever imagine. It would be impossible to keep the torch going on and on. So Julia came to the conclusion that the secret of a good marriage was that her husband love her more than she loved him, that they have some mutual interests and cohabitate without too much bickering.

"Have you really made up your mind and want to get married to this guy?" asked her sister Caroline.

"Yes, why not, he is a good catch, he loves me, is very dependable, amusing, wealthy and mentally stimulating. I am learning a lot from him, and he does not bore me. He will make a good husband. I am tired of running around, meeting losers," was her reply.

"But you don't really love him."

"So what, what is real love? The type of love you have with your husband is one in a million. I thought I had it with David but it was not meant to be. We were too young."

"You are still young, you're only twenty-nine. It is not as though you are forty and running out of time."

"Yes, you're right. I still have time, but a bird in the hand is worth two in the bush, sis. I have made my decision. I will marry Bernard unless I meet a better candidate in the foreseeable future, which is the next twelve months. That's as long as I will wait."

Bernard had been to the best French schools and had a PhD on the subject of employer/labor relations in the Soviet Union (she could not imagine how that would work in a communist society in the 1950's). He had gone to Moscow to study there. He was an unusual man, rather eccentric. She did have a few orgasms with him and faked the rest. She did not like it when men worked too hard on her to provoke an orgasm. Either she got aroused quite fast and had one, or she did not. She liked spontaneity and, in any case, it was all mental for her; she got aroused with her mind and not with her sexual organ. Her mind was her most erogenous zone. She heard so many stories from her girlfriends about their partners' sexual habits. Some complained that the partner could not get it up; others said that they could not get aroused, so the partner worked on them for hours on end. How boring. She was very realistic in that domain and did not expect much from any one man. All she expected at this point in her life was that he be a good husband and a good father, be interesting and intelligent, have common interests and that she would not suffer boredom with him. Sex and passion became secondary in her criteria.

Bernard was considered *un bon parti* (a good catch) in the aristocratic circles in Paris and many women were after him. She had sneaked around in his desk drawer and read some of the letters from women inviting him here and there.

"One of the reasons I love you is that you don't see me only as a good catch like women in my circle of friends do," he told her one day after making love. Julia realized that he had chosen her because she was so different from the girls in his milieu and also because opposites attract, she thought. *Well, Bernard I also think you are a good catch, but I just don't show it so obviously.*

Bernard introduced her to his mother (the only woman he had ever introduced to her) and they were engaged for over three years now but had not yet set a date to get married. He gave her a beautiful diamond ring; he loved showering her with jewelry. He was very comfortable in their relationship but was dragging his feet in setting a definite date. Bernard had the habit of procrastinating in everything. Julia did not mind it. He was not going anywhere. She had him. Maybe he was waiting for her to get pregnant in order to take the definite plunge, but she was not so eager to have children yet. He was thirty-nine years old and wanted an heir to his fortune. She was twenty-nine years old and babies were not in her immediate future plans. He thought she was off the pill and, as she was not getting pregnant, he suggested that they go to a fertility clinic. She was on birth control pills, unbeknownst to him, because she was in no hurry to fall pregnant. She wanted to have fun before being bogged down with a child. So she postponed the fertility clinic idea indefinitely. She realized she was being deceitful but she did not want to rush towards the baby world. They did a lot of travelling and she knew that this would stop once they had kids. They could afford to have a nanny but that was not the point. A mother did not really have fun. Julia always assessed the life of her married friends; they were full of excuses for not being able to do things they wanted because of the children, so she postponed pregnancy. She went into this relationship with her head and not her heart.

The most important thing about Bernard was that he did not bore her, and they got along most of the time. They hardly ever quarreled. She was easily bored, and this was the longest relationship she ever had had with a man since her divorce. She liked being with him because he was not controlling and left her quite free to pursue her own interests. He thought she was very talented and encouraged her in her artistic endeavors. Her quest for passionate love was not foremost in her prerequisites at this time. In any case, passionate sex does not last long with the same man, she told herself. Passionate sex happens at the very beginning of a relationship. One would have to change lovers every so often to get that continuously. The initial passion would not last and it would be followed up with the comfortable, predictable married sex, in the same boring, missionary position, over in ten minutes tops. There would not be the languorous, lengthy foreplay of the beginning.

She had come to the conclusion that it was almost impossible to find a man who was both fun and husband material. It was either one or the other.

She was now resigned with her choice. No need to look any further. Actually, in a way, dragging on the engagement period suited her quite fine because, who knows, she might meet someone with whom she could actually fall in love before her biological clock hit her in the face. It annoyed her that she had never really been in love, whatever that means. She got attracted to men, had had several boyfriends who were convenient and amused her but she never really loved any of them. She was the one who always ended the relationship for one reason or another. She continued to remain just friends with them until they found other pastures to graze on. But one particular man refused to remain friends with her. "I can't just be your friend," he had said. "I desire you too much. I would go crazy not being able to touch you." That statement boosted her ego, of course.

Bernard had planned an interesting New Year's trip for them to tour the principal cities in Morocco. He was on a mission to Nigeria with the United Nations, so it was decided that she would fly down to Casablanca alone, and he would join her a couple of days later after the termination of his mission. She did not particularly like the idea of arriving by herself in a Muslim country, a woman alone going through passport control under the leery eyes of men, who would wonder what an unaccompanied woman was doing, coming to their country. She did speak Arabic though, but not the same Arabic as the Moroccans. Nevertheless she enthusiastically agreed to go on this trip and thought it would be exciting touring the main cities of Morocco, seeing the old towns, the quaint bazaars, the different types of architecture and desert landscape. She adored all things oriental.

She arrived in Casablanca on a nice balmy afternoon and checked into the hotel where he had reserved a suite for them. At the reception desk she was told it was customary to leave one's passport at the desk for registration purposes, and so she did. There was an older man hanging around the reception area, talking to the other clerk, and she noticed that he was checking her out. He looked quite ordinary, so she did not pay much attention to him.

She went to her room to unpack and, fifteen minutes later, there was a knock on her door. It was the reception manager returning her passport *Why would the manager personally return her passport and not give it to one of the clerks?*

"Madame" he said, "the gentleman who was at reception while you were checking in also happens to be from Switzerland, and he would like to invite you for a drink at the bar of the hotel."

She looked at him incredulously. The guy, whoever he was, must have bribed the manager to have a look at her passport. How else would he have known she was from Switzerland? She declined the invitation. She would perhaps have accepted it out of curiosity had she found him interesting and appealing at first view.

Ten minutes later there was another knock on her door. This time, it was room service bringing her a bottle of champagne and a small bowl of caviar, with compliments of the gentleman in question. Hell, why not accept this? She loved champagne and caviar and they were being offered to her *sans le monsieur en question*. The guy was being persistent, she thought, but she was still not interested in befriending him. She was absolutely certain of that. Bernard was arriving in a couple of days and, in any case, it was not proper to accept invitations from unknown men in foreign countries. She accepted the tray though and told the waiter to thank the person who sent it.

The next morning in the breakfast room, she saw the man again. This time she scrutinized him. He was of medium height. He had a squat, swarthy figure, salt-and-pepper hair and piercing beady, grayish eyes. Not her type at all, just an ordinary-looking, middle-aged man.

He got up from his table, came over to hers and introduced himself as Carlos Francisco Ortega, told her he was Argentinian, lived in Gland—a lake town not far from Geneva—and was a grain merchant on a business trip in Morocco. "We are practically neighbors in Geneva," he said. She did not ask him to sit down and, to make it clear that she was not a lonely woman seeking adventure in a foreign country, told him that she was waiting for her fiancé to show up in a couple of days and that they intended to tour Morocco by car. "Thank you for the champagne," she added.

"Oh, so you are not alone. What a pity. Actually, it rather surprised me that an attractive-looking woman like yourself would be travelling by herself in Morocco. By the way, do I stand a chance of getting to know you?" Getting to know her? He certainly did not have a chance. She was not attracted to him at all. Accepting the champagne must have given him the wrong idea. She regretted doing so. She had to get out of this situation without hurting his feelings.

"Not really," she said laughing, "you already know the reason," and stood up to leave the table when he told her that he would be giving a cocktail reception in his suite in honor of some Moroccan dignitaries that evening and invited her to join them. As this was a cocktail invite along with other people and, as she had nothing better to do but watch boring Moroccan TV in her room, she accepted his invitation. It would be interesting to meet some locals and socialize.

She dressed up very elegantly for the occasion and, at about 5:00 p.m., she went to his suite in the penthouse of the hotel which was built on a hill. It had an adjoining large terrace overlooking the ocean. The view was magnificent. She was spellbound by the sunset that cast golden ripples on the ocean. There was also a pianist belting away famous, melodious tunes. The guests were all on the terrace where a mild ocean breeze was blowing. There were quite a number of people all dressed up in elegant clothes—a mixture of Europeans and locals, the former indulging in alcoholic beverages and the latter drinking fruit juice or Coca-Cola. She ordered a gin and tonic from the bartender and was introduced around as a guest from Geneva.

After Julia chatted with several people, Carlos asked her to follow him to the study adjoining the living room. He invited her to sit on the sofa, and he sat across from her on an armchair. He wanted to know a little more about her besides what he had learnt from her passport. He did admit looking at it.

"So, how do you like Morocco so far?" he asked.

"I have just arrived. I have not seen anything yet. But I love the scenery and the atmosphere."

They chatted amicably about banal things, like the weather, Moroccan food, the landscape, the enchanting bazaars, life in Switzerland, etc. It was quite a friendly conversation, and he did not come on to her—yet. He then told her that, very recently, he had separated from his wife.

"One day she just walked away with our chauffeur, or rather drove away and did not come back. She abandoned our six children," he said. This had enraged him to no end. In his opinion, the woman was a slut. But why tell her? Julia asked herself. She was a perfect stranger to him. She guessed he wanted to unburden himself to a "soul mate" from Switzerland.

"Can you imagine a woman abandoning her children, the youngest only one year old, and going with another man—a chauffeur for God's sake?" he asked her angrily, frothing at the mouth with his spit going in all directions. Luckily she was sitting far enough not to be splattered with it.

"Yes, I can imagine that," she said. "Ingrid Bergman, for one—you know of her don't you? And a Swedish friend of mine who abandoned her three children to go with an Egyptian guy she met on a plane from Stockholm to Cairo. This kind of behavior is not that unusual."

"Women do not seem to have any morals anymore," he retorted. He was beside himself, consumed with rage and pacing back and forth in the room, going on and on about his unfaithful wife who was, it seemed, very beautiful even after having had six children.

"She is Argentinian, not Swedish. She acted like a whore and she humiliated me. I cannot get over it. It is so degrading," he spat out. "And then she has the audacity to send the chauffeur to pick up her jewelry from the house. I kicked him out, of course, and would have killed him right on the spot but restrained myself on time." Actually he had felt like killing both his wife and the chauffeur but had reminded himself that he could not afford to go to jail as he had to take care of his six children.

Again, she wondered why he was telling her all this. She surely did not seem to have given him the impression that she was interested in his predicament, but she listened politely while letting out a few yawns from time to time. She hoped he would stop monopolizing her time with his ranting but, as this was not likely to happen, she got up to leave.

"I sympathize with you very much Carlos, but I have to go now because I am really very tired. Thank you for inviting me. I enjoyed meeting your friends."

As she was getting up from the sofa, Carlos made a sudden movement and opened a drawer of the bureau next to his armchair. The gesture startled her. She thought for a minute that he was taking out a gun to do some shooting right there and then.

The drawer must have contained more than a hundred pieces of jewelry. It was full to the brim.

"You see these? This is all the jewelry I bought for her over the years. I brought it with me because I don't trust her—she may come back to the house and steal them. I have changed the locks of course but, you never know, she might hire a thug to break in." He picked up a very ornate gold bracelet from the pile and threw it at her. She caught it in time before it fell on the floor.

"Here," he said, "this is for you." *What the hell was the matter with him, throwing jewelry at her?*

"I certainly cannot possibly accept this, Carlos, here take it back," and she tossed it back to him.

"Why not?"

"First of all, I am engaged to be married and—"

He cut her short. "So what? This is just a small gift. Engaged to be married doesn't mean anything, you are not married yet."

"I can't accept this kind of gift from anyone except my fiancé and look, I have nice jewelry on, all given by him, and I don't need any more. I suppose I should not have accepted the champagne you sent to my room because that must have given you the wrong idea." Who was she kidding, a woman always needed more jewelry but not given to her in this manner and certainly not by a stranger. Accepting the gift would mean she was willing to start something with him and she absolutely had no intention of doing that. First of all, she was engaged to Bernard and secondly, Carlos did not appeal to her at all.

"You are being stupid, you can have the contents of this whole drawer if you would leave your fiancé and come with me. You will have anything you want, a mansion, trips all over the world, servants galore and a chauffeur, and children, if you want. You will also be free to pursue any interest you fancied."

What was this all about? What was wrong with this guy? He hardly knew her. Was she so desirable? Why was he acting so desperate? In a way, she was flattered, but she thought he must be on some type of drug.

"Oh, come on, Carlos, you are being ridiculous. I would certainly not leave my fiancé for you or anyone else. You are a perfect stranger to me. You are some guy I met in a hotel who is trying to buy me. How can you make sure that I will not run away with the chauffeur too? You make me laugh, really." She also wanted to add that he did not appeal to her at all physically or otherwise with or without the jewelry, but she did not want to hurt his feelings.

"I am tired of being with whores all the time. I liked you the minute I saw you and, when I found out you were from Geneva, I thought this was a chance to get to know you better and have a meaningful relationship for a change." (Meaningful relationship, my ass. All he wanted was to sleep with her. Men said such asinine things sometimes.)

"My dear Carlos, this is really going too far, you're acting like a spoiled teenager who wants to get everything he sees immediately. This is not the way to get a woman interested in you, not that I would be interested in the first place. I belong to someone else." (Belong? What a stupid word she had uttered. She did not belong to anyone and would never be.)

"Everybody has a price, my dear. What's yours? I'll give you anything you want. I'm being absolutely serious here. Just name it."

Why was he so desperate? "You are acting like a jerk, you know that? For your information, my fiancé can certainly give me anything I want. I don't need anything from you or from anyone else."

"'My fiancé, my fiancé,' I am tired of hearing the word *fiancé*. You are a beautiful woman, very smart but very stubborn. Most men don't like smart women, but I do. Actually, I would like to meet that fiancé of yours. He is one lucky bastard. How about if I invited you both to dinner with my children when he arrives tomorrow evening?"

"I am afraid he will be very tired and not in the mood for socializing since we will start touring Morocco the day after tomorrow."

"Okay, how about having dinner on New Year's Eve with my friends and children in the night club on the roof of the hotel?"

"I'll ask him."

Julia thought Bernard would get a kick to learn of this encounter and the invitation and that he would probably want to accept it. Bernard was quite the eccentric. He liked unusual situations. She also liked that about him. Of course, she would tell him everything beforehand. He always liked the idea that other men desired her. It kept him on his toes. He was rather strange that way. He knew he could not possess her entirely. She was too much of a free spirit, but he felt proud that she had agreed to marry him.

"What are you doing tomorrow?" he asked.

"Nothing, I am planning on hanging around the hotel swimming pool."

"I can lend you my car, and you can go to one of the fabulous beaches on the coastline all by yourself. No strings attached, don't worry, I will not be joining you."

"Really, you will not drive me yourself?"

"No, you are free to take the car and go on your own. I have some business to take care of. I am not on vacation."

"Okay." She agreed on an impulse. How on earth was she going to drive by herself in the streets of Casablanca? Well, she would manage somehow.

Bernard called that evening. "Oh boy, do I have things to tell you," she said.

"I cannot wait to be with you. I miss you terribly," he said.

"Me too."

"See you tomorrow, ciao, ciao sweetie." And they hung up.

The next morning, she got a phone call from one of the clerks at reception telling her that the car was ready whenever she was.

She picked up her beach bag, hat and dark sunglasses and went downstairs, thinking this was a trick and surely Carlos would be there to drive her. But no, he was true to his word. He was nowhere in sight and the doorman was holding the car door open for her. Wow, the car was a convertible white Cadillac with red leather interior. She asked the doorman a few questions about the functioning of the car and directions to the best beach location and finally, pretending that she was in complete control, drove off to go to one of the luxurious hotels on the beach.

She felt very conspicuous with her hat and dark glasses, driving a white Cadillac down the main avenue of Casablanca. A lot of the local people in the street were looking at this young unaccompanied woman in a convertible driving all by herself. She was a little scared but it was broad daylight, and surely nothing could happen to her. She was also reassured when she saw a few policemen hanging around. She went to the private beach club of the hotel recommended by reception and saw that almost all the women wore bikinis, so she felt quite in place. This seemed to be a European hangout. She recognized a few French actors and actresses lying around on their beach chairs, tanning themselves to a crisp toast.

She lay on a beach chair for a while before going swimming. She then got up and went to the bar to get herself a drink. A good-looking man materialized next to her. He smiled and said hello. She said hello, and then she recognized that it was Jean Marc Perrier, the famous French actor, an older guy who was known to be a womanizer although he had a very beautiful and talented wife, also an actress.

"May I offer you a drink?" he asked.

"No, thank you, I already have one," she said and proceeded to go back to her chaise longue.

"Why are you in such a hurry to leave? Would you like to go to the TV room and watch *Les Celibataires?*" This was a French film that she had not seen. "It's going to start at 3:00 p.m."

"No, thank you," she said. "I am not in the habit of watching TV during daytime and especially not when it is such a beautiful day." Was this his pick-up line? She knew exactly what would happen in the TV room. He would put his arm around her and give her a few squeezes, whisper some nonsense in her ear and start to fondle her, thinking she would succumb and accept to go to his room and go to bed with him. Stupid, arrogant idiot. He probably thought she would go for it just because he was a good-looking, famous actor. She walked away. He had a surprised look on his face but got the hint and did not follow her. She hated arrogant men who thought they could get any girl just because they were famous.

After a couple of hours at the beach, she found her way back to the hotel without too much trouble, left the car in the parking lot and left a little thank-you note at reception for Carlos and went up to her room.

Later that evening, Bernard arrived and, during dinner in the hotel dining room (Carlos was not there), she told him of her adventures. He laughed, making some cynical comments and, being the curious type, he told her that he would like to meet this Carlos fellow and to go ahead and accept the dinner invitation once they got back from their tour.

The next day, they rented a car to tour the principal cities of Morocco. They had a fabulous time in Marrakesh, Fez, Tangiers, and Rabat.

First stop was Marrakesh, a major exotic city, blending the old with the new. They walked around the main square and were fascinated with the Medina, the star attraction of Marrakesh, where they saw the snake charmers and an array of odd-looking objects for sale. They did some bargain hunting.

Fez was also very interesting with its medieval architecture which they admired as they walked up and down the narrow arched alleys of the old city made only for pedestrians. Donkeys and hand-pulled carts provided the only mode of transport. The souks were fascinating. They took a lot of photos.

Next stop was Tangiers, famous for its bazaars and oriental architecture. She bought quite a few djellabas in brocade and exotic tops of embroidered cotton and some oriental jewelry. They also bought a very original handmade carpet, after extensive bargaining, for their future home in Geneva.

Rabat, capital of Morocco, was just a modern city. They visited the museums and historical attractions and also the famous Kasbah, which was built in Andalusian style.

They got back the day before New Year's Eve and visited Casablanca, which is the most European of all the Moroccan cities, with its panoramic ocean views. They had a wonderful time and came back exhausted. The drive in the desert was quite tortuous, but Julia enjoyed the desert landscape and took quite a number of photos to use as ideas in her paintings later on. Upon their return, she left a note for Carlos at reception saying that they would accept his invitation for New Year's Eve dinner.

Bernard looked good in his dark-colored suit, and he told her that she looked drop-dead gorgeous in a little black number with a plunging back, a slit on the side, and a stunning Ilias Lalaounis necklace (a gift from him on her twenty-seventh birthday). Her flaming hair fell in cascades over her shoulders.

They went up to the roof, and she introduced Bernard to Carlos who, in turn, introduced them to his friends and his older children. The three boys (age 16, 19, and 21) were very good-looking, unlike him, so they must have taken after their mother. The conversation went very smoothly and she was happy that Bernard was enjoying himself. There was an excellent band playing all kinds of dance music and she got up to dance a slow dance with Bernard. Unfortunately, Bernard did not know how to dance the Latin dances very much in vogue in Morocco that year. She was dying to dance those and, if it were in Europe, she would have gotten up and danced by herself, but this was a Muslim country, so she refrained and just did some dance movements sitting on her chair.

Carlos shouted from across the table, "Hey, Luis"—to his oldest son, the twenty-one-year-old—"why don't you ask Julia to dance with you?" and to her, "Luis is a very good dancer, you won't be disappointed. You don't mind, do you Bernard?"

"Of course not, go ahead Julia."

Luis had been very quiet during dinner so she did not know how things would go while dancing with him. He was very attractive, tall, broad-shouldered, with intense dark brown eyes and wavy black hair, long at the nape. She liked what she saw. She got up to dance just when the band was doing a series of intoxicating mambos. Luis just pulled her to him and they started gyrating to the sensuous beat. He was indeed an excellent dancer. They were both unleashed and were performing an incredibly sensual number, *Dirty Dancing* style. He put his hand between her breasts and slid it down to her tummy. This guy was hot. She had not danced this well with a partner since the time when she was with her ex-husband who had also been a very good dancer. She was enjoying herself immensely trying to keep up with him. The band switched to a tango—the "Cumparsito," her favorite tango tune. She was thrilled to be dancing the tango with an Argentinian. They did a very sexy version, her leg coming out of the slit on the side, brushing his leg. He almost grabbed her buttocks in one dance move but restrained himself at the last minute.

Suddenly it was midnight; the lights went off for just two seconds and Luis pulled her to him, bent her backward, and kissed her right smack on her lips, forcing them open with a little tongue action going on. *Wow, what was that all about?* She wondered and was stunned but liked it. She tingled in all the right places. He had a rock-hard body and it felt good, pressed against hers. This was quite a passionate kiss, the likes of which she had not had in years. *It is always better with a stranger,* she thought. The lights came on and she did not know where to look. Her heart was aflutter and she was tittering as he accompanied her back to the table without saying a word.

She caught Carlos' eyes and he was grinning like a Cheshire cat. He winked at her. The old geezer must have guessed how she felt. Was it that obvious? She held his gaze until he looked down on his plate. She then looked at Bernard who looked daggers at her with his ice-cold blue eyes— hurt or jealous, maybe for the first time. He started rearranging the food on his plate. The other guests were fiddling around on their plates also, and the two other sons were looking at each other with raised eyebrows and snickering.

Julia put on a haughty "I don't give a damn" look and sat down demurely in her chair, although she was not calm at all. She thought she was having A-fib and that she would have an attack and collapse any minute; then she would end up in a miserable foul-smelling, germ-infested Moroccan hospital and would probably die of a horrible infection. She collected herself by taking deep breaths and pretended there was nothing wrong. She could feel Bernard's seething rage but this was not apparent to the others. It was a good thing he was not the explosive type, otherwise there would have been a scandal right there at the table. She took a sip of water to calm her nerves and tried to relax and put on a nonchalant air. She dreaded the moment, however, when she would be alone with him. What would he say?

She realized she was attracted to Luis. She took another sip of water and took a sneak peek in his direction. She noticed that he had a naughty glint in his eyes and he winked at her. She smiled discretely and he smiled back. She then looked around to see if anyone had seen them smile. No, they were too stunned by what had transpired on the dance floor to notice anything else. They were still fiddling around with the food in their plates, except for Bernard who was acting very cool and looking at the dance floor at the other dancers as though nothing of importance had taken place. Carlos was shaking his head and chuckling while sipping his wine. There had been no conversation between Luis and herself while dancing, and there would be none now. The only thing she knew was that he was attending university in the United States and was in Morocco to be with his siblings and his father. She had heard Carlos explain to Bernard what his sons did.

Luis was also very attracted to Julia and thought she was quite flirtatious but he knew that he did not stand a chance of going any further. Firstly, because of his age and what with his father devouring her with his foxy eyes and ready to pounce on her, and Bernard suddenly acting very possessive and proprietary toward her, putting an arm around her shoulders, intimating, "This woman is mine, and I am the one who is going to end up in bed with her tonight."

Luis fantasized carrying her off to his lair, where he would strip her down naked and lay her down on the mattress with her flaming hair spread all around her face. He would then open her thighs wide, and she would be offering him her wet pussy. He would caress her and kiss her all over, including the most intimate parts, and she would groan and moan and say, "More, Luis, more, Luis." After several orgasms, they would lie together like a pair of octopi, all legs and arms intertwined.

He woke up from his erotic reverie with a colossal hard-on and heard his father asking him to get up and fetch the waiter who had not yet taken their dessert orders. Well, he could not possibly get up so he asked his younger brother, Eduardo, to go and call the waiter. A rapid conversation in Spanish ensued between them, and Luis informed his brother of his anatomic malfunction and why he could not get up. The brother took a sneak peek in Julia's direction and guffawed. Carlos barked at Luis.

"What the hell is the matter with you, Luis? Go and get the waiter." Eduardo whispered in his father's ear, and Carlos also glanced in Julia's direction and grinned.

Julia guessed that the conversation was somehow related to her. But what was it about? She, on the other hand, had a different fantasy. She visualized Luis sitting next to her, his hand caressing her thigh under the table and going farther up. She felt an electric shock run through her body, imagining this. She was flushed and she quivered. She glanced at Luis but he was no longer looking at her and was busy with his food.

"What's the matter?" asked Bernard, thinking she was shivering. "Don't you feel well?"

"I'm fine, thank you, I suddenly felt cold."

"Do you want my jacket?" the ever-thoughtful Bernard.

"No, thank you. I'll be fine."

The sumptuous dessert arrived, and they ate it in relative silence. Shortly thereafter, everyone wished each other Happy New Year, and Bernard said he was tired and wanted to retire early. They excused themselves and went back to their suite.

When Bernard was nervous, he would try and compose himself by taking deep breaths. That's what he did now upon entering their suite. She braced herself for what was going to come next.

"How come he kissed you?" he asked.

"What do you mean how come? It was midnight on New Year's Eve. People kiss each other at midnight."

"And so you kiss anyone at midnight on New Year's Eve? That was a passionate kiss, not just a little peck. You should not have encouraged him. And all that *Dirty Dancing* stuff that you both performed, copied from the movie, I guess. And then the sensual tango was the icing on the cake. He was feeling you all over, and you were stuck together like superglue. You were now and then brandishing your leg and running it up his thigh. I know that is a tango move, but I was embarrassed looking at you gyrating and almost making love on the dance floor. You seemed to enjoy this sensual exhibition with a complete stranger. I felt very humiliated."

Dancing sensually with a stranger is always exciting, she wanted to say but only said, "It is not that at all. The music was very stimulating, and you know my passion for dancing. I've always been a sucker for Latin music. Just because you don't like that kind of dancing does not mean I should refrain from doing it."

"Actually, you should have been kissing me at midnight. I am extremely upset. I could not believe my eyes. Your behavior was pretty scandalous and outrageous, to say the least. You acted as though I did not exist."

"First of all, I did not kiss him, he kissed me, and secondly, I did not encourage him. It came out of the blue, and thirdly you were not next to me at midnight."

"It was very impertinent on his part kissing you in that passionate manner, knowing you are engaged to me. He disregarded me completely, the arrogant bastard. And the worst part is that you publicly encouraged his behavior. He is an upstart and a cheeky young man who thinks he can get away with anything just because he is young and handsome. I hate to think what Carlos' friends thought of you."

There we go again—what will people think. That's what her mother always asked her when she did something not quite appropriate.

She rolled her eyes. "What was I supposed to do? Create a scandal on the dance floor by pushing him away? Don't tell me you are jealous of a twenty-one-year-old kid? You did not act jealously when, at the party you had in your house last month, your friend Patrick made a pass at me and wanted to have my phone number. In fact, you felt quite proud that another man desired me and you laughed it off when I told you."

"That is not the same. Patrick did not kiss you, he only asked for your phone number."

"Forget this kissing incident, it meant nothing to me," she lied. It had been a very memorable and exciting moment, and she still tingled and felt chills going up and down her spine when she thought about it.

One good thing about Bernard, he never shouted or got verbally abusive. He retained his calm but she knew he was seething inside. They had sex that night, of course, to celebrate the New Year. She fantasized about Luis while having sex and Bernard was very happy with her orgasmic moans.

They packed the next day and left for Geneva. She did not want any more comments about what had happened so she pretended to be asleep on the plane.

He nudged her. "You're very quiet."

"I am very tired, I really don't feel like talking."

"Okay, we won't talk about this incident anymore." She readily agreed. She could not forget Luis, however. She kept thinking about him for days until such time as her life resumed with work and social engagements. She wondered occasionally whether she would ever run into him one of these days, weeks, or years. It was such a far-fetched thought, though.

Soon after Bernard and Julia came back from their Moroccan vacation, Bernard was transferred to Belgium to head a team of experts in labor relations. He suggested that they get married and move to Brussels. Julia did not feel like moving to Belgium; she considered it too dull, too rainy and too provincial compared to the international atmosphere of Geneva and told him that she was not eager to make a move. She suggested that he should go first and see what it was like and that they would commute and then eventually they would take an appropriate decision. Bernard was quite disappointed and tried to entice her with the things she could do there with her artistic career. But Julia was not convinced and did not feel like leaving the cocoon-like atmosphere of Geneva, where she was quite known in artistic circles.

"Where will we go skiing?" she asked. "Where will be go swimming? Here, I have the mountains and the lake. Also, it is too cold and rainy over there and I don't know anyone. I will have to start all over again, make new friends, contacts, etc." Had she really been in love with Bernard, these things would not have been deterrents. But obviously she did not love him enough.

Quite reluctantly, Bernard went by himself and came back every other weekend or she visited him when she felt like it, but their relationship started to fizzle.

"Why don't we get married in the summer?" asked Bernard on one of his weekend trips.

"This summer?"

"Yes, this summer, what other summer are you thinking about?"

Julia did not answer. She had grown distant from Bernard and, somehow, she could no longer envisage marriage to him. She had started to get cold feet and realized that Bernard was really not her type. At the beginning of the relationship, she had thought that he was the perfect choice for a husband—he had all the required credentials, but the lack of passion seemed to weigh on her lately.

"Let's give each other some space," she suggested.

Bernard was heartbroken; he loved this woman, and he did not need any space, but he agreed halfheartedly to her suggestion. He was definitely ready for the plunge and did not understand why Julia was hesitating. He unwillingly agreed that they do not see each other for a couple of months. After that, things did not improve; the relationship was in a tepid state and Julia told Bernard that she had decided against getting married. Bernard was quite surprised by her decision. He did not understand it. He thought that their getting married was a fait accompli. He kept calling her and writing love letters, hoping that she would change her mind, but Julia did not budge from her decision.

"You're right sis," Julia told Caroline, "I am still young so why settle down now. I'll continue looking around." So she started dating other men, but they were all unsatisfactory until she met Jean Claude.

La Belle (the Beauty)

Chapter 3

Jean Claude

During the autumn of that year, Julia met Jean Claude at an art vernissage curated by the PBSU Bank in their fabulous state-of-the-art atrium of their headquarters in Geneva. The bank's functions were always very elegant affairs catered by the best restaurants in Geneva. Besides looking at art, people went to look and be seen. Julia always looked forward to this quarterly, social, artsy-fartsy event to meet new people and prospective clients for her art. This event came at the right time. She had not had a boyfriend for over three weeks now and she was getting antsy. She usually did not dump one before finding a new one, but the last one after Bernard was such a loser that she had to let him go. These past three weeks had been a dry period for her, and she was thirsty—for men, that is. She had not touched a man or been touched by one, and it was about time to remedy that situation.

On this occasion, she dressed up with great care in a sleek short burgundy dress with a plunging V neckline. She looked at herself in the mirror and liked what she saw. She had a trim figure and wore no bra. She went to the vernissage accompanied by two of her girlfriends.

The first thing she did when she entered the magnificent atrium was approach the buffet to get herself a drink; then she started scouring the hall, looking at people and at men, in particular. This was her priority during the evening. The bank's event was the perfect hunting ground. Its important clients were always invited to this function. She was on the prowl and she looked around the already crowded hall for eligible prey. Her eye caught a group of banker-type men and a well-coiffed, meticulously made-up, rather attractive woman in one corner, engrossed in a discussion. She looked the men over and one stood out in particular. He was imposing-looking, tall, broad-shouldered, with sun-streaked brown hair, good profile, and he seemed to exude a lot of power—male power. He was not facing her, however. She had a side view of him, but what she could see looked quite interesting. He could be a plausible candidate to ensnare.

Julia had psychic powers, or so she thought. She had the habit of staring at a person's back and willing him or her to turn and look at her. Her hypnotic powers usually worked and it did this time. The man turned his head sideways in her direction and their eyes met. He had a chiseled face and a strong jaw. She held his gaze while sipping her champagne. He turned back to his group and resumed the discussion. Julia told herself that if he turned around to look at her again, she had him hooked. He did in fact turn and gazed at her. He sort of smiled. She smiled back coyly, then walked over to the hors d'oeuvre table to get something to eat and lingered there, hoping he would follow her.

"That's the guy I want to meet," she told her friend, Laura. Laura was married to a PBSU employee and knew everybody and all the current gossip at the bank and in most of Geneva.

"That's Jean Claude du Barry, a big-shot financial consultant at the bank. He is French, of course, with that kind of name," she said, "and the hawk-eyed woman is his mistress. She is married to Antoine Catala, an important client of the bank, but they have an open marriage. He goes after bimbos, and she also plays around—well, she did until she found Jean Claude. She does not mind her husband's philandering as long as he keeps her in the style she is accustomed to. They have been married for about fifteen years. She's got Jean Claude in her well-manicured claws and, I assure you, you'll never get him away from her. He is a kind of a mystery man at the bank. People never know what he is thinking. He is not transparent. He is considered one of the most eligible bachelors at the bank but, since his wife's premature death about twenty years ago, he has not had a long-lasting relationship with any woman. He has had several short-term meaningless affairs until he met Isabelle Catala. This one seems to be going on for a long time, well, over a couple of years perhaps. Personally, I don't know what he sees in her. Maybe it is because she is considered *safe* and will not want to hook him into marriage as her husband is ten times wealthier than he is. Anyway, don't waste your time, you'll never get him."

"Watch me," Julia said.

From the corner of her eye she saw Jean Claude approach the hors d'oeuvres table. She turned and looked at him. He was indeed very good-looking and commanded presence in a casual way. He was tanned, had deep-set brown bedroom eyes, sculpted lips, and a dimple on his chin. His sideburns were sprinkled with gray. She loved men with dimples on their chins. It made them look vulnerable. There was a crowd at the bar but somehow he managed to squeeze by and stand next to her. While turning around to face him, she was shoved and collided with him and her drink spilled on the floor.

"Oh, I am so sorry," he said. "Let me get you another one." His voice was deep and melodious and his eyes crinkled at the corners.

"I should be the one to be sorry, I turned abruptly," she said, looking up at him.

"No problem."

He got her another drink and introduced himself as Jean Claude du Barry from the bank.

"Julia Chamoun," she said and also introduced her friends who had followed her and were standing around, trying to get drinks.

"How do you like the exhibition?" he asked.

"I just got here. It looks quite interesting from what I've seen so far." Her friend, Grace, said, "Julia is an artist."

"And what kind of art do you do?" asked Jean Claude.

"I mostly paint imaginary couples intertwined, sometimes with child, sometimes with a cat or an apple. It is mostly the Adam and Eve theme. Mind you, I'm not an amateur."

He laughed. "I am sure you're not," he said, appraising her up and down.

"And what is your function at the bank? This is where I do my banking by the way."

"I am a financial consultant to international clients," he responded, "and I am also in charge for curating this exhibition. I owe that position to my passionate interest in art. Also, I collect art from promising artists."

Grace then came out with an asinine statement, "Julia is a promising artist."

Julia brushed Grace's comment aside, "Don't pay any attention to her," she said and looked daggers at her friend. She then told him that she would look around the exhibition and tell him her opinion if he was interested to know.

"By all means. I am interested to hear the opinion of such a charming, promising artist. In fact, I'll go along with you if you want company, and I'll give you the inside information on the artists and their work, if you like."

Would she like that? Of course, she would like it, but she did not readily show her enthusiasm. It was not good practice to show a man she was eager for his company.

"That would be great," she said coyly. "I'd love to hear what the curator has to say."

They walked along and he commented on the various paintings, and she liked the way he spoke and his point of view. This man was very knowledgeable in art and quite charming and witty. He had an overpowering presence, and she got quite enthralled by him. Too bad her two friends were in tow. Somehow, she did not feel free to be on a more personal ground. She wanted to know more about him. Laura had said he was an eligible bachelor. He looked about forty-five. As they were walking from one painting to the other, Julia noticed that the woman who was in his group did not look too happy and was looking at them with piercing eyes. Laura was right; she had him in her claws. She certainly would not give up Jean Claude easily, but Julia was very confident of her power over men. If she wanted this man, she would somehow get him.

After about fifteen minutes or so of looking at the exhibit, Jean Claude took his leave saying that unfortunately he would have to go and mingle with other people, although he was very much enjoying the company of this charming artist. He gave her his card and said, "In case you need my services," and then "Do you have a card?" he asked.

"Yes, of course, here it is," and she handed him her business card with a photo of one of her paintings. Jean Claude put it in his vest pocket and walked away talking to people on the way and the woman, Isabelle, came and joined him.

"Who is that young person you were chatting away with?" she asked.

"She is the daughter of a guy I do business with," he lied. He was not going to tell Isabelle that he had spent time with Julia because he was attracted to her.

Julia looked at Jean Claude's card before putting it in her purse. *That's it?* she asked herself. How was she going to meet him again? She certainly was not going to call him as she did not need his services, not being a hotshot international client. She had given him her card but had not asked him to contact her. *Well*, she thought, *if he is interested in me, he'll contact me*, but she did not want to leave it to chance. She had to strike while the iron was hot. She had never left an opportunity go by in her whole life and this time was no exception. She had sensed his interest in her. She had to do something to encourage him. She went around the hall meeting other people and chatting, but she kept her eye on Jean Claude the whole time. Her friends were talking to her but she was not listening. Her mind was on Jean Claude. She had to do something before she left.

"So what do you think?" asked Laura.

"He is very doable," she replied. "I am interested, and I don't care if he has a woman friend. I will make it happen, you'll see."

Julia noticed that Jean Claude and the woman were in a heated discussion. "Excuse me," she told a group of people she was standing with and walked over to where he was standing and brazenly said, "I congratulate you for having put on such an interesting exhibit. I enjoyed it very much."

Jean Claude introduced Julia to Isabelle.

"I hear your father and Jean Claude are in business together," Isabelle said, appraising her from head to toe in a haughty manner.

Julia was surprised at this comment and arched an eyebrow and looked at Jean Claude who did not flinch. Her father was in Egypt and did not do any business with Jean Claude or Swiss banks as far as she knew.

"Yes, big business," she said and took a sip of her drink not knowing what else to say. It was an awkward moment.

"I plan to look at your website," Jean Claude said.

"I like a man with a plan," Julia said as she wet her upper lip with her tongue and winked at Jean Claude. She noticed that Isabelle looked ready to pounce on her and strangle her for sure. *Who cares? If I want him, I'm going to get him,* she told herself, *Isabelle or no Isabelle.*

Julia had always got the men she wanted. As she had never failed, she had developed a self-assurance. She had a way about her. "Come and get me if you can" was her look. She did not care if they had girlfriends. Wives were another matter. She did not encourage married men. Admittedly she was a big flirt, but she never flirted with married men who lived in Geneva. On the other hand, visiting married men were not out of bounds to just have fun with. She liked being wined and dined. Businessmen did like to fool around and sometimes it was just innocent fun and, at other times, it went further. She never pursued a man openly but somehow aroused his interest to pursue her. After all, man was the hunter and she was not about to take that instinct away from him.

"What was that all about?" asked Isabelle after Julia had walked away. "She is very cheeky, winking at you while I'm standing right next to you."

"I suppose she likes me."

"For God's sake, Jean Claude, she is young enough to be your daughter."

"I wouldn't mind having a daughter. It would not be such a bad idea after all." He continued to tease her while sipping his drink and watching Julia walk away moving her buttocks provocatively in her tight little dress.

"You are gawking and I don't like the way this conversation is going."

"Isabelle, give me some space, for heaven's sake. You always make such a fuss when you see me talking to women. You know very well that our relationship is not exclusive. First of all, you are married, don't forget that, and I don't like it when you get possessive. See you later." And he walked away to mingle with the guests.

A few days passed after the bank function, and Julia eagerly waited for a call from Jean Claude. *Will he call? Of course, he will call. Be positive,* she told herself. She was sure of herself and the impression that she had made. She had felt some positive energy pass between them. And indeed, after about a week, while she was working in her studio, Jean Claude called.

"Allo, Mademoiselle Chamoun, this is Jean Claude du Barry from PBSU, remember we met at the bank exhibit?"

Of course, she remembered. How could she forget? She had been eagerly waiting for this very moment.

"Oh yes, Jean Claude, I can call you Jean Claude, can't I? Please call me Julia."

"And how are you, Julia? I looked at your website, and I liked your paintings, they intrigue me. You have a lot of talent. I would like to see them in person if I may."

Yippee, he was interested. That was the first step.

"Thank you, you're very kind, you can come to my studio/gallery any time you wish." Her studio was in the back of her gallery.

"Could you please give me the address and can I come this afternoon, if it is okay with you?"

That was moving too fast, she thought. Was she ready for him? She wanted to play hard to get, but she decided against it. She was dying to see him again. She took a couple of seconds before replying, "Um, let's see, would 3:00 p.m. suit you?" And she gave him the address.

"I'll be there."

Julia quickly went home, changed clothes, put on a little makeup, and fluffed up her hair.

Jean Claude was eager to meet this young woman again. She appealed to him and he was drawn to her; he did not know why. Granted, she was very attractive, vivacious and a good artist from what he could surmise from her website, but there was something else that he could not put his finger on. She intrigued him. Was she available? He hoped that she was not seriously involved with any man. At 3:00 p.m. sharp, he showed up at her studio with a box of chocolates wrapped up in gold paper with a bronze ribbon.

"Oh, thank you, Jean Claude, you needn't have done this," Julia said, smiling coyly.

He was casually dressed in a light-colored suit with an open-necked shirt and no tie. He looked dashing. His eyes were dreamy. She adored dreamy eyes. *They are a mirror to the soul, and he must have quite a soul with eyes like that,* Julia thought.

"Playing hooky from bank business?" she asked.

"Sort of. I had nothing important lined up for this afternoon, and I was curious to see your paintings after having looked at your website. So here I am. Please show me what you have and what you are working on now."

Julia wanted to make a good impression on him. She showed him her paintings and they discussed them thoroughly. He seemed to be very knowledgeable about techniques and style and genuinely interested. He made a few positive comments going as far as correctly interpreting her feelings while she had painted them. She was impressed. She then offered him coffee "to go with the liqueur chocolates," she said, and made coffee from her espresso machine. What a good idea her sister had had, suggesting that she get such a machine in her studio to be able to offer coffee to potential clients and guests. She had a small corner set up in her gallery with a high table and two barstools, and they sat down and chatted about art and artists. He was indeed very au courant about everything concerning the art world. Julia liked the idea that the men she went out with knew more than her. She felt a little self-conscious though. Did he really think she was good? She was indeed attracted to Jean Claude and felt that the feeling was mutual. Why had he come up with the comment to Isabelle about her father being in business with him? She knew this was a ruse to perhaps assuage Isabelle's doubts regarding the time he spent with her at the vernissage. She did not bring up the subject of her father's fictitious business with him. She did not want to embarrass him. She would comment about his statement some other time when she got to know him a little better.

Before leaving, Jean Claude asked Julia whether she would like to go out to dinner with him sometime.

Yippee, she had him. What about Isabelle though? Wasn't she his attitrée woman friend?

"I would love that," was her reply.

"How about tomorrow, are you free?"

"Actually, I have something planned for tomorrow," she lied, smiling up at him. She did not want him to think that she was available at such short notice.

"When would you be free?" he asked.

"Let me see now," she said, "I'll look up my agenda," and walked to the back of the studio pretending to look up her agenda. There was no agenda at the back of the studio. After a couple of minutes she came back and faced him.

"How about Thursday evening?"

"That would be fine," he said "I'll pick you up at 7:30, then?"

She gave him her home address and they shook hands to say good-bye. "Julia, I really enjoyed looking at your paintings and I have already made a choice to buy one. I'll tell you about it Thursday, or maybe you can guess which one it is."

"I think I can," she said. "We'll talk Thursday."

Julia was excited. Things looked to be very promising. She called up Laura and told her what had transpired.

"I got him, you see?"

"Good luck," said Laura. "I don't know how he will manage this. Is he going to see two women at the same time? Isabelle will surely find out, you know. After all, Geneva is a very small town. People will talk."

"I don't really care. We'll see what happens."

Julia dressed with great care on the evening of her dinner date. She chose a flowing chiffon print dress that matched the color of her red hair and showed off her bosom. She donned high-heel shoes. She was not short, but Jean Claude was very tall and she did not want to appear like a midget next to him. She put little makeup, emphasizing only her eyes, some gloss on her lips and a dab of eau de toilette Joy, her favorite scent. She had to act and appear natural. She did not think men like Jean Claude would go for artificial women, although that Isabelle did not look too natural to her. Well, maybe he was ready for a change.

Jean Claude picked her up in a dark blue BMW which matched his navy blue suit. He had no tie on, and she could see a thatch of hair through the opening of his shirt. She liked men with chest hair. She did not care for the young ones who had the habit of shaving them off. They looked too sleek and shiny. He drove her to a restaurant in Carouge, a quaint, artsy suburb of Geneva.

The setting was quite intimate and informal, which is what she preferred. She disliked sophisticated restaurants with waiters hovering around all the time.

The dinner conversation went very smoothly. Jean Claude told her that he had been with the bank for over eighteen years, had been married quite young, and his wife had died of a rare disease and they had had no children, a fact that he regretted immensely. She could see that he was pained talking about it. He talked to her about bank developments, his travels (he was an avid traveler), liked exotic places, mountain climbing, trekking (the last two she did not go for). He was also very much into French and English literature, movies, classical music, and of course, art (things that interested her). They also discussed skiing and swimming, two sports which she loved. At least there were things they could do together, if this would develop into a relationship.

All in all, things looked very promising to Julia. She then proceeded to tell him a little about herself, her early marriage, her life in New York, subsequent divorce, and her move to Switzerland. Just after dinner Jean Claude told her that he would like to buy the painting entitled "Les Amoureux". He wanted to know how much it cost. She told him the price.

"I'll pick it up sometime next week and will transfer the amount to your bank account. Please give it to me."

She opened her purse and took out a business card on which she scribbled her bank account number and handed it to him.

"What is your ethnic origin?" he asked. "You have a charming accent that I cannot place. I can tell from your last name that you are Middle Eastern, but from where?"

"I am a mixture, Lebanese from my father's side and Greek from mom's side."

"I like Middle Eastern women," he said. "They have big beautiful eyes and captivating smiles and they have a certain oriental mystery about them. You are quite fascinating," he added. His gaze briefly wandered down to her chest, then quickly back up again. Julia caught that.

"Do you know that you have a four-thousand-year-old profile?" he said, making her laugh.

"Yes, I am rather ancient."

The food was very good and Julia enjoyed his company. She was sure he was attracted to her because of the way he looked at her with obvious interest in his eyes. She thought he was almost fawning on her. She knew how to attract men just by looking at them in a certain flirtatious way and by being a very good listener. She was an expert in that domain. Men became infatuated with her because she was pretty and lively. *There is something to be developed here,* she thought, as he led her by her elbow out of the restaurant and to the car. He took her home and accompanied her to the elevator. He gave her a peck on the cheek. "You smell nice," he said and held her hands, looking into her eyes. He had a powerful grip, and she liked that.

"I had a wonderful evening, and I would love to see you again," he said. She expected more physical contact, but she guessed he was taking his time.

"I had a wonderful evening too."

Jean Claude was very taken in by Julia. She had awakened his senses that had been dormant for quite some time now. He felt like touching her and kissing her and taking her to bed right there and then, but he decided to go slow with this woman. He wanted her to desire him as much as he desired her. With any other woman, he would perhaps have made the move but not with this one. She was different and he did not want to frighten her away.

"I'll call you," he said and walked away to his car.

She had almost asked *when* but restrained herself. She did not want him to think that she was eager and easy to get. She wanted him to pursue her. She had always believed that men liked the chase and that they did not like eager beaver women, who were so readily available and tried to leech on to them immediately. She was giddy with excitement at her conquest. This looked like a very good prospective lover and she was eager to try him in bed. She liked his smiling eyes, his sculpted lips and his powerful built. She felt like rubbing herself against his body. How come he did not grab her and kiss her like most men would have done on the first date? She reported the outing to Laura and wanted to know her point of view.

"Well, I suppose he really is interested in you, but I don't know how far it can go. How is he going to handle Isabelle? Is he suddenly going to drop her?"

"I am hoping he will—in fact, I'm positive" said Julia with a laugh.

After a few lunch and dinner dates, they ended up in bed. In a way, she appreciated that he had not rushed her and had taken his time. It meant that he was serious about her. She did not like it when men were too eager and wanted to have sex the very first night. She compared some men to panting dogs in heat. During their dating they had done some mild kissing in the car, but she had never invited him for a nightcap, and he had not suggested that they go over to his place. Julia was a little surprised that he had not made the move to take her there. She had not yet seen his house. According to Laura, Jean Claude lived in a fabulous house in Cologny, the most chic and affluent suburb of Geneva. She was very curious to see it.

Their first time in bed was quite ingeniously orchestrated by Jean Claude. She did not see it coming. When he was driving her home after having had lunch in the country one Friday, he suddenly asked, "How about spending the weekend in Annecy?"

She loved Annecy. It is a quiet, lazy, picturesque town in nearby France, on the border with Switzerland, with a fabulous clean lake, and people from Geneva often went there for day trips or weekends.

"Weekend in Annecy?" she repeated.

"Yes, let's drive there right now."

"Right now?"

"Yes, right now."

"But I don't have anything with me."

"We'll buy what you need over there. Be adventurous, Julia. Don't you like that?"

"I guess I do," she said, but she felt quite embarrassed. They had not even done any heavy petting, and they were going to spend a weekend together? How was that going to work out?

Jean Claude could feel her discomfort. "If it will make you feel more comfortable, we'll take two rooms," he suggested and put his hand on her thigh to reassure her.

"Don't worry too much," he said. "I am not kidnapping you." The touch of his hand was warm and she liked it.

"Okay."

During the rest of the trip, she was silent. A thousand thoughts passed through her head. What if she did not like his lovemaking? It had happened to her once when she was very attracted to a guy but then, after having gone to bed with him, she had not liked his lovemaking and had not wanted to see him again. That had been easy. When he had called, she had pretended she was busy, and he had finally got the hint and left her alone. But spending a weekend? How could she get away if things did not work out? She was excited but felt trapped.

"The cat ate your tongue?" he asked. "I hope I have not made you too uncomfortable."

"No, it is okay as long as we have two rooms," she said and looked at him sideways to see if he really meant it.

"You worry too much," he said, patting her thigh again, and laughed.

They arrived in Annecy, and he took her to a charming boutique hotel and asked for two rooms. The innkeeper was surprised but did not show his reaction.

"Let's go buy what you need," he said after checking into their rooms.

They went to a couple of shops and Julia picked out a nightgown, bathing suit (they planned to go swimming, of course), and toiletries. Jean Claude did not let her pay.

"After all, it was my idea to whisk you off without having you go home first," he said.

She felt like she was his mistress already. She then wondered how come he did not buy anything for himself. She had the answer to her question when they got back in the car; she noticed that there was a duffle bag in the back seat. So this was not so spontaneous after all. *Cunning man, this Jean Claude,* she thought.

They had a wonderful candlelit dinner in Talloires, a tiny resort village next to Annecy, at the renowned Père Bise restaurant, which was in the Michelin guide, then came back to the hotel. Julia felt very apprehensive during the dinner, wondering the whole time what Jean Claude was up to. He accompanied her to her room, drew her toward him and, putting his arms around her, he kissed her gently at first, then quite passionately. He had a rock-hard body, and Julia liked the feel of his arms around her. She closed her eyes, put her arms around his neck and kissed him back. He kissed the hollow of her throat, behind her ears, and stroked her back, running his hands up and down. He had powerful hands, and she felt electric shocks passing all through her body. She had a burning desire to be *taken* by him.

"Sleep well, Julia," he said, letting her go. "If you feel lonely, I am next door," and he winked. She laughed. He walked away. Julia was surprised. She thought he would have come in her room and continue where he left off. She was aroused and wondered how this cat-and-mouse game was going to unfold. She went to bed, took up a book but had a hard time concentrating on what she was reading. She wanted Jean Claude's body and his kisses. After a little while, her phone rang.

"Do you feel lonely?" he asked.

"Not really," she lied, and giggled.

"Well, I have a bottle of Bailey's with me, and I could come over and we could have a digestive. Would you like that?"

Would she like that, what a silly question, but she did not want to sound too eager. "I like Bayley's" was all she said.

"I'll be good, I promise you, I won't pounce on you, you don't have to worry. I'll keep my hands at my sides."

"I am not worried, but I have a faint suspicion that you're lying," she said and felt giddy with anticipation.

A few minutes later, he knocked on her door. She put on the bathrobe provided by the hotel over her nightgown and opened the door. He was in a pair of jeans and a T-shirt and was carrying the bottle of Bailey's and two glasses in one hand. He looked so handsome and desirable. She resisted the impulse to hug him. He put the bottle and glasses down on the table next to the door and closed the door with his foot. He held out his arms to her.

"Come here," he said, and she went to him. He embraced her.

"Um, you feel good," he said. He held her at arm's length and just looked at her with desire in his eyes; then he pulled her toward him again and crushed her against him. They kissed quite passionately, and Julia had to free herself to get some air. He made her feel breathless.

"Aren't you hot with this bathrobe?" he murmured in her ear.

"I guess I am."

"Let's take it off then," he suggested and untied the belt. She sighed. He removed it from her shoulders, and it slid down to the floor. She was in the skimpy nightgown that they had picked out together at the lingerie shop. He crushed her to him again and his mouth came hungrily down on hers. "I love your scent," he murmured in her ear. She felt her nipples harden against his chest. It felt so good to be in his arms. They were so powerful; she felt like a limp doll. He held her face in his hands and kissed her again and again. She returned his kisses and entwined her fingers through his wavy hair.

"I've wanted to do this from the very first moment I saw you." His lips then nibbled her earlobes as his hands caressed her body. She loved the feel of his warm, exploring hands. She was almost purring like a cat.

"But I won't insist and I won't pressure you. The ball is in your court. If you don't want to, I'll stop right here and go and take a cold shower."

His sheer sexual energy and virility were overpowering but she did not say anything; she just looked at him provocatively. She returned his kisses, matching his ardor. Her decision was obvious; she wanted him also. She could feel the warmth of his skin through his cotton T-shirt. He stroked her with a lingering slowness, arousing her even more. She felt herself floating.

"Oh Julia, Julia," he kept repeating while caressing her body; then he held her at arm's length as his gaze followed the outline of her breasts against the thin fabric of her nightgown. They were so inviting. He glided his hands up and down her arms brushing his thumbs against her nipples while doing so. She let out a sigh and drew her head back. He then kissed her neck and the hollow of her throat and cupped her breasts and fondled the hard nipples through the thin fabric of her nightgown. Her breath drew in sharply and shivers ran up and down her spine. He felt her shudder and he lowered the straps of her nightgown to expose her breasts. Her nipples were erect, and he looked at them with unabashed desire.

"Your nipples look so sweet and pink, just like pearls." His voice was husky. He took one, then the other, in his mouth and nibbled them. Electric shocks went through her body, and she dug her nails into his back. He drew her closer; his body was hard and virile, and she could feel his manhood pressing against her belly. With one swift movement, he picked her up and lay her down on the bed and continued caressing and kissing her face, her lips, her throat, her breasts, sucking and pulling at her nipples. He then took off his shirt, and she caressed his muscular shoulders, arms and his smooth back. He had such a powerful body, and she felt herself drowning in the heat that radiated from it. His warmth enveloped her and she wanted to stay in his arms forever.

Jean Claude felt his excitement rising with Julia's youthful body lying next to his. It set him on fire but he took his time. He wanted their first time to be slow and languorous. He lowered her nightgown down to her hips and pulled it off her. She had her panties on, but nevertheless, she felt completely naked as his eyes devoured her. He kissed her breasts and his lips travelled down to her belly button. He rubbed his cheek on her belly then ran his hands down her stomach, sliding his fingers inside her panties and stroked her sex gently. He took her panties off slowly, and his lips played with her pubic hair. She was moist. She sighed and her nails dug into his shoulders.

"Please turn off the light," she said. "I feel self-conscious. You are staring at me. I feel like an object in a China shop."

"You are indeed. You can't imagine how desirable you are," he said, his eyes full of lust, "You don't know the power you have over me," and turned off the light. Her eyes shone in the semidarkness, and he felt completely under their spell.

She could feel his hard sex against her body. He wanted her to yield, and she did as his hands and mouth were all over her, kissing and caressing her passionately in all the intimate places. He was obsessed with the smell and touch of her skin. It was so smooth, silky and tantalizing. She was such an enticing woman and he was intoxicated by her sensuality and femininity.

Julia was also extremely aroused and rested her face against his chest to feel his warmth. She loved his masculine smell, mixed with lavender soap, was it? He had such strong hands, yet his touch was so gentle. He slowly parted her thighs and kissed her sex. "You are so wet," he said and started licking it and darting his agile tongue in and out of it and gently biting her flesh while kneading her breasts. She was whimpering and digging her fingers into his powerful shoulders. She moaned and arched her back, rubbing her breasts against his chest; he kissed her nipples again and again with a hunger that made her squirm with desire, and it brought her almost to an orgasm. She was whimpering. His sexual expertise overwhelmed her. His touch was gentle yet commanding. No man had ever made her feel like this. She was almost melting and was completely powerless in his embrace. She wanted him to possess her.

Jean Claude loved to watch Julia's face as he gave her pleasure.

"Are you okay?" he asked.

"Yes," she groaned and climaxed with a moan.

He then removed his trousers and his shorts, took out a condom from a pocket, put it on, and entered her very gently at first, stopping himself intermittently, prolonging his pleasure, moving in a circular motion then his thrusts became rhythmic and forceful and he went in deep, his movements going faster and faster until he climaxed with a wild groan. He collapsed beside her and hugged her.

"You're adorable," he said. "Where have you been all my life?"

She just held on to him and rested her head in the crook of his shoulder, breathing in his masculine scent. He was so cozy, like a teddy bear. His broad chest was so inviting, and his embrace so protective that Julia never wanted to get out of bed. She felt like a cat, and she almost purred.

"Are you okay?" he asked her again. She liked that he was so considerate about her well-being. She was more than okay. She was in heaven.

"I have been fantasizing about you ever since I met you," he said, "and the reality is better than my fantasy. At the vernissage, your dress with the slit V neckline was so tantalizing that I had a hard time taking my eyes away from your chest. I wanted to put my hand in there and grab one of your breasts and watch your shocked reaction."

"I feel fine," she whispered and buried her hands in his hair. They slept together that night.

She rarely slept with a man after making love for the first time, but she wanted to this time. It was a strange feeling for her. She usually asked them to leave after sex, but it was different with Jean Claude. She wanted him to stay. When she woke up in the morning, she noticed that he was spooning her with one hand on her left breast. She tried to pry it away to get up.

"Leave it there," he said. "Something is coming alive."

"We'll see about that," she said. "Let me go to the bathroom first. I don't think that the something will die soon."

She came back in bed into his waiting arms and they came together with an unbridled passion that exhausted them both. Jean Claude was an expert lover and phenomenal in foreplay. He knew exactly what to do to arouse her. She felt like a musical instrument in his hands and felt extremely fortunate for having found him. Sex with him was so very gratifying. It was the best ever. He took his time in foreplay and he gave her pleasure before his own gratification. He did not jump on her bones like some guys whose only thought had been of penetrating her as soon as possible. She had finally found the man she was looking for. She was sure he would be good husband material. That was important to her. Bernard would have been a devoted husband and father too, but he lacked the passion of Jean Claude. She was glad she had not married Bernard after all. Jean Claude was the man for her. Was Isabelle going to be a problem though? Finding the right partner had been very difficult. Her quest had been time consuming, and success was not guaranteed, up until now. She had almost given up. But the impossible had happened and she had found Jean Claude. She was absolutely sure, without any doubt, that he was The One. She reveled in her good luck.

"Is she your woman friend?" she asked out of the blue.

"What?"

"You heard me. Is she your woman friend?"

He knew she was talking about Isabelle. "Do I have to answer that right now?"

"Yes."

"Sort of."

"What do you mean sort of. It's either yes or no."

"Yes."

"Then what are you doing with me?"

"Isn't it obvious?" and he started playing with her pubic hair. "I am cheating on her."

"All men are sneaks and cheats," she said and laughed. She ran her hands down his chest and offered him her pouted lips. He came down on them and kissed her hungrily while stroking her womanhood.

"You have bewitched me," he said.

"So what's your next move?" she asked.

"My next move is to devour you," he said.

"I'm not kidding, what's your plan with Isabelle, Mr. Plan Maker? Am I going to be a mere diversion?"

"Don't worry your pretty little head. You'll never be my diversion or anyone else's diversion, I can guarantee that. I'll take care of it. What about you? How come you're available and don't have a boyfriend, or are you cheating on him? A beautiful woman like you cannot possibly be without a man."

"I left my last boyfriend a few weeks ago. I had no one when I met you. You got me when I was free and available. Aren't you lucky?"

Jean Claude decided then and there that he had to get rid of Isabelle. Their relationship was only a convenience to him and lately it had been very strained anyway, and he had wanted to distance himself from her. His meeting Julia came at a very opportune moment.

They had breakfast in bed and, before leaving the hotel to go sightseeing, Julia told Jean Claude that it was ridiculous to be paying for a second room if he wasn't going to use it. "I like a practical woman," he said and told the reception clerk to cancel the second room for that night. The clerk wondered what game this couple was playing. He had seen plenty of games during his career at the hotel.

They went to the lake again, took a pedalo (floating raft) and went to swim far out. They kissed in the water and fondled each other and acted like two mischievous kids. He did not seem to get enough of her. After lunch they went to an antique market in another town close by, bought a few trinkets, had dinner there and came back to the hotel. They went straight to bed for their last sexual tryst of the weekend.

Jean Claude had not enjoyed himself so much with a woman for a long time, actually since the death of his wife. He had had all these mindless sexual romps with lots of women but his heart and senses had never been involved. Julia was so feminine and captivating and so sensual in bed that she had brought out his own sensuality, which had been stifled and hidden all these years.

Sunday morning was spent at the lake again; then it was time to return to Geneva. It had been a wonderful weekend. Julia was ecstatic. She had to tell Laura all about it.

"Did you enjoy yourself *bichette*?" he asked.

"Of course, I did. You had a very good idea to whisk me off to Annecy to get me to bed. Your two-room suggestion was only a ploy to get me to accept going away wasn't it, admit it. You knew we would end up in one room and in one bed. You had your bag already in the car. Were you so sure that I would accept going?"

"I was not sure at all, but I succeeded, didn't I? That was the only way to get you. I'll call you tomorrow," he said as he dropped her off in front of her apartment and kissed her good-bye. "I hate leaving you," he said, embracing her.

"Me too." She couldn't believe her luck. She needed a couple of days to assess the situation.

She needed space. Too much of a good thing all the time would lose its spontaneity and kill desire. She hoped he would understand this and not ask to see her every day. Nevertheless, she decided that Jean Claude was a keeper. She also had to talk about her good fortune to her sister who was away on vacation.

The following week, they went out a few times around Geneva and then to his house, where she spent the night a couple of times. Jean Claude's house was beautiful; it was nestled against a slope and quite private. It was full of art, paintings and sculptures. It was a very masculine place, quite sparsely furnished except for the art. It had a swimming pool and Jacuzzi where they sipped wine and frolicked. Surprisingly she did not find any tell-tale signs of Isabelle at his house. She wondered whether he had talked to her and broken up with her.

Jean Claude had not called Isabelle since he had come back from Annecy and had avoided her phone calls. He knew he had to deal with her soon but waited, thinking perhaps she would get the hint and not pursue him.

In the meantime, Isabelle had found out that he had been seeing that artist girl. Geneva was a small town and word got around at the tennis club, where they were both members. People were gossiping. She was furious. She was going to give him a piece of her mind.

Complications

CHAPTER 4

Jean Claude and Isabelle

Soon after coming back from Annecy, Jean Claude decided to put an end to his relationship with Isabelle. He had never been entirely satisfied with the arrangement anyway. It had just been a convenience. After his wife had died, he had been very depressed and had had several unsatisfactory relationships. The women were either too eager to get married or he did not care for them enough. He went from one woman to the other having mindless sex. He then met Isabelle who was the wife of a very wealthy BPSU client. Her husband had mistresses and Isabelle was left to tend for herself so she also played the field. She did not mind her husband's philandering as long as she was kept in style. Jean Claude had met her at the tennis club, where they were both members. She had made the first move. The husband's peccadillos were common knowledge at the club so Jean Claude went along with her advances. He thought she was fair game as the husband did not care one way or the other.

She was quite good-looking in a flashy sort of way, was fun to be with, and men were attracted to her. She also played a mean game of tennis. It was easy to start a thing going with her. And he was sure she would not want to divorce her husband and give up her luxurious lifestyle for a banker whose financial worth was much less than her husband's. He had been seeing Isabelle for over two years now, and lately he had begun to feel that she was getting more and more possessive. He had made it clear to her from the start that there would be no future with him. But Isabelle was very stubborn, and Jean Claude knew that it was not going to be easy trying to tell her that their affair was over. He knew she would not let go quietly, that he was sure of. There would be war.

She had called him a few times after he came back from Annecy, but he had found excuses—too much work—for not being able to see her. He avoided going to the tennis club so as not to have a confrontation over there until he was ready to do so. But with Julia in the picture now, it was no use procrastinating any longer. He decided he would have to call her soon. The tennis club was their meeting place and they had many friends there. Some of their friends had seen Jean Claude and Julia together and were suspecting that things were not going well with him and Isabelle. They gossiped and rumors of Jean Claude's liaison with Julia reached Isabelle's ears. She was furious.

About a couple of weeks after getting back from Annecy, Jean Claude came home after a very harrowing day at PBSU. They had had a highly confidential meeting to discuss the latest IRS demands concerning Swiss banks and their important American clients. He could not postpone the confrontation with Isabelle any longer and decided to call her the very next day, meet for coffee, and break up with her. He was very tired that evening and wanted to take a hot shower and go to bed. His doorbell rang. He looked through the peephole, and there was Isabelle. Speaking of the devil. He opened the door and she barged in like a fury.

"So you are having an affair with that two-bit artist woman. For how long do you think you were going to keep it a secret from me? Everyone at the tennis club is talking about it. How does that make me feel? I feel like a discarded piece of rag."

"Actually, Isabelle, I was going to call you tomorrow to talk about ending our relationship."

"You want to end our relationship after almost two years, just like that, because you are having a roll in the hay with this Julia girl who is young enough to be your daughter?"

"No, it's not just like that. I have been thinking about it for quite some time now and I have realized the futility of our affair. Admit it, it was never serious, it was just a need we were fulfilling in each other."

"Nonsense, I don't believe that." She walked past him into his bedroom and threw herself on his bed.

Jean Claude followed her and asked, "What are you doing?"

"I will lie on your bed in your favorite position for your favorite pastime." And she took off her coat under which she was stark naked and lay down on his bed with her arms outstretched and spreading her legs wide open, exposing herself.

"Come and lie next to me Jean Claude, and I will give you a good time as usual. Forget that skinny broad."

Jean Claude was shocked and looked at Isabelle, at her large enhanced boobs with the dark aureoles and large erect nipples, and glanced down to see that she had completely shaved her pussy. Isabelle started playing with herself.

"You have always liked me to play with myself while you watched. It made you horny, so come over," she coaxed.

A sudden wave of disgust came over Jean Claude and, very calmly, he said, "Isabelle, don't do this, it is very undignified. Please put your coat on and leave." He could not stand the sight of her lying there naked, violating his space. He could not understand how he had had a liaison with that woman for such a long time. Had he been blind? But then she had not always been like this. He felt revolted and disgusted with himself. He was thoroughly pissed.

"What, what's come over you? Don't you want to have some raw sex? You always did. You never had enough of it. You always panted for more."

"No, Isabelle, I don't want any sex, raw or otherwise. I am asking you to please leave."

She got up then in a huff and came and stood in front of him pressing her naked body against his. "You have a temporary condition of being smitten by that two-bit artist. It will pass, I assure you," and she put her hand inside his trousers to grab his penis. Jean Claude pushed her hand away brusquely.

"What is the matter with you? You used to come to me like a horny dog in heat and were all over me, begging for kinky sex, and I did accommodate you very generously. Have you forgotten?"

"Stop it, Isabelle," said Jean Claude, pushing her firmly away.

She then slapped him. "Don't you dare push me away and discard me like a used rag."

Very calmly and, without losing his temper, Jean Claude grabbed her coat and gave it to her.

"We are finished. I was temporarily insane hooking up with you, and I realize the stupidity of my actions, but now I have come to my senses, and it is over. I do blame myself, and I apologize. We are finished, Isabelle. Finito. Try to get over it. I am sure you can find plenty of other men to accommodate you."

Isabelle was almost foaming at the mouth and spat at him. She then put on her coat.

"It is not over as far as I am concerned. You have not seen the end of this. You will regret your actions, you'll see," and she walked out the door.

Jean Claude wiped the spittle from his face, tore off his clothes and cursed to himself. *What a horrible and stupid mess I got myself into,* he thought. *How on earth did I ever get involved with this woman?*

When Isabelle, a married woman with a sort of open marriage, had presented herself to him after his many failed unsuccessful relationships, he had thought that she was the perfect solution. A woman married to a wealthy philanderer would not likely give him any problems. The sex had been good and she was a good companion, quite witty and a lot of fun. In any case, he had never wanted to get married again. The death of his wife had been too painful. But this situation was even worse than some unmarried woman pursuing him. This was a woman scorned. He realized how wrong he had been to have hooked up with her. He should have seen it coming. He had been too busy with work to pay much attention. She had been very convenient, with no strings attached. And the husband had not presented to be a problem because he had been too busy pursuing his bimbos.

He went in the shower and stayed a long time under the hot water, trying to get rid of all memories pertaining to Isabelle. He had a hard time erasing his folly. First of all, he realized that he did not like sexually aggressive women, did not like big tits and did not like shaved pussy either. Wow, a lot of dislikes. How come he had gone for them? Temporary insanity, that's what it was. He craved for Julia and her delicate, lithe, feminine body, her silky skin, and her discreet feminine odor.

He got rid of the bedcover on which Isabelle had lain, and threw it on the floor. He reminded himself to get rid of it first thing the next day. He flopped down in between the sheets and thought of Julia and yearned for her. He picked up the phone and called her.

"Hello," he said, "I had a horrible day and wanted to hear your voice." He sounded very tired and his voice was cracked.

"Oh, hello, Jean Claude, are you okay? You sound funny."

"I'm fine. Would you like to have dinner at my place tomorrow? I'll come and pick you up after the office. It will be around seven. Why don't you stay over the weekend? Bring a few things with you. I miss you."

"Miss you too, see you tomorrow. Sweet dreams."

"Ciao, my darling, sleep well."

He picked her up the next day, embraced her tenderly then he kissed her passionately inhaling her scent. He drove her to his home. His *employée de maison* had laid out a very nice table on the terrace. There was a fresh vase of *fleurs des champs* and candles on the table.

Jean Claude put some Chopin on the stereo and got a bottle of chilled white wine from the fridge. They sat on the terrace and sipped the wine. The gentle evening breeze and the music were very soothing. The stars glistened in the pitch-dark sky and Julia's eyes had silvery glints in them as she looked at him. They mesmerized him.

"You don't look too well," remarked Julia. "Is anything wrong?"

"I broke off with Isabelle yesterday. It was ugly."

"Do you regret it?"

"Are you kidding? It's the best decision I have ever made. I have you, and that's all I want."

Julia looked at him lovingly and patted his hand.

"That's what I like to hear," she said.

Jean Claude had the uneasy feeling that Isabelle would create trouble. He did not want to burden Julia with his misgivings. Their dinner consisted of a scrumptious salad, baked salmon with veggies and tiramisu for dessert.

"Blanca is a good cook," Julia remarked.

"She is priceless."

They made plans for the weekend and the coming week, and Jean Claude started to unwind. He felt so good with Julia.

After dinner they lay together on the large hammock on the terrace, just gazing at the stars and kissing intermittently and tenderly touching each other. They lay together for a long time, listening to the music and caressing each other. Eventually Jean Claude became more ardent in his embraces and his fingers started toying with the buttons of her blouse. He inserted a hand in her bra and he could feel her nipples harden at his touch. She moaned faintly and arched her back. He brought his mouth down on her breasts.

"I can't sit still when I am next to you," he said and carried her over to his bed. He lay her down devouring her with his eyes. She looked so desirable with her flaming hair spread out on the pillow. He liked her air of abandon. She reached out and touched his face, looking at the intensity of the desire in his eyes. They tore their clothes off and he caressed her bare flesh tenderly with his lips travelling up and down her body. She felt tremors going through her thighs. He brought his head down and hungrily kissed her wet sex. Her spasms grew more intense and she gingerly touched the tip of his penis. He took her hand away and entered her gently at first, then more feverishly until they both climaxed at the same time. They were both drained physically and fell asleep in each other's arms until the following morning, when they made love again.

Julia spent the whole weekend at Jean Claude's house. They swam in the pool and frolicked in the Jacuzzi and watched TV. He was reluctant to part from her but had to take her back on Sunday evening because he had an early meeting at the bank in the morning.

Reflections

CHAPTER 5

Julia and Isabelle

Isabelle was seething when she came out of Jean Claude's house. *He cannot treat me this way. I'll fix both their asses. I have to think of a way where I can hurt him most and take her out definitely,* she told herself.

She had forgotten Julia's last name but, by asking around, she found out her phone number and the location of her studio. She had to talk to her and get her out of the picture. No one was going to get Jean Claude away from her. It's not as though she loved him, but he was convenient to have as a lover and she enjoyed his company and the sex. And now this bitch of an artist had come and spoiled her cushy existence. She had to put an end to this before it got too serious. She had quite a few sleepless nights but then decided on a mode of action. She was going to confront Julia and tell her to lay off her man. She called her.

"Mlle Chamoun?"

"Yes, who is this?"

"This is Isabelle Catala, we met at the BPSU vernissage, remember?"

"Oh yes, of course."

"Jean Claude has been talking so much about your art, I'd like to see it too. Could I visit your studio some time? Do I have to make a rendezvous?"

Julia was taken aback. She never expected this. She did not think Jean Claude would have talked about her. *There was something wrong here,* she thought. *This woman was up to something fishy. But what?*

"No, you don't have to make a rendezvous. My studio is open in the afternoons. I am closed on Sundays."

"May I come now?"

"Yes, of course, you know where it is?"

"Yes, I do, *tout de suite,* then."

Julia was perplexed. What did this visit mean? She did not like it at all. This woman had sized her up and down during the vernissage, and she could tell that she did not like the fact that Jean Claude had spent time with her then. Jean Claude had told her during their weekend that he had broken off with her. Or was he continuing on seeing her? Julia was disturbed at the thought. Had Jean Claude lied to her? She did not look forward to this visit.

A half hour later, Isabelle sauntered in the gallery, dressed to kill and, after initial greetings, she said, "We both know why I am here."

Julia feigned ignorance. "No, actually I don't."

"I am here to tell you to lay off Jean Claude. He belongs to me and nobody takes away what belongs to me."

Oh-oh, thought Julia, *this woman means business.* "I think you have come to the wrong place, Mrs. Catala, and you're talking to the wrong person. You'll have to talk to Jean Claude to find out whether he wants to be one of your belongings."

"You two-bit slut. You think you can take him away from me? Who the hell do you think you are? Jean Claude and I have a long history together. We belong to each other. He may have strayed temporarily, but I assure you it is very temporary."

"I tend to disagree with you, and I will ask you to leave now. I have only one thing to tell you, Mrs. Catala, go take care of your marriage."

"My marriage has nothing to do with this. My husband and I understand each other, we have an open marriage, everyone knows that, so don't you start threatening me."

Julia was shaking inside but appeared very calm and went resolutely to open the door of the gallery. "I have nothing to discuss with you, so please leave now and don't ever come back."

"I will leave but not before warning you that if you do persist in seeing Jean Claude, some very bad things will happen to you." And she walked away clicking her high heels in a self-assured manner.

The encounter had perturbed Julia immensely and her heart was pounding. She hated this woman and her haughty airs. She meant trouble, big trouble. How could Jean Claude ever have been involved with this type of woman? She did not know what to do. Should she call Jean Claude and tell him what had transpired? Had she read him right? Did he really mean it when he told her he had broken off with Isabelle? Or was he just saying it and wanted to keep her on the side? She decided to call him and get things out in the open. She picked up the telephone. She was breathless and agitated on the phone. She was told that he was in a meeting and could not be disturbed, so she left word that he call her back. She was scared stiff of Isabelle who had looked capable of eating her alive.

Jean Claude called after about an agonizing hour's wait.

"Julia, what is so urgent? I was told you were very distraught on the phone."

"Jean Claude, please come quickly, something happened. Isabelle came by to see me and she started to—" She could not finish the sentence and started crying on the phone.

"Julia, please calm down, I will be right over."

He rushed to the gallery, breaking the speed limits in town, and was there within fifteen minutes. Julia was so glad to see him. She ran into his arms and hugged him, crying uncontrollably. He embraced her and stroked her hair, trying to soothe her.

"What happened, Julia? Talk to me." Julia then told him about her encounter with Isabelle. Jean Claude cursed under his breath.

"Julia, calm down, I will fix things, don't worry. You do believe that I broke off with her, don't you? She can't hurt you and will never hurt you, I promise." He patted her back and comforted her. Julia felt relieved and tried to calm down.

How dare she threaten her? Jean Claude resolved to take matters into his hands right there and then. *She cannot do this to Julia, I will not allow it.*

Julia felt so protected by this adorable man. She loved him so much, as much as she could love any man. She, who had thought that she would never meet a man she could really fall in love with, had in fact found him. She felt reassured and confident.

"I am so afraid," she said.

"Just don't worry, okay? I'll come over later tonight after I take care of this matter."

He left her, went back to the office, called Isabelle and asked to see her at a coffee shop near her house. Isabelle guessed Julia had talked about her visit and she was prepared for a showdown with Jean Claude. When she entered the coffee shop, she saw that he was already seated at a corner table in the back and was sipping his coffee. He got up to greet her and pulled back a chair for her.

"So have you come to your senses, Jean Claude?"

"Yes, I have come to my senses and I am here to tell you once and for all that I am through with you for good. How dare you threaten Julia the way you did? Who do you think you are? I am warning you, Isabelle, if I ever hear that you have harmed her or have anybody harm her in any way, I will divulge to the IRS all the secret bank accounts that your husband has all over the world. You are both American citizens besides being Swiss, don't forget. As you probably know, the IRS has demanded that American citizens worldwide declare all their offshore bank accounts. As you very well know, your husband has not done so and he risks very big penalties. I know you love money more than anything in the world and that you would not want to give up your lifestyle. Your husband risks losing a big chunk of his money in penalties if I divulge his holdings, so think twice before taking any action against Julia. I have two words for you. Lay off." And with that said, he paid for the coffee and got up and left.

Isabelle was stunned. She realized she had lost him forever. Well, she would find other fish to fry. Jean Claude was not the only man in town. He was right, she could find plenty to replace him. What she did not like is that she had lost face at the tennis club, where they were known to be a couple. *What the hell, shit happens,* she thought. She would take a lengthy vacation and be away for a while and find another lover when she came back or maybe even meet someone on her holiday. Who knows? She would handle this humiliation. It was not the end of the world.

Promesse (Promise)

CHAPTER 6

Julia and Jean Claude

Julia and Jean Claude became an item in Geneva. They went out for dinner, to the movies, to art and antique shows; he taught her quite a bit about antiques. He introduced her to his friends. They made a handsome couple and her friends envied her, while his friends thought Jean Claude may be doing the wrong thing going out with such a young woman. They pulled his leg telling him he was robbing the cradle because Julia looked so very youthful. His friends thought she was in her early twenties. They also thought that it was a midlife crisis for Jean Claude and that the relationship would not last. "She is thirty-six," he told them. "Fifteen years difference is not a hell of a lot."

"And what about Isabelle?" Matt, his best friend, asked. All his friends knew that after his wife's death, Jean Claude had been playing the field and had not had a serious relationship with any woman. They guessed that Isabelle had been a convenience, being already married and not in the market to hook him into marriage.

"I'm through with Isabelle, it was a temporary aberration. I am keeping Julia. She is the best thing that has happened to me in a very long time," he told Matt. "I feel alive again, exhilarated and rejuvenated. She has such a vibrant personality and is so different from any other woman that I have known. She keeps me on my toes. I am in love again, Matt. I did not think that would ever happen to me again."

They went on long weekends to Paris, London, Rome, and spent a week in Tuscany, at the beach, and explored quaint little towns. She was eager to go on skiing trips with him in the winter. He had been the junior champion of Switzerland and could have trained for the Olympics had he not had a very serious accident that had prevented him from pursuing his passion on the slopes. She could not believe her luck that she had actually found a guy that she loved and loved being with him. She was never bored.

She introduced him to her mother, her sister and her brother. They all liked him, so did her sister's overcritical lawyer husband. They all came to the conclusion that Julia had finally met her mate and that she would settle down and stop her constant wanderings.

"Don't mess this up," her sister told her. "He seems like a very decent, mature man who, I can tell, adores you. You have no time to waste anymore if your dream is still to have a family and children. I hope you won't discard him like you usually do when you see someone else on the horizon. Be content with what you have. You have found The One, I hope." Yes, indeed, she had.

Jean Claude introduced her to a gallery in Carouge, which was called Galerie Bleu, and she had an exhibition there with all imaginary ocean themed paintings. The title of the exhibition was *Blue Reveries*. The gallery looked like a fish tank. It was a great success, and clients started pouring in.

Summer and autumn seemed to float by and, when winter came, they went to Crans-Montana, an exclusive ski resort in Switzerland, for a long weekend to ski with the first snow of the season. Jean Claude was an excellent instructor and her skiing improved. They usually skied in the morning, had a late lunch up on the slopes, then took a nap, went for a stroll in the afternoons, went for drinks, then on to dinner.

As they were lying down in bed the first night, naked under the covers, in front of the TV after having had sex, Jean Claude got up and said, "I have a surprise for you." Jean Claude never paraded nude in front of her. She liked that about him. He was not an exhibitionist. He put a towel around his waist and went toward the bureau.

She watched and admired his back and his broad shoulders—he did not have an ounce of fat on his body. He went to the dresser, opened the top drawer and picked up a small package and came back to bed, holding it behind his back.

"What is it?"

"You'll see."

He then took her in his arms, looked deep into her eyes, and popped up the question, "Will you marry me, Julia?"

"Wow, Jean Claude, what's this all about?"

She had been waiting for this but had not shown any eagerness. She had not wanted him to think she was pursuing him. Men liked to do the chasing, so she had left him at his pace. Of course, she wanted to marry him. That had been her plan all along. She was finally in love with a man who was husband material and, she was sure, would be a great father material also, and she enjoyed his company very much. He treated her with respect, was very considerate and kind, made a very good living, and was an excellent lover, and she was never bored with him. What else did she want? He then opened the little black box and presented her with an engagement ring. It was a gorgeous ring, twin emeralds surrounded by pear-shaped diamonds set in white gold.

"I bought the emeralds in Brazil on my latest business trip and had the ring made in Geneva. Hope you like it."

"It is absolutely beautiful. Of course I like it and of course I'll marry you. When?" And she hugged him.

"Whenever you want."

"Okay, let's see, how about after my father manages to get out of Egypt and joins us, which I hope will be soon." (Her father had problems getting out of Egypt because of the regime.) He put the ring on her finger and they kissed. Then she got up, wrapped herself up with a towel and pranced around the room giddy with joy.

"Take off the towel," said Jean Claude. "I like seeing you dancing around naked."

"If you see me naked all the time, you'll get bored with my body."

"The day I'll get bored seeing you naked is the day that I am dead."

She flopped down next to him on the bed and gave him a wet kiss. She was like a child with a new toy. He liked that about her. She then nestled against his shoulder and he hugged her. She closed her eyes and brushed her body against his.

"You are like a cat," he said. "You want to be caressed all the time, and I love doing it."

"Yes, I am like a cat. You've made me very happy. I have to call my sister and tell her the news." She got up to do so then she changed her mind. "It can wait till we get back."

She then lay face down on the comforter, and he massaged her back. He ran his hands down her back to her gleaming buttocks and kneaded them then he bit them.

"You have the most gorgeous ass. I want to pinch it but I can't, it's so damn firm," he said, "the best ass in Geneva." He kissed the nape of her neck, and his lips travelled down her spine to the small of her back and down to her sex. He adored her femininity. He kissed her warm flesh, and she squirmed with pleasure.

"Is that why you are marrying me?" she asked, "because of my ass?"

"Yup, that's one of the reasons, the other being you have the most perky breasts with the most delicious pink nipples. And, of course, you have the most tantalizing, sultry, almond shaped eyes. Other than that, you are just ordinary," and they laughed and played around. They kissed again and again. They were both insatiable. She liked lying in abandon and having him play with her body and kissing her in the most intimate places. She whimpered with pleasure as he took her from behind. His penis pressed against her G spot. It was a different sensation.

Yep, life was good, very good indeed, she thought when she woke up the following morning, looking at Jean Claude peacefully sleeping next to her. She liked watching him asleep. He looked so vulnerable yet very masculine. She bent down and gave him a kiss. "Hm," he muttered, "continue." She stroked his face, his chest, and his arms, giving him little kisses here and there. She loved his muscular body, his back, his shoulders and his masculine odor.

"Come here you witch," he said. "I want to possess all of you. Would you like an erotic massage before I devour you?"

"I always like a massage, but an erotic one, I don't know, I've never had one." So she lay down on her back with her arms above her head, fully naked and exposed, while he worked on her body. She had lost all her inhibitions with him by now. He started with her face, neck, then her arms, stroking and kissing them, then his hands came down to her breasts. He massaged them and flipped her nipples with his thumb and forefinger, and took them between his lips, licking and biting them very slowly, sending her to ecstasy. He moved down to her belly button, which he also kissed; his hands then roamed down the inside of her thighs while she was squirming with desire. His tongue explored her mound, and she writhed and groaned clutching his arms.

"This is not a massage," she said. "I did not know a massage involved licking and kissing. I cannot stand it anymore, Jean Claude," she said.

"I enjoy so much teasing and arousing you, but you always want me to hurry up," he said and continued kissing and gently biting her wet vagina while massaging her thighs.

"Basta," she screamed. "Now, take me now, Jean Claude, now," and she dug her fingers in his shoulders.

"Not yet," he said and kept teasing her. She arched her back, let out one big moan, and she climaxed.

"There, now it is basta," he said as he rubbed his penis gently against her clitoris, then entered her and slowly moved inside her. After a few vigorous thrusts, he also climaxed with a wild groan. He loved and desired this woman so much. He was consumed by her. He had had lots of women, but he had never felt this way about anyone before. He had come to the realization that he was obsessed with her. He was "bewitched, bothered, and bewildered" like Frank Sinatra's song. He had to check his desire sometimes and give her small doses of it, lest she gets overwhelmed and cringe away. He was afraid he might lose her with his unbridled eagerness. He knew that Julia liked to be chased but too much of it would drive her away. He wanted her to always ask for more. He also realized that she had quite an independent personality and did not enjoy it when a guy fawned on her too much. She was a delicious creature and, although he desired her all the time, he had to be careful to restrain himself. He was sure she loved him but things would have to be paced. It was when *she* wanted it. He had found out early on that she needed her space. Just like a cat. A cat came to you when it wanted to. He did not want ever to be rejected by her saying "not now" or "I'm not in the mood tonight." He had to be in tune with her moods and, up to now, things were working out quite well.

He never found out why she had left Bernard, her ex-fiancé, after three years of being together. She was quite evasive about it, and he did not persist in wanting to find out the reason.

Christmas came and they went to Club Med in Guadeloupe for ten days and had a wonderful time. Jean Claude wanted to get married in the spring but Julia wanted to wait for the arrival of her father. He was having a hard time trying to get out of Egypt even with all the affidavits they sent him.

Reveries

CHAPTER 7

Luis

Spring was in full bloom in Geneva, and Julia was sitting with her sister on the sun-drenched patio of their cabana at the InterContinental Hotel swimming pool in Geneva (her regular summer haunt), watching Jean Claude swim some laps. He did have a great body. She felt very lucky for having finally found the love of her life. She was at peace with herself and was living a life of contented, heavenly bliss with him. She no longer felt the need to constantly look around searching for the right man. She had found him. They had not yet set a date for their wedding as they were waiting for her father to manage to get out of Egypt. Exit visas were not granted easily in those days. There was no rush, however, as she already had the ring.

Her life had been very pleasant in Geneva up to now. She had her own studio located close to her apartment, where she usually spent every afternoon painting. Now it was spring, and in the mornings she went to the pool of the hotel to swim. Sometimes she had lunch there with Jean Claude or her sister and the kids or friends. They would go out for dinner in the evenings, or he would come over and have dinner at her place and watch a movie and go to bed, or she would go over to his house, watch a movie and go to bed. They went out to parties, art and antique shows, movies, conferences, etc. They also had fabulous long weekend trips all over Europe, and they had done a lot of skiing in winter. Geneva was a perfect location for this. It was so close to ski slopes in Switzerland and France and central to all major European cities.

"You have found your man," said her sister, Caroline, seated next to her on a lounging chair. "I'm so happy for you, so now you can finally relax and concentrate on your painting. No more man hunting."

"Absolutely right," Julia said, soaking in the sun with a contented smile on her face. "I'm so happy with Jean Claude. He's so kind and considerate and understands me and loves me and takes care of me. He's almost like a father/lover. Our father never took care of us. He was a child himself and I have always felt the need to have a strong man by my side. Jean Claude takes control and I like that. He envelopes me, if you know what I mean. I feel like I'm in a cocoon surrounded with love. It is such a great feeling. My ex-husband was not bad, but he was very young. Heck, we were both very young when we got married. It was doomed to failure. I had too much curiosity and wanted to experience other relationships."

Her sister suddenly nudged her. "Hey, look at that good-looking hunk coming this way."

Julia looked in the direction pointed out by her sister and whispered under her breath, "Oh my God. It can't be." The color drained off her face, and her heart skipped a beat.

"What, what is it? It's like you've seen a ghost."

"Yes, it's him, it is Luis from Casablanca."

"Who on earth is Luis?"

"Remember the young guy I told you about when I was in Casablanca with Bernard, the guy I danced with and who kissed me? We had not even exchanged any words with each other. And Bernard had been thoroughly pissed? Don't gawk. He is coming over. What on earth is he doing here?"

Luis sauntered over to the cabana with a slow masculine, feline grace.

"Ola Julia, remember me?" She pretended to be startled and looked up. It was, in fact, Luis, more handsome than ever, a grown man, taller than he was in Casablanca. She looked in his mischievous deep dark brown eyes with the long straight lashes. *God, he is so handsome with that stubble,* she thought. His body had also matured, broad chest, wide shoulders and narrow hips. A real stud. It also looked like he seriously worked out. He was wearing light-colored chino pants and a black T-shirt. A silver medallion hung around his neck. So very Latino-looking.

She was flustered and looked up at him. "Um, no, I don't think so," she lied.

Luis then knelt beside her lounging chair and said, "It's Luis, Carlos' son, remember Casablanca? We danced together on New Year's Eve?"

Did she remember? Of course she remembered, it was one of the most exciting, memorable evenings ever. He seemed very self-assured; gone was the silent young man she had danced with and who had not uttered a word but who had dared kiss her at midnight. A masculine power oozed off him, kneeling beside her and looking at her with a quizzical smile.

"Oh yes, of course, now I remember you." What a liar she was! "How are you, Luis, fancy meeting you here. What are you doing in Geneva? I thought you were in the States or in Argentina."

"I live and work here now. After I finished my studies in the States, my father asked me to come and run the Geneva office. Actually I live just across the street and was having lunch with friends and Eduardo, my brother, remember," gesturing toward the hotel patio's dining area, "when I thought I recognized this beautiful woman sitting at a cabana. You have not changed much." His gaze took in her scantily clad body in a stunning white bikini. This woman had haunted his memories way back eight years ago, and here she was now, and she still had the same effect on him. "So I came by to say hello. You live in Geneva, don't you?"

She suddenly felt self-conscious with the way Luis was looking at her body and then bringing his gaze straight up to her eyes. It rekindled memories from that famous New Year's Eve dinner in Casablanca. She stood up and wrapped herself in a pareo and sat down again.

"Yes, I often come to this pool to spend the day, swim, have lunch and relax. Meet my sister, Caroline."

"Caroline, this is Luis. We met in Casablanca ages ago."

"Would you both like to have coffee with us?" he asked.

"No, thanks, Luis, actually we are here with my fiancé."

"Your fiancé? The same fiancé of eight years ago?" He was smiling mischievously.

"No, another one." She laughed and felt stupid saying it. It seemed as though she had an array of fiancés lined up.

"He is swimming at the moment." She pointed him out.

"Not bad," he commented, "powerful strokes. Too bad you have a fiancé or good for you or whatever. So besides getting engaged again, what have you been up to?"

"Oh, same old thing. I am an artist, you know. I have a studio and gallery not far from here. I paint and give exhibitions."

"I would like to see your art. Give me the address and I'll stop by one day."

"One second," and she stood up, picked up her handbag, took out a business card and gave it to him. "All the information is on here, my telephone number, address, my website, etc." Why was she being so precise? He could read couldn't he?

"Perfect. I'll call you. In the meantime though, would you like to have dinner with me some time?" Just like that, he blurted out of the blue.

"Dinner with you?" Julia asked, taken aback. This invitation took her completely by surprise. She was at a loss for words. He knew she was engaged, yet he was asking her out to dinner.

"Yeah, dinner. We never talked when we first met, so maybe we could catch up. Actually, how about tonight?" His bottomless dark brown eyes were twinkling, almost daring. The invitation was quite brazen and very tempting to Julia.

"I cannot possibly do that, Luis. I am engaged to Jean Claude, that is his name by the way."

On the one hand, she very much wanted to go out with Luis. It would certainly be a fun evening. He was a gorgeous specimen of the male gender. But it was completely out of the question. She looked at her sister as though asking for her advice or approval. Her sister was engrossed in her book, and Julia sensed that she did not approve of this conversation at all.

"Come on, Julia, I am sure it can be arranged. There is no harm in a dinner, is there? I would very much like to get to know you."

First, the father and now the son. Forget the father, she liked the son. How could she manage this? Why would she go out to dinner with Luis in the first place? Jean Claude met all the criteria she was looking for in a man, and she loved him as much as she could love any man. There was no more need to look for other men or go out with them. She had never been tempted to do so since she was with Jean Claude. But Luis looked so irresistible, so charming and full of life, so Latino. Her mind was working a mile a minute. She was so very tempted to accept this dinner invitation. And if she did, what reason would she give Jean Claude for not seeing him that evening? Luckily they did not live together, but still. Her mind kept racing. She would think of some plausible excuse. She certainly did not want to jeopardize her relationship with Jean Claude by doing something stupid, but she did so want to go out with Luis. She looked at her sister again who had kept a stoic face during this exchange but was thinking, *Here goes Julia again. She is interested in this man, she is crazy; she should certainly not accept the invitation.*

Julia was hesitating. If she did accept the invitation, Jean Claude should never ever find out. After all, there were not too many marriageable men around who were husband material—she had not met any—and her biological clock was around the corner. She could not lose Jean Claude, but a dinner with Luis was so tempting and would be so exciting. She did not know what to do. What harm was there in just a dinner?

"How about it, Julia?" he persisted.

"You are crazy, you know that," she said, laughing. "Okay, I'll have dinner with you," she added trying to hide her eagerness.

Her sister looked at her aghast and shook her head.

Julia was giddy with excitement. She was the crazy one going out with a guy seven years her junior. There was no sense in this, but she was tempted. Carpe diem. That had always been her motto. She felt reckless today. She should think about her life more seriously one of these days but not today. Today adventure beckoned her. It boosted her ego and she was quite flattered to have a much younger guy asking her out. They made arrangements for him to come and pick her up at 7:00 p.m.

Her decision to go out to dinner was indeed a very precarious one. If Jean Claude ever found out, it would be the end of their relationship, and she would be back to square one trying to find a man who was husband material. Luis would never be considered as such; first of all, he was too young and too good-looking to be bogged down with one woman at this stage in his life. Luis was fun material. In fact, now that she thought about it, why can't a woman have two men, one who is the husband, fatherlike, and provider and the other as a backup for some fun and crazy stuff? Actually, Jean Claude *was* a lot of fun, and she was in love with him, no doubt about that. So what was she looking for? Nothing except she suddenly had the urge to be reckless.

"This is a dangerous game you are playing, sis," said Caroline. "You are always doing this. You jump from one man to the other. This time it's not a game. Jean Claude really loves you, and I suppose you love him too in your own crooked way. Don't jeopardize your relationship," she advised. "Be reasonable and cancel your dinner. It's not worth your taking the risk of being found out."

"It's only a dinner, for God's sake. What harm can one dinner do? Jean Claude will never find out. I want a little adventure in my life, not that I don't have any, but I find Luis very charismatic. Did you see his hands? Such long sinewy fingers and those bottomless eyes and that wavy jet-black hair down to his nape and his sideburns and oh, his stubble. He's adorable. And don't forget his butt. Actually, I am very much looking forward to this evening."

"Don't come and cry on my shoulder when the shit hits the fan," Caroline warned.

Julia had had a series of boyfriends and lovers since she had left her first husband, but she had never really cared for any of them, and they were not really marriageable. There was Bernard, but somehow they had not really clicked. He had been very good to her, and she had enjoyed his company, and their sex life had been quite satisfactory, but there had been something missing. The passion. So when she had finally met Jean Claude, she had decided this was it. She fell in love with him. He was much older than she; he was fifty-one, and she was thirty-six, but they were very compatible in many ways; they complemented each other, and the sex was terrific. She had never been carried to such orgasmic heights as with him.

But love had nothing to do with her decision to get married although it helped in this instance. What was love anyway? She had learnt her lesson the first time around. Love only brought heartaches. In fact, she had never loved anyone after divorcing her first husband. He had been the love of her life, but she had left him on a whim. She had been young and stupid then. So after that episode, she had decided to choose a husband with her head and not her heart. When she found Jean Claude, he was everything that she had been looking for and she fell in love again and she made the choice with her heart again. He was good-looking, elegant, suave, worldly, affectionate, caring—the adjectives could go on and on. He took care of her emotionally, and he understood her or thought he did. Sometimes she did not even understand herself.

Jean Claude came out of the swimming pool and sat down next to her and gave her a peck on the cheek. He ordered drinks for them. Luis had already gone away to join his friends—one of them a pretty blond woman—was she his girlfriend? He raised his glass from afar, tipping it at her.

"Who was that guy you were talking to?"

"The son of a friend of the family," she blurted out. *Here goes the first lie,* she thought.

"What do you want to do tonight?" asked Jean Claude.

She fiddled with her hair, trying to concoct a reply. "Nothing, I would like to stay home and have an early night."

"Okay. I'll come over and fix us something to eat." Jean Claude was also a good cook among his other attributes.

"Actually, I don't think I'll be hungry. I ate too much at noon, so I'll just have some mint tea and crackers and go to bed early."

"Don't you want some company?" asked Jean Claude with a sheepish grin.

"No, not tonight, Jean Claude"—sounded like Napoleon's 'Not tonight, Josephine'— "I am really tired." She felt horrible lying to him. She hoped he would not persist in coming over. She would then have to cancel her dinner date. He did not persist. She was relieved.

"Okay, then, I'll call you tomorrow." Oh, that was easy. She was free to go out with Luis. She felt a hot flush coming on and was excited at the prospect.

Out of earshot from Jean Claude, her sister warned her for the last time. "Don't be stupid, cancel the date. Don't say I did not warn you if a catastrophe happens. You are so fickle. I can't believe you are doing this."

"Nothing will go wrong, I am sure of it. I'm just going to have a little harmless fun."

She went home and prepared to get dressed for her dinner like a teenager on her first date. How should she act with Luis? Flirtatious or reserved? She threw a whole bunch of clothes on the bed, trying to decide what to wear. Not too sexy, not too demure. She created a mountain of clothes and then she threw all of them on the floor with exasperation. Why was it so difficult to decide? For God's sake, this was not the very first date in her life. She finally picked up a short, tight white silk dress with a decent neckline. She did not want to be provocative. She felt like a sausage trying to get into it, though. She must have put on some weight, damn it. She reminded herself to starve for the next couple of days and work out more at the gym. She donned murderous white high-heeled sandals, a pearl choker around her neck, brushed her long red hair away from her face and put on very little makeup. You never know, she thought, if there was going to be any smooching later at night, she did not want her kohl and mascara messed up. She would then end up looking like a raccoon. Did she actually think there would be smooching? Was she crazy or what?

She looked at herself in the mirror and liked what she saw. She had a petite compact body with curves in the right places. She did not look thirty-six. She looked very youthful. She had always been told that she did not look her age. The doorbell rang but she did not rush to open the door. She made him wait. It rang again. "Coming," she shouted.

She opened the door, and there was Luis in a pair of midnight blue trousers and a matching blue shirt, open at the neck, with a sweater casually draped over his shoulders, Italian style. He was so dashing, so handsome. She loved his stubble and his mischievous eyes. He exuded an irresistible masculine virility.

"Hi, gorgeous," he said, letting out a cat whistle. "Are you ready?"

"Yup, let me get my purse." She was giddy with excitement.

They stepped into the elevator and his closeness made her uneasy. She could feel his pure male heat, and she could smell a very faint aftershave. She liked that. She disliked men who doused themselves with overpowering cologne. They walked to his car, a dark blue convertible Porsche that matched his attire. She did not particularly like sport cars, however. They were very uncomfortable and claustrophobic; they had a ridiculous sitting position, one almost had to lie down on the seat, and it was not easy to get out of. She got in with difficulty, trying to keep her tight dress not rising up to her crotch. Her thighs were exposed, and she noticed that he was looking at them as she managed to put herself in a comfortable sitting position in the car. She was glad they were tanned. While he put the car into gear, she thought his hand hovered above her thigh and that he was almost going to touch her. She was imagining things. He did not touch her, of course.

"Where are we going?" she asked.

"What did you tell your fiancé?"

She smiled and looked at him sideways without replying. It was none of his business.

"You are not answering my question."

She still did not reply. She looked at his hands at the wheel—they were strong hands with tapered, sinewy fingers. He had rolled up the sleeves of his shirt and she noticed that he had powerful forearms with a small tattoo on one, but she could not decipher what it was. She felt like touching him. She imagined him holding her tight and having his hands all over her body doing all sorts of sensual things. She was really crazy to have these thoughts. But she could not control them. She had always had a very fertile imagination.

"Okay, so you don't want to answer me. I am taking you to a cozy restaurant across the border in France. They have a flamenco guitarist playing there. Do you have ID with you?"

"Yes, I do." An ID was needed to cross the border into France.

She could sense that Luis was glancing at her once in a while. She felt a little awkward, having a fiancé and going out with another man. *A little awkward?* That was a colossal understatement. She hoped he did not think she was a wanton, frivolous woman. Of course, she was wanton and frivolous. Her accepting the dinner date confirmed it. It was not the right thing to do. She wondered what he thought of her. She felt guilty and suddenly burst out "Luis" she said, "you know I'm quite uncomfortable with this situation. Maybe this was not such a good idea after all, perhaps you should take me back home. I am sorry I cannot go out with you. This is madness."

"Oh, come on Julia, we are only going to have dinner. What's the harm in that?" He desired this woman. He had desired her eight years ago and he desired her now. He did not want her to change her mind. He had the faint suspicion that she might also be attracted to him. Why would she have accepted going out to dinner with him otherwise?

You think it's only going to be dinner, she thought. *I bet it will be much more than dinner.*

"Okay, let's make it an early night, then," she said.

They went to a restaurant that she had never been to before. It was dimly lit and had a very romantic atmosphere. The guitarist was already playing smooth flamenco.

"It is a new restaurant and I hope the food is as good as they say it is," said Luis.

"It looks quite charming, and I love the music," was her reply.

He had made reservations in a corner booth. Candles on the tables were the only lighting. They sat down across from each other. She still felt uncomfortable. She looked around to see if there was anyone she knew. It was difficult to see in the dark. Luis sensed her preoccupation.

"Are you trying to see whether there is anyone you know who might recognize you?"

"I am trying to but it is very difficult to do so with this dim lighting."

"Well then, you're lucky, nobody can see you either. Just relax and enjoy the music and the company, I hope?"

He had to get some wine in her fast to make her relax otherwise the evening was going to be hopeless with all her feelings of guilt. He wanted to make her forget she had a fiancé. He hoped he could achieve that. He had never felt this eager to be with a woman before. Was it because she was not really available? That he wanted to test his powers of seduction on her? To take her away from her fiancé? No, it was not that. He would have been eager even if she were unattached and available. She was a very delightful and enticing woman. *She is so flirtatious but does not realize it,* he thought, *but how far would she go?* He did want to conquer her. He had never had any trouble getting women, but this was different. It might be rather difficult to seduce her. It's not only wanting to seduce her, he wanted to keep her. But how? He had a difficult task ahead of him. It was a challenge, but then Luis never did balk in front of a challenge.

They ordered wine and paella for dinner. After their glasses had been filled, he raised his glass and said, "A toast to us, chin-chin."

"Why to us?" she said, but she clinked her glass to his anyway.

"To our reunion, of course," he said, looking at her intensely.

"I'll drink to that," she said flirtatiously.

After having a glass of the smooth Bordeaux wine, she relaxed somewhat but was still uneasy about the situation. They talked about their lives. Carlos had sent the three older boys to boarding school in the United States as he could not care for the six children without the mother. She told him she knew the story of the mother. He felt quite uncomfortable talking about it. He told her that he had done his undergraduate studies in Business and French at Columbia University and had also gotten his MBA from Columbia. He was a partner in his father's grain import/export business. They had an office in Geneva, where they also did their banking. Of course, where else would hotshot businessmen do their banking if not in Switzerland.

"And so, now you are engaged again. Are you never available? Is that your life ambition, to collect fiancés? What does he do, this fiancé of yours?"

"He is a financial consultant at PBSU."

"And you are a famous artist."

"Well, I am an artist, but famous is too big a word. I try to exhibit here and there. I like living in Geneva. It is such a quiet place after having lived in New York with my first husband." He raised an eyebrow at this statement.

"You were married before?" he asked.

"Yes, I was married to my childhood sweetheart at a very young age, which led to divorce. Then I got engaged to Bernard, as you know, and now I am engaged to Jean Claude and am going out to dinner with you. I don't even know why I am doing this. Very funny, ha-ha. Does it boost your ego?"

He reached across the table and took her hands in his. "Don't fret so much, it will be okay, relax and enjoy the music." His touch sent electric shocks down her spine. Why did this guy fluster her so much? She moistened her upper lip with her tongue. He let go of her hands. *This guy is so cute,* she thought. *I wouldn't mind getting kissed by him again.*

"No, it is not okay. Jean Claude would leave me if he found out, and I absolutely don't want to lose him. He is one of the few decent men I have met, and he loves me. How would you feel if you were engaged to be married and your fiancée went out with another man?"

"I hope I will be able to keep my fiancée chained to me so that she would not wander around," he chuckled.

"Well, you see Jean Claude did not chain me."

"Are you in love with him?" he asked.

"I don't really know what love is, it is complicated." Then she blurted out "Yes, I am in love, I think, and I do have a very satisfying relationship with him because I know exactly where I will end up, married with a couple of children and raising them in Geneva with a man who loves me. But then I thought the same thing with Bernard, you know the other guy I was engaged to. But this is different, I am more in tune with Jean Claude than I ever was with Bernard. We are good friends, by the way, Bernard and I. Hell, I am also good friends with my ex-husband."

"But you have not exhausted all the possibilities yet. How can you be so sure that Jean Claude is The One? He may end up to be an ex too if I ever move up your ladder and be your present one, your *amant du jour,*" he said with a grin, looking deep into her eyes. Her sensuality was so appealing, and he liked the idea that he flustered her. She tore her gaze away, lifted the wine glass to her lips, and sipped it.

"Ha, you make me laugh. I would never take up with you, a man seven years younger than myself. It would be a disaster for me. I am not a cougar, you know. It is better to be an old man's darling than a young man's slave—I am quoting my mother here."

"Who talked about being my slave? I may end up being your slave, and for your information, I would like that a hell of a lot," said Luis with a sheepish grin on his face.

"You don't look like you could be anyone's slave. Why did you ask me out anyway? You want to add an older woman to your list of conquests? Don't you have a girlfriend or girlfriends?"

"As a matter of fact, I do kinda have a girlfriend, but the relationship is dwindling. It has gotten to be tepid, and it is on its way out," he lied. "Also, I do not make conquests, and I am not trying to make you one. I find you very attractive and very vivacious, quite out of the ordinary, and I am curious to know more about you. You intrigued me in Casablanca and you intrigue me now. There is a certain exotic mystery about you. You are an enchanting seductress. Actually, I was quite smitten by you in Casablanca, but I was too young to make a move on you then, nor did I have the occasion later on. You had your fiancé in tow, who was taking on very possessive airs, and my lecherous father was devouring you with his hungry eyes, getting ready to pounce. What chance did I have? And now you have another fiancé. It is not fair. I have not been given the opportunity. I am heartbroken," he said lightheartedly.

"Yeah right, heartbroken, you must have a million girls after you. I certainly am not trying to seduce you, by the way. Why do you say I am a seductress? It looks more like you are trying to seduce me," she said, moistening her upper lip with her tongue and looking at his sensuous lips.

"Oh yes, you are a seductress without trying to be one. You give out signals of which you may or may not be aware of. You have very flirtatious eyes, and you have the habit of licking your upper lip sometimes, and then you pout and slightly part your lips, which is very provocative." She flushed as his gaze moved down for a fraction of a second, lingering on her bosom under her tight bodice.

She looked so inviting to him. He wanted to grab her and kiss her. He could visualize her naked and he felt aroused at the thought. Her face was so expressive, and she exuded such a mystic illusion in him that he felt the urge to dominate and possess her sexually.

"Wow, I did not know all this. I don't give out signals, you're imagining things. All right, let's not discuss me and my fiancés or you and your designs on older women. Let's talk about some banal ordinary subjects, like what films have you seen? What books have you read? What do you enjoy most? What are your hobbies? What sports do you practice? Where have you been lately?"

Luis was smiling and shaking his head.

"What are you shaking your head for? The subjects I mentioned are part of a normal conversation between two people getting to know each other."

"Yes, we should indeed have a normal conversation to give us more time to ponder whether it will lead to anything else later on."

"That's where you're wrong Luis. It will never lead to anything else other than this dinner. If that is your ultimate goal, to take me to bed, take it out of your head once and for all because it ain't happening."

She wished it would happen, though. His vitality and obvious virility were drawing him to her like a magnet. It was always the same with her. She met someone, dated him, slept with him, and after a while, she got curious and looked around. But this was not the case as far as Jean Claude was concerned. First of all, she was not bored with Jean Claude, and she had not been looking around like she was with Bernard. Jean Claude kept her very much on her toes. He was a force to be reckoned with. Luis just happened to come into her life again out of the blue and, undoubtedly, there was a powerful current between them. Why did he have to turn up at this moment in her life and try and spoil her plans of a stable future with Jean Claude? Actually, it was her fault. She liked men too much.

It dawned on her that she had liked men all her life ever since she was a kid. At the end of WWII, her father had brought one of his GI buddies to have dinner at home. She remembered being very attracted to this tall blond GI. She was six. He was twenty-six. She could still remember his name. In fact, he was in one of the photos in her album. She is sort of leaning against him, sitting on the couch with all her family.

Luis told her a little about his life, his hobbies (he played the guitar), the sports he practiced. He was a black-belt karate expert besides playing competitive tennis and, of course, he liked dancing. Well, that was one thing they very much had in common.

During this dinner, she started toying with the idea of being married to Jean Claude and keeping Luis secretly on the side. It would never work out, of course. She had such stupid wandering thoughts. Jean Claude would eventually find out, and it would be catastrophic. Her marriage would go down the drain. She had to remind herself that she was getting on in years and a woman had her biological clock. It was time for her to have children. She could not afford to fool around forever like some men do. And, in any case, Luis might not want to be kept hidden in the sidelines. He was too attractive not to have a steady paramour. And why was she even thinking about such a stupid scenario. *Jean Claude is enough for me,* she kept on repeating to herself.

"Was the blond girl sitting with you at the hotel restaurant your girlfriend?"

"Yes, her name is Claire, but as I told you before, she is of no consequence. As for going to bed with you, we shall see, my dear. Never say never. I would never push you or insist, but I do think it will happen. It is inevitable. I am attracted to you, and I think the feeling is reciprocated," he said almost humbly. "Otherwise I don't think you would have accepted my dinner invitation."

He looked straight in her eyes, took hold of one of her hands and brought them to his lips, and kissed the fingertips. She felt her nipples harden, and she flushed as his gaze dropped down to her neckline for a fraction of a second. It was enough for him to ascertain that she was not wearing a bra, and he could see her nipples poking through the thin fabric. It aroused him and he wanted to touch her breasts. She held his gaze and did not move her hand away. She could feel the rapid pounding of her heart. He had such sexual charisma and she was mesmerized by his bottomless dark eyes with the abundant straight lashes and his chiseled, kissable lips. He exuded a sexual power so intense that she felt like jelly. She should never have accepted going out to dinner with him. The evening was getting out of hand.

"The feeling is not reciprocated," she blurted out. "I am just having dinner with you, and that's all."

His eyes then held her gaze. "Whatever you say, but your eyes are giving you away," he said.

Are my thoughts so transparent? she wondered.

What was it about her that made her so desirable? Luis asked himself. It was undefinable. He was smitten big-time. This was so unlike him. He had known and slept with many women but Julia seemed so different. She fascinated him and excited him. She finally tore her gaze away. The air between them was charged with such sexual electricity that it overpowered him, and a shudder went through his whole body. He felt like a fifteen-year-old boy out on his first date. He was again sexually aroused by this creature just like in Casablanca. He composed himself and lifted his glass of wine to his lips and sipped it slowly, still looking at her.

Julia, on the other hand, was in a state of chaos and confusion, and she felt powerless.

The evening went on quite smoothly after that, and they laughed a lot. He was very good company, witty, and oozed of incredible charm. He amused her and teased her. And then it was time to go home. Almost everyone had left. They had not felt the time go by. She felt quite tipsy walking toward the car and she almost stumbled, but he held her just in time and kept her close to his side. He had such a strong presence, and his masculine smell filled her nostrils. It made her dizzy. Yes, she wanted this man, but she had to pretend to resist him and play hard to get. They were silent as he drove her home. She wondered what he was thinking about. She was certain he would make a move, but how would he make it? They arrived at her apartment building, and he opened her car door and walked her to the door of the building. She fumbled for her keys and could not find them.

"Here, let me get that for you," he suggested.

"I can manage by myself, thank you," she retorted. She was intoxicated by his closeness and it annoyed her for being so vulnerable. He was watching her intensely. She found her keys, opened the door and turned around to say good-night.

He looked at her quizzically. "No good-night kiss?" and he stepped on the threshold of the building after her.

"Oh, all right," she said and turned around offering him her cheek. In so doing, she stumbled and fell forward. He caught her in time and held her steady against the wall, facing him. They looked at each other. Their bodies were touching. His body heat was so overpowering; it sent thrills up and down her spine. They just stood there without moving and looked at each other. His look betrayed his desire.

"Is that the best you can do?" he asked, "offer me your cheek? We did better than that eight years ago." She looked at him, and her heart was beating wildly.

"By the way, thinking back to that evening, what was Bernard's reaction when you went back to your room?"

"He was mad, of course, but things resumed between us, no great harm was done."

"Are you scared of me?" he asked.

"No, why do you say that?"

"Because your eyes are darting back and forth and you look like a trapped animal."

"Yes, you're right. I do feel like a trapped animal, stuck against the wall like a lizard. Oh, fine, kiss me and let's get it over with. I am sure you are dying to try your powers on me and find out whether I will succumb to your charms and melt in your arms." She knew this was exactly what was going to happen. She was weak with desire and she would certainly succumb if she did not take control of herself immediately.

"Oh, by the way, did you know that kissing is the beginning of cannibalism?" she asked.

"Are you quoting Georges Bataille now? Julia, I am neither a beggar nor a grabber. You either want to kiss me or you don't. Make up your mind and let me worry about cannibalism."

Why was he making things difficult for her? Of course, she wanted him to kiss her but she knew it would not stop there. She was too attracted to him. And if she kissed him back, it also meant that what she had said during dinner about not going to bed with him would be a downright lie. She hoped that he did not sense that she wanted him desperately.

He had a confident air about him and he was taking his time, waiting. Then he stepped closer, held her face in his hands, and started to kiss her very lightly on the lips. His stubble was gently scraping her cheeks. She loved it. She was tingling all over. Not sensing any objections, he grasped the nape of her neck, bringing her face closer, and slid his tongue in between her parted lips. He started kissing her slowly and deliberately. He did not want to frighten her away. He was afraid that if he showed too much passion, she would make him stop and cringe away and the opportunity of going any further would be lost forever. He lifted her chin and looked into her eyes. "That's better," he said. She was tongue-tied and did not say a word. His virility, his scent, his touch and his stubble were driving her insane. She wanted him to continue. What was the matter with her? Jean Claude's face came into her vision and a little voice in her head was telling her to stop the madness. But she did not listen to that voice.

"I'll accompany you to your door," he said, and he guided her toward the elevator and they went up to her apartment in silence. She opened her door, and he followed. She did not object. He closed the door with one foot and pushed her gently against the wall and stepped closer. Their eyes locked.

"Now what?" Julia asked.

"It all depends on you," was his reply. She did not move. She felt frozen in place. Luis took that as a sign that he could continue. He raised her arms above her head, pinned them against the wall, his hard body pressed against hers, and started kissing her more forcefully and passionately. The heat emanating from his body was electrifying, and she could feel the hardness of his penis against her body. She was on fire. She wanted this man badly. She gave a little sigh and returned his kissing, banishing all warnings of the little voice. He nuzzled her neck with his stubble, nibbled her earlobes and kissed the hollow in her throat. He then brought his lips down to her cleavage and kissed her between her breasts. He was aware of a faint moan coming out of her throat.

Julia thought she should stop him but she did not want to, and yet she had to pretend she wanted him to stop. What would he think of her if she let him continue? She had to somehow show some resistance. She could not let him think that he was overpowering her with his sexuality. She had never lost her self-control with men, ever—this was a first for her, and she hated her loss of power over him. She did not want him to think that she was some sex-starved woman who would go to bed after a first date and, on top of that, being engaged to another man. What was wrong with her? She was not sex-starved. She had had sex with Jean Claude the night before, for God's sake. She felt trapped and vulnerable, burning with desire for this young man but somehow she absolutely had to regain her self-control. But how? She felt so limp and helpless.

"No, stop, I can't continue doing this, it's very wrong, you have to go now." He let go of her arms and stroked her cheek, then touched the upper mounds of her breasts gently. She could feel her nipples harden and push against the fabric of her dress and she was aching for his touch.

"That's not what you want, Julia," he said, his gaze on her breasts. "Don't resist, go with the flow."

God, his body was so hard as he pressed himself against her and his chest pressed against her nipples. She felt weak in the knees, and her resistance was melting away very quickly. The sensation was so unbearably erotic. She inhaled deeply, trying to recover herself but she could not. She was pinned against the wall, and she could hardly breathe. Luis, on the other hand, had a very even breathing and was looking at her, waiting for her response. She had to pretend to resist him. He was watching her with intense desire in his eyes, but she did not want him to witness the power he had over her. She hated him for that. Hated him to think that he could overcome her resistance so easily. Hated him for dominating her. Although she wanted to be dominated and possessed by him.

"You can tell me to stop anytime and I will, if you really want me to," he said.

She did not reply, but the response was in her eyes. He exuded a magnetic sexual power that she could not resist.

"Oh, what the hell," she said and gave in by putting her hands around his neck and entwined her fingers through his hair, arching her body toward his chest. He then very slowly parted her neckline, revealing her high, firm, youthful breasts with erect, pink nipples.

"Beautiful," he remarked as he bent his head down, hovering his lips on her breasts but not touching them. Her breath drew in sharply.

"No, stop," she said.

"Stop? You really want me to stop? Your nipples are erect and dying to be caressed," he said. "You don't want to deprive them, do you?"

"They are erect because I am cold."

"There is a solution for that."

"And what would that be, pray?"

He showed her his hands. "They are here to warm them. You have the breasts of an eighteen-year-old, small and perky," he added. "I could already tell what they looked like through your bikini top at the pool."

"They are not small. I wear a size 34B bra."

"I don't care about numbers. I know what I see. I can cup one in one hand, that's your size. You cannot imagine how I am dying to make love to you," he whispered in her ear. "I have fantasized about you since we first met," and he brought his mouth down on hers hungrily and kissed her again. He then drew away and watched her expression but could not really tell whether she also wanted him as desperately as he did.

"You mean dying to have sex with me," she said.

"A man would have to be a eunuch not to want to make love, oh sorry, have sex with you."

He held her by her shoulders and began kissing around her breasts. She felt her nipples harden again and electric shocks shot down to her groin. He was teasing her. He had not touched her nipples yet and they ached for his touch. She moaned and groaned and arched her back, flaunting her breasts toward his mouth. She was in extreme arousal mode.

"What are you waiting for?" she asked.

"Why are you in such a hurry? I am taking my time, enjoying you little by little. Desires that are immediately fulfilled are not appreciated in the long run. There is no need to hurry," he kept repeating.

No need to hurry? She was exploding with desire and spasms were going through her body. He brushed her breasts with his stubble, and she could feel his hot breath; she quivered and kept her eyes closed, yearning for more. He then almost growled and finally cupped her breasts and caressed her taut nipples with his thumb and forefinger. He then started to nibble on one, then the other, very playfully, and she was gasping for breath. He started sucking hard, and her pussy was throbbing uncontrollably. He then slowly slid one hand under her dress and it crawled up her thighs. He caressed her slowly, lingeringly and adeptly until his hand rested on her sex. She pushed his hand away.

"No, don't," she said. The intensity of his desire overwhelmed her.

Luis yearned for her body and his fingers grabbed at her panties and tried to pull them down.

"No, don't," she repeated.

"You are so wet," he said huskily, touching her pubic hair and fondling her delicately. "Is it also because of the cold, or is it because of me?"

"Stupid idiot," she said. He resumed his caresses. Her skin was so soft and tantalizing and he had a hard time restraining himself.

Julia held her breath. Her heart was beating erratically. Luis could feel the twitching of her vagina under his fingers. He then knew she wanted him as badly as he wanted her.

"I wonder if it is also as pink as your nipples and your lips. They say the three go together color wise."

Her preoccupation at that moment was that she did not want him to think that she was a sex-starved, wanton woman who would have sex with perfect strangers. She was not sex-starved so why was she doing this? Was he that irresistible? Yes, he was, incredibly so.

"This is so very wrong," she said. "You must think I am a wanton woman."

"Possibly."

"And a slut."

"Probably."

"And that I go to bed with other men while I am engaged to be married."

"Perhaps that is also true," he said, tightening his embrace and kissing her over and over, pressing his chest against her naked breasts. She wished he would take his shirt off. She wanted the flesh-on-flesh feeling.

"I should not be unfaithful to Jean Claude. He is such a decent person and he loves me, and I love him too, and I am going to get married to him. Why am I doing this? My moral compass is completely out of whack, and I hate myself. How would you feel if your fiancée ever did this to you?"

"I can't imagine that situation. Did you know that fidelity is not in the actions but in the heart?" he asked her.

"No, says who?"

"Some French author, I don't remember which one. So, Julia, are you being unfaithful with your body or with your heart? If it is only with the body, it does not count, but if it is with the heart, then it is more serious. So which is it?"

"How do I know? I am so mixed up now. I just met you. I don't really know you from Adam. All I know is that I should not be doing this behind Jean Claude's back."

"Okay, how about this? Let's get him over here and I'll tell him, 'Listen, Jean Claude. Julia does not want to be doing things behind your back, so please turn around and watch her getting laid by a stranger she met eight years ago.'"

"Jerk," she said and put her arms around him and drew him closer, lacing her fingers through his sleek long hair. The top buttons of his shirt were open and she could smell his skin. It aroused her even more. She trailed her fingers down his chest to his hard stomach. He had such rock-hard abs and she loved the hair on his chest and rubbed her cheeks against it. The sensation was unbearably erotic.

Julia's touch aroused Luis even more and he took her face in his hands and kissed her again and again. He was ravaging her, and she loved it. He kissed her hands, the inside of her arms and her armpits.

"I am sweaty," she said.

"I like that," he said and cupped her breasts and brought his mouth down on them, suckling and gently biting the tips. This thrilled her and she was intoxicated by his lips and his hands. Her heart started to beat erratically. Her legs felt weak and she felt herself melting. She wanted him to dominate her completely. She was almost quivering and she hated herself for succumbing to the sexual power emanating from him. She was burning with uncontrollable desire and felt incapable of moving. She also felt like this with Jean Claude but the difference was that this was clandestine. She was delirious. *The added thrill is in the forbidden,* she told herself. He pulled her against him and she could feel the hardness of his manhood. She hoped that he did not have a huge penis. His feet were big, and men with big feet have big penises, she had read somewhere.

Luis wanted to possess her there and then but he restrained himself. He was going to take his time and prolong the evening.

"Do you have something strong to drink?" he asked. "Not for you though—you already had too much to drink. You might lose all your self-control and be my slave and I will be able to do all sorts of things to you, and you may regret doing all sorts of things to me. A strong drink makes me think clearly and I need a clear head very badly at this moment."

"In the bar over there, but first, help me get out of this dress. I feel like I have a large bandage around my body. There is a zipper in the back."

He carried her to the bedroom and after taking off her dress, he lay her down on the bed, with her flaming red hair sprawled around her face and wearing only a thong. He wanted to jump on her; she was so beautiful but again, he restrained himself. There was a painting of a naked woman in utter abandon on top of her bed, and she reminded him of it. He guessed that it was one of her own paintings. It was like a scene repeating itself on her bed. Her exquisite body was in the same abandoned position as in the painting, and he adored it.

"What is this?" he asked, fingering her panties. "Are you wearing dental floss now?"

"Jerk," she said again. Luis fixed himself a drink and came and sat at her side, his eyes taking in her nakedness, and he was aroused just by looking at her.

"You have such a youthful body. You are so lucky to have the body of a young girl. Your friends must envy you," he said and took off his shirt. He was tanned, and his chest was magnificent, so taut and lean. She looked at it and at his broad shoulders and she drew him to her putting her cheek against his chest, inhaling his scent. He stroked her face and hair, and she was almost shaking.

"What am I going to do?" she asked.

"I don't know what you are going to do, but I am going to have sex with you. I am afraid you'll have to deal with the problem of Jean Claude by your little old self. I am no help there. It is your decision."

"I will not drop Jean Claude. He is the man I love," and she let out a nervous laugh as he played with her nipples and grazed them with his teeth. She was so wet, and she kept on talking.

"What I feel for you is pure lust and I don't know where it will lead me. At least, I know with Jean Claude, it is love. He loves me, wants to marry me, and I love him and I do like having sex with him and I want to have his children. Does that sound silly to you? I don't know what I am doing. It is as though I am two people. Why did you have to come into my life and tempt me?"

"Am I going to be your secret lover, then? Everyone knows clandestine sex is more exciting."

His lips were on her breasts, and one hand was stroking her sex, driving her insane. He was like an expert puppeteer and she, the obedient puppet. He was touching her erogenous zones with his lips and fingers all at the same time.

"If you want to. Sorry, Luis, but I cannot decide on the spur of the moment how I am going to handle this new situation. This is a very important decision for me. So it's up to you. My brain says you are bad news for me, but my heart says otherwise. I am so very confused. I cannot think straight. You have to give me time to think."

"You need to think while you are having sex?"

"Yeah, to determine whether I am doing the right thing."

"But it is obvious you are not doing the right thing. You are having sex with a man while you're supposed to be engaged to another."

"Oh, shut up. It feels as though tonight is a dream and I am going to wake up to reality and realize that all this never happened to disrupt my comfortable life."

She cuddled against him. There was so much electricity between them. He took off his trousers. He was wearing a pair of black jockey shorts, and it was bulging. She again wondered about the size of his penis. Did she dare touch him there? No, not yet. They embraced for a very long time. He then took off her panties. "Ridiculous-looking thing," he said, "and you are a real redhead, somehow I did not doubt it." He looked down at her mound with trimmed reddish pubic hair. There was raw desire in his eyes and he liked the sensations he was experiencing. She felt so exposed and tried to cover herself with her hands.

"Don't," he said, "I like looking at you. I am glad you have not had a full Brazilian." He stroked her mound and played with her pubic hair. He brought his mouth down and kissed the inside of her thighs and rubbed his stubble against them. She was ecstatic.

"Why are you crossing your legs? Are you hiding the goodies? Please open your legs, Julia, I would like to taste you."

"It is too intimate."

"You think what we have been doing up to now is not intimate?"

"I just don't feel comfortable exposing myself to you in that way. It feels like I am at the gynecologist." She gave out a nervous laugh.

"The gynecologist? You're kidding." He did not want to press her. She was one strange woman and he wanted her to be comfortable with him. He kissed her stomach and her thighs, but she still kept her legs crossed at the ankles. He then knelt down at the foot of the bed and started licking her toes. This tickled her and, with a moan, she involuntarily uncrossed her legs and exposed herself to him. Her pussy was throbbing wildly. He looked at it.

"Pink, as I thought it would be," he said huskily, touching her sex. He felt it twitching, and he went wild with desire. He drew her legs around his neck, and he kissed her most intimate place which was wet, very gently at first. She was on fire, and she groaned and pulled at his hair. He took his time kissing her hungrily. He parted her labia with his lips and licked her, darting his tongue in and out and putting a finger inside her. She writhed with pleasure, whimpering faintly and dug her nails in the sheet. She was delirious which aroused him even more. He was extremely pleased seeing the effect he had on her.

The nude painting above her bed was somehow distracting him. The woman on the bed was the same woman in the painting. It was very exciting.

"Your pussy is like the delicate petals of a rose—reminds me of a Georgia O'Keeffe painting."

"You are killing me," she said.

"Softly, I hope," and he went on caressing her.

She was floating with a wonderful erotic sensation and whimpering as he gently moved his finger around.

"You're ready," he said, and he lay down on top of her, cupping her buttocks, lifting her and he entered her gently while nibbling her ear lobes. He finally took her with several fervent thrusts. They both climaxed feverishly at the same time and collapsed panting. Julia was grateful that he had a normal-sized penis. She clutched him and did not want to let him go. His body was so desirable and his skin so young and taut. He was just perfect. He reminded her of a panther.

"You can stay the night if you like," she said. She regretted saying it but she was so intoxicated by him that she threw caution to the wind. For the rest of the night she forgot all about Jean Claude.

He stayed and after having had sex a second time, "I cannot get enough of you," he told her. "You know I fantasized about you in Casablanca, and now you are here in my arms. I can't believe it. I think I am dreaming and that I shall wake up any minute and find myself alone in my bed."

"Or in the bed of another woman. I really should not be doing this, Luis, it is absurd. I am with Jean Claude. What am I doing with you? This is ridiculous. It should not continue. This was an aberration."

"Hush. Will you please stop talking and repeating yourself when I am trying to make love to you? Enjoy the moment and don't let your mind wander in all directions." He brought his mouth down on hers and kissed her hungrily and passionately. She reciprocated. She was hooked; there was no denying it. Her mind was in utter chaos.

"This is very disturbing to me. I am leading a double life." She then nestled against him and let out a little giggle.

"Why are you giggling?"

"I am laughing because I was afraid to have sex with you, thinking that you had a huge penis, judging by your feet. They say that a man's foot determines the size of his penis."

"Ha-ha, you should have checked it before going to bed with me, querida. What if I had a huge penis, would you have refused to have sex with me?"

"Yeah, I would have. It has happened to me once, and it hurt for three days. I declined to see the guy again. But everything turned out to be normal with you. Lucky for you." She flung one leg across his legs and tried to fall asleep. After a little while, they were aroused and had sex again. She was so tired yet hungry for his lovemaking. She wanted to fall asleep but it seemed that he never lost his hard-on. She had never had sex three times with any of her lovers before. Twice, yes, but never three times. They were both insatiable and very exhausted and eventually fell asleep in each other's arms.

She woke up in the morning to a rude awakening. Luis was in bed next to her, spooning her under the duvet. She could feel his hard-on. Just then the phone rang. She looked at the clock—it was 9:00 a.m. She picked up the phone. It was Jean Claude. *What the hell. She had forgotten that he was supposed to call her in the morning.*

"I have some croissants 'ma biche.' I am parking the car. I suppose you are awake and would like to have some breakfast." Oh my God. What was she going to do?

"It is Jean Claude," she nudged Luis to wake him up. "You have to leave immediately, he is coming upstairs, he has a key."

"Well, the bed is hot and ready for him."

"Don't joke about this. Please gather your clothes and leave immediately." Luis was stunned for a second and shook his head trying to wake up.

"Luis, please hurry up, don't you dare spoil things for me."

"Okay, okay, I am going." He picked up his clothes in a jiffy, got dressed, and closed the door behind him and was down the two flights of stairs and out of the building. *You lucky bastard* thought Luis as he watched Jean Claude getting out of his car.

Jean Claude used his key to get in the apartment and found Julia in bed.

"Ah, just where I want to find you," he said. "I'll make us some coffee, and then I'll join you for breakfast in bed."

"Oh no," she said, getting up and not looking at him. She felt so guilty and slutty. She knew Jean Claude would want to have sex with her after breakfast but she could not possibly do it after three times with Luis the night before. How was she going to get out of this dilemma? She wondered whether Luis had dropped the used condoms on the floor next to his side of the bed. She did not remember him getting up to discard them. What if Jean Claude saw them? Disaster loomed ahead. She felt panicky.

"Why not?" asked Jean Claude, looking at her with surprise.

"I just had my periods and have to wash up."

"But you had your periods about two weeks ago. Is something wrong with you? You look distraught." *Jean Claude and his sharp memory.* He looked over to the bed. It was rumpled and reeked of Luis, but luckily Jean Claude was not close enough to smell it.

"You seem to have had a restless night," he remarked. "The bed is messy. You usually sleep on the right side and do not move too much. What happened?"

"Yeah, I was quite restless with my periods and all," and she threw the bed cover on top of the bed to hide any trace of Luis, if any. She got up and walked naked to the bathroom.

"Since when do you sleep au naturel?"

"I don't know why, I felt so hot. I was perspiring so I took off my nightie."

He had a puzzled expression on his face and she felt awful lying to him. She came up to him, pressed her naked body against his, and gave him a passionate kiss. She hated the idea of kissing Jean Claude so soon after having slept with Luis. She needed time in between. She really felt awful deceiving him like this. She felt like a whore. She could not possibly jump from one man to the other with no time in between. She had gotten herself into a very awkward situation.

She then went to the bathroom, took a shower, and had breakfast with Jean Claude in the kitchen. She was eager for him to leave so that she could change the sheets, look for the condoms, and think hard on her next move. The future looked very complicated. Could she handle two men at the same time? Was Luis going to become a fixture in her life? What was she going to do? The sensible thing to do, of course, is not see Luis again.

Jean Claude finally left, and they made a date to go out for dinner in the evening. The excuse of having told him she had her periods would buy her some time for about three days of not having sex with him. And then what? Have sex with two men at intervals? What kind of schedule? *This is ridiculous,* she thought. *Why am I doing this?*

As she was clearing the dishes, her sister called, curious to find out the details of her dinner with Luis.

"I hope you have satisfied your curiosity, and it was only a dinner."

"Well, no, I . . . um . . . well, I went to bed with him."

"What? Are you out of your mind? What did you do that for?"

"It just happened, I could not resist him. He is much too cute and sexy."

"You're so stupid, Julia, you are a real masochist, you are jeopardizing your relationship with Jean Claude. Why would you do that? Isn't Jean Claude satisfying you in every way?"

"I had a couple of glasses of wine and—"

"Couple of glasses my foot."

"And then I could not stop his advances. It was as though I was hypnotized. I let myself go, I just—"

"You just what? Are you so sex crazy? Why am I even bothering to ask? Of course, you are sex crazy. You don't know your limits."

"Look, Caroline, everyone is not as logical and sensible as you are and in control of one's emotions and actions. I happen to be very sensual and it was impossible to resist him. I tried, though. We did it three times, can you imagine? Three times. He was like a puppeteer, pulling the right strings all the time. He is such an expert lover and so sensual."

"So what are you going to do now? Are you going to continue to have sex with this guy? And what about Jean Claude? Come to your senses and stop this madness."

"I will certainly not leave Jean Claude, don't worry, but I think I want to continue with Luis for some time at least."

"Stop it, Julia, don't do this. It is sheer stupidity and very dangerous. This is not a game, and you certainly can't handle it. You are not in a movie."

"I know it's sheer folly, but I think I can handle it. Jean Claude will never find out."

"Yeah, right."

They hung up after Julia promised her sister she would not do anything stupid. She went out to dinner with Jean Claude that evening. She looked at him and tried to evaluate her feelings toward him. No, her feelings toward him had not changed after going to bed with Luis. She still loved him and wanted him. They kissed passionately before parting but they went back to their separate homes. She was supposed to have her periods, so no sex.

She did not hear from Luis for four days. *The bastard*, she thought, *he used me as a one-night stand. He got what he wanted and now I'm screwed and humiliated.* Well, she was not going to call him. She would not humiliate herself any further. *He can go to hell*, she thought. She would forget about him. Could she though? The sex had been out of this world. She called her sister and told her that Luis had not called and she was seething.

"I told you not to do it," Caroline said. "He seduced you and used you and you fell for his Latin charms. I must admit he is a very good-looking guy but forget about him, concentrate on Jean Claude. You are lucky to have such a good man. Don't lose him."

During the four days after the incident with Luis, her life went on as usual with Jean Claude as though nothing had interrupted it. She tried to forget Luis. On the fifth day of not having heard from him, which happened to be a Monday, she got out of bed, took a shower, wrapped a large towel around her body, and was just going to prepare herself some breakfast when the doorbell rang. She looked through the peephole, and it was Luis. She froze. What should she do? Should she open the door and ask him to go away or should she invite him in? She was undecided. The doorbell rang again.

"I know you're there, Julia, so open the door please, I have to talk to you."

She opened the door with the chain on. "I don't feel like talking to you, go away," she said and she closed the door.

"Open the door Julia, you don't want the neighbors to hear us, do you?" She opened the door again as far as the chain would allow.

"I have nothing to say to you."

"I have something to tell you."

She took the chain off and opened the door. "What do you want?"

"May I come in? After all, you don't want the neighbors to hear a lovers' quarrel."

"You are not my lover." She let him in anyway, closed the door, and stood facing him. "You bastard, you did not call me for four days. Who do you think I am? A one-night floozy?" and she slapped him.

"Perhaps a floozy," he said with a grin, "but not a one nighter. The reason I did not call you is because I was very angry with you for dismissing me like you did the other day. You treated me like a used-up toy."

"Dismissing you? Of course, I had to get rid of you and fast. Jean Claude was coming upstairs, for God's sake. What was I supposed to do? Leave you naked in my bed and, when Jean Claude came in, introduce you as the guy I met eight years ago in Casablanca who kissed me on new Year's Eve and I accidentally ran into him at the pool yesterday, and I agreed to have dinner with him and then I got laid. 'But don't worry he is leaving now, he is going to take a cold shower to take care of his erection and you can take his place in bed. This was only a stupid meaningless fling I had, and I am so sorry I lied to you, but I only love you.' There, does that sound better to you?" She turned her back to him and started to walk away.

"Come here," Luis said and grabbed her by the arm. Her bath towel fell off on the floor. She was naked, of course. She picked the towel up to cover herself.

"Don't bother, I've seen it all," he said.

"Well, the sightseeing is over, you can leave now, the door is right behind you."

"Do you really mean that?"

"Yes I do."

Luis then turned around and went out the door, leaving her naked staring at him. She regretted telling him to leave. What next? Was he gone forever? Two minutes later, the doorbell rang again. Luis must have returned. She wrapped herself in the towel and opened the door. There was Luis on his knees in front of her door with a pastry box in his hands.

"I forgot something in the car, *pains au chocolat* for breakfast."

She was disarmed and laughed and looked at him, shaking her head, and let him in.

"I'm so sorry I didn't call you, I was so angry. Please forgive me. You can never be a one-night stand, you surely know that."

"You are forgiven this time. Do you want some coffee?"

"Before or after?" he asked. She looked at him and laughed again. He was too much. "After" was her reply. He dropped the chocolate buns on the table, picked her up in his arms and lay her on the bed.

"Let's resume where we left off." He tore the towel off her, got rid of his clothes, and jumped into bed alongside her.

"Lie spread-eagled," he said. "I want to ravish you." He spread her arms and legs wide, and his mouth and hands were all over her. She lay in abandon and let him play with her body. She felt like a doll.

"Don't move," he said. "I'd like to do all the work." He then kissed her face and her lips, caressed her breasts, and put his head between her legs and used his tongue on her labia. She was panting and writhing with pleasure and did not want him to stop. He finally entered her and they climaxed together. They lay back breathless and almost fell asleep. She was in another world. She watched him as he had his eyes closed with his arms behind his head. She gently caressed his chest and underarms.

"Um, that's good, continue." Her hand slid down over his taut stomach down to his penis that was flaccid but which immediately came to life.

"Don't stop," he said.

She held him in her hand and caressed him.

"I am glad you don't shave your underarms," she said. "Did you know that some women get excited by the odor of a man's armpits?"

"No, I didn't know that."

"Well, it's true, and I am one of them."

"You are one crazy broad, do you know that?" He raised her arms above her head and kissed her passionately then his lips hovered over her breasts. Her breath drew in sharply.

"So sweet and pink." His voice was husky. His lips pulled at her taut nipples, and he nibbled at them. This was a sign he was going to start again but she said she was hungry and jumped out of bed.

"After breakfast, maybe," she told him, and they sat down to have breakfast. She then got up and said she was going to take a shower.

"Would you do me a favor?" he asked.

"If I can."

"I would like to have some honey."

"So have some honey, it's right in front of you."

"I know where the honey is, but I would like to eat my honey off your cute little tits."

"What?"

"Yeah, lie down on the floor, and I'll take care of the scenario."

"You are absolutely loony, you know that, don't you? Loco."

She laughed and lay down on the carpet with her robe on. He opened her robe, rubbed honey on her nipples, and licked them off while stroking her sex at the same time. She was in ecstasy and she got wet again, and her pussy was throbbing.

"You are boob crazy," she said.

"Yes, I am, it is not every day that I can find such delicious ones with pink pearly nipples. Would you like me to give you a nipple orgasm one of these days?"

"And what on earth is that? Another one of your wacky ideas?"

"It's not a crazy idea, you're the right candidate. I fondle and kiss your nipples until such time as you have an orgasm."

"I don't think that can happen," she said.

"You'll see, if you want to try it one day. Something to look forward to."

"One other thing," he said, "some honey on your pussy."

"Yucks, now you're really nuts. I'll be all sticky and gooey."

"I'd love that."

He cleared the table and lifted her on top of it and drew her legs down to the edge.

"What are you doing?"

"I'm going to have more honey."

He spread her legs open and rubbed some honey on her sex, then wrapped her legs around his neck and licked the honey off her labia, which were sticking together. She started to pant and was gasping for air until she had an orgasm. Then he took off his clothes, wiped her with a wet napkin, and raising her buttocks, entered her slowly; then with rapid thrusts, he also climaxed. She loved it; she loved his hard body crushing her to him. She loved everything about him. He was a sex machine, and she had become one too. They were having a fuckfest.

They went in the shower and played around some more, taking their time. It was lucky that Jean Claude was on a business trip and there would be no intrusion like last time.

"I am late for work. I have to go now." He started to get dressed. "Call me when you can fit me in between your busy schedule with Jean Claude. I will not call you because I don't want to hear any excuses. I want to hear from you only when you can see me. Ciao, bella," he said, blowing her a kiss, and he was gone.

She was stunned. She was hooked by this guy. She had completely lost control of her emotions and actions. This had never happened to her. She had always been in perfect control of herself with all her lovers. But with Luis, she was helpless. He completely controlled the situation and he dominated her sexually. She liked the idea of being dominated sexually, but she had to have the upper hand in their relationship; otherwise she would feel like a slave. The problem was that he was so irresistible.

Usually she had sex with Jean Claude once or twice a week. How was she going to handle this new situation? She wanted to keep Jean Claude. She needed him desperately but she did not want to give up Luis. There was going to be too much sex in her life by having both of them. She had to reorganize her schedule of getting laid. It was going to be difficult but she had to manage it somehow. Maybe two times with Jean Claude and only once with Luis, but not more; otherwise she would be completely worn out. She already felt like a limp rag. She did not think that Luis would be satisfied with having sex only once a week though, and she supposed he would have another girlfriend. Well, she could do nothing about that.

She called her sister and told her of the recent developments.

"You have completely lost your mind, Julia. Are you a sex maniac? Stay away from that guy. He will bring you nothing but misery and lots of trouble and, at the end, you'll find yourself heartbroken and alone. Don't do it. Get away now, when it is still the beginning."

"I can't do it. I am obsessed with him. He carries me into another world of excitement and erotic sensations that I have never felt before. No, that's not true. I have actually. I feel it with Jean Claude too. I want them both."

"Nonsense. You are always like this at the beginning of a relationship, very elated and infatuated, and then you come down to reality. I know you too well. Drop him now, before you create unwanted complications and lose Jean Claude. Is it worth it? This young stud is using you. He has you hypnotized and, when another prey comes his way, he'll drop you like a hot potato. Leave him before you are dumped. Don't be stupid. Listen to me."

"I can't and I won't. I love Jean Claude, but I lust for Luis. Why should he be using me? He can find lots of girls."

"Well, you see you are the unattainable one or you were unattainable. He just wanted to conquer you. You were a challenge to him, and now he has you, and you're fucked, literally."

"We'll see what happens." With that said, she hung up.

Rapport (Relation)

Chapter 8

Cannes Film Festival

The days went by and Julia juggled her schedule to fit in both men. It needed a lot of planning. One day, as she was having dinner with Luis in some faraway restaurant, in order not to run into any of Jean Claude's friends, he asked her, "Do you want to go to the Cannes Film Festival?"

"The Cannes Film Festival? Of course, I'd like to go."

"Well, we'll go then, it starts next week."

"How can I manage it? I cannot possibly go away with you. What will I tell Jean Claude?"

She racked her brain for a few seconds and came up with the perfect solution. A very good friend of hers, Marianne, who was a journalist and a film critique, always went to Cannes to cover the festival for her newspaper. She would tell Jean Claude that Marianne had invited her to go along. She would also tell Marianne that she was going to the festival with Luis (Marianne knew of her relationship with him), so that, in case Jean Claude would question her, she would know what to say.

It seems Luis had been invited by a producer friend of his. He had anticipated going and had made a reservation at the Hotel Martinez. She had been to Cannes several times in the past but had never been to the film festival, and she was very excited at the prospect. Luis advised her to pack all her sexy clothes because they would be invited to lots of parties.

They arrived in Cannes on the afternoon before the festival and the town was already in full swing, studded with celebrities from all over the world. The weather was warm and sunny which was a welcome change from gray and gloomy Geneva.

The hotel was completely booked up by stars, starlets, producers, agents, and the movie buffs. Julia and Luis were a very attractive couple and were often taken to be celebrities, which enchanted Julia to no end. The town was brimming with glamour and excitement. Wherever they went, paparazzi swarmed around them, clicking on their cameras and asking for their names. Luis ignored them with a haughty manner, and Julia followed suit. She loved the attention but worried, lest segments of the videos would be shown on Swiss and French TV, and Jean Claude might recognize her in the crowd of people if he happened to watch the news of the festival. She doubted it, though. He never watched this kind of reporting.

On the first morning after their arrival, they went to the beach of the hotel and lay down on beach chairs cramped close together with semi-nude female bodies in topless bikinis, showing off their enhanced breasts, accompanied by young or older men, basking in the sun. Julia looked around and was about to take her bikini top off when Luis restrained her by saying, "Don't even think about it."

"Why not? Everyone is topless."

"You are not everyone. I'm lying down so close to you. I'll get an erection if you take yours off."

"How come you don't get an erection by all this abundant array of boobs and ass?"

"Those boobs and ass are attached to bodies that don't interest me. Yours are different, yours wet my appetite. I am even getting an erection now just talking about them, so forget it."

"You get excited too easily. Actually, I should be grateful because I don't have to work on you."

"I doubt very much that you have had to work on any guy, my dear."

If I don't take my bra off, I will get tanned with a bra mark on my chest and it won't look good when I'm naked. It will look as though I have a carnival mask on."

"In my opinion, it is sexier to have white boobs on a tanned body."

Julia pouted, put on her sunglasses and a hat and lay down next to Luis.

"Your bra is already very skimpy. It barely covers your nipples. As for your bikini bottom, it hardly covers your pubic hair. I see some sticking out on the sides. You better keep your legs closed."

"Oh, for God's sake, since when did you get so prudish?"

"Shh, be quiet," he said, "and just enjoy the sun," and he took her hand, kissed the fingertips, and held it close to his side.

After a while, he suggested that they take a pedalo and go out in the open sea. They rented one and went far out, swam around the pedalo, fondling each other and giggling like two kids. They came back ashore and ordered some drinks from the waiter, who was taking orders on the beach.

"Why do you always ogle at other women?" Julia asked when she saw Luis casting a sidelong glance at some pretty young topless girls not far away. "You have such roving eyes."

"To assess the competition my dear, and make sure that I made the right choice in hanging out with you."

"Bastard. You always do that, and it makes me feel uncomfortable. It gives me a complex."

"You complexed? You have nothing to worry about. Who are you kidding? You're the most gorgeous piece of ass on this beach. I'm sure you've had men swarming around you like bees all your life."

"How would you feel if I looked the men over in your presence? There, I see one good-looking blond hunk right there. He is well-built and has pecs to die for. Look, he is raising his arms above his head and stretching. I like his blond underarm hair. I bet you he has curly blond pubic hair, which I'd love to twine around my fingers."

"*Salope*, stop right there," Luis growled jokingly. "I thought you did not like fair-skinned men. He is tanned now, but he'll lose it when he gets back to civilization."

"I don't intend to keep him that long," said Julia. "He'll do for the summer. I'll try to squeeze him in between you and Jean Claude."

"Slutty bitch." He picked up her hand and put the tip of each finger in his mouth and licked them. "Relax, babe, you're the only one for me, you should know that. I am getting aroused just licking your fingers because I am visualizing licking some other things. I am a one-woman man at any one time, which I am sure you don't believe. However, that's not the case with you. You have Jean Claude ensconced in your life, and I hate the thought of his hands and lips all over your intimate parts. Damn it."

"There we go again. Forget Jean Claude. I am with you now."

But *she* could not forget Jean Claude. He was always present. Her steady, strong, trustful Jean Claude. She felt guilty all the time. They loved each other and she was being unfaithful to him, but she could not let Luis go. He was too charismatic and magnetic, and she lusted for him. Jean Claude was also very sexy and passionate, but the two men were so different. She questioned herself all the time as to why she was behaving in this way. She was stuck, that's all. Why did both men have to be gorgeous? She could not find fault with either of them. It made life more difficult for her. She was leading a very dangerous double life, and she knew it. She knew she had to come to a decision one day, but she postponed it. It was always "I'll think about it tomorrow."

They went back to their room in the afternoon and had a session of sex, then another one after dinner. All in all, they spent four days in Cannes, and the ritual was always the same. Beach, parties and sex. They went for rides along the magnificent coast, had dinner in charming little bistros, visited Juan Les Pins and St. Paul de Vence, a couple of museums, local artisan markets, and returned to Geneva well satisfied with their escapade.

When next time he saw her, Jean Claude asked her if she had enjoyed her stay. She felt horrible lying to him but she looked straight into his eyes and did so without batting an eyelid.

Le Temps d'aimer (Time for love)

CHAPTER 9

Julia and Luis

Julia had to arrange her schedule in such a way that Jean Claude would not guess that she was seeing another man. She felt so guilty about the whole thing, but she was obsessed with Luis and could not let him go. On the one hand, she absolutely loved everything about Jean Claude, his personality, his character, his physique, his lovemaking, and she could not understand why she was being such a bitch and being unfaithful to him. Why was not one man enough for her especially since she was convinced that Jean Claude was the man she had been looking for all her life? She hated herself for always wanting to try someone else. She thought of going to a psychiatrist to find out what was wrong with her.

One thing that facilitated her double life was that Jean Claude was extremely busy with the bank's involvement with the IRS demands and was often absent, going to Zurich for the day and returning late at night or having meetings that lasted late into the evening. She was also very busy arranging for her next exhibition in Nyon (a small town twenty miles away from Geneva), so they were not seeing each other as often as they had in the past. Therefore, the scheduling for the next couple of months was going to be relatively easy.

She would consecrate her weekends to Jean Claude, unless he was away on a business trip, whereupon she would spend weekends with Luis. And the weekday evenings would be shared between the two of them. Outings with Jean Claude would be in the open, but going out with Luis had to be clandestine and needed some careful planning. She was not only hiding from Jean Claude but also from their mutual friends. No one except her sister and Marianne knew of her double life. They would meet in Luis' apartment and not hers—she did not want a repetition of the first time with Luis when Jean Claude had almost walked in on them. Dinner outings would preferably be in nearby France or small towns away from Geneva. Her life was going to be quite complicated and very risky. She surmised that most of the excitement lay in the fact that Luis was her secret lover and that their passion was enhanced as a result of their affair being clandestine. She had one nagging thought, though. What would Luis be doing on the evenings and weekends that she was with Jean Claude? She did not think he would sit home quietly by himself. He was a social animal and she was sure he would be with his girlfriend, relationship dwindling or not, or maybe even with several girlfriends. She could not see Luis committed to one woman only. He was too young, too handsome and eligible.

Luis introduced Julia to his friends and acquaintances at a private party on a yacht moored at the marina in Geneva. The party was hosted by his best friend Patrick. Julia was dressed to kill in a billowing white dress with a plunging neckline, and conversation almost stopped when she got on the boat with Luis. Everyone wondered who was this attractive woman with Luis. She was introduced all around, and she mingled quite easily with the guests. Patrick took Luis aside and asked him whether he had left Claire.

"Not exactly," was his reply.

"What? You're screwing two chicks at the same time?"

"The problem is that Julia is engaged to someone, and she sees me on the side, so to speak."

"You, a backup? Wow, that's quite a novelty, I can't believe my ears."

"I'm working on the problem," Luis replied.

There was a good band playing, and Julia and Luis danced the night away. They were the talk of the evening. *"Luis has finally found a matching dance partner, is she his new girlfriend? She is gorgeous. Where did he find her? Lucky Luis. He always gets good-looking chicks."*

At one time during the evening, Julia was surrounded by three men, and she was joking and laughing with them and also flirting a little bit. Luis was at the bar with a drink in his hand, watching the scene with amusement. He went over on deck and watched the black waters of the lake under a moonless sky. He was deep in thought. His thoughts always involved Julia. What to do about her? He had to have her. Jean Claude had to go. Julia came over and joined him after a while.

"Did you have a good time flirting, my dear?" Luis asked.

Julia pressed her body against his and, looking up at him, asked, "Are you jealous?"

"Not really, I'm the one who will end up in bed with you tonight. I feel almost like Bernard did that fateful evening in Casablanca when he put his arm around you after the kiss and took a proprietary air, making everyone well aware that he would be your bed partner that night."

"Are you sure you're the one ending up in bed with me tonight, Mr. Ortega?" she asked, teasing him, leaning even closer, and grabbing the bulge between his legs.

"Positive."

"What are we waiting for then, let's go," and she increased the pressure of her hands on his package.

"My, aren't we getting to be audacious." He took her by the hand and they disembarked. They spent the night in his apartment.

Sometimes she saw Luis in her gallery. They would lock the door, put the Closed sign on and go in the back of her studio and have sex on the daybed that she kept there for short naps.

Luis came by unannounced one day when she was trying to finish a painting.

"I'm very busy now. I really don't have much time for you," she said without stopping her work. "I've got to finish this painting, it's a commission, and the client wants it in a couple of days."

Luis just came behind her while she was painting, put his arms around her waist, drew her to him and nuzzled at her neck. "I love your smell," he said. "Um . . . you're so delicious." He handed her a gift wrapped in some sexy packaging.

"Happy Valentine's," he said.

She turned around and gave him a peck on his lips. "You remembered. What am I going to do with you now?" she asked, gazing into his eyes flirtatiously.

"Whatever you wish, querida. I'm all yours."

"What's in the package?"

"Open it." Julia opened the package, and there in the pink box was a red lace bra and matching panties. "Wow, sexy," she said.

"Try it on and see if it fits."

"How did you know my size?"

"Well, when the saleslady asked me for your size, I sort of cupped her breasts and said, 'That's about it, that's her size.'"

"Very funny, ha ha." Julia then went in the restroom and removed her clothing and put the lingerie on and came around to the back and posed in front of Luis.

"You're some gorgeous piece of ass," said Luis, ogling her.

"It barely covers my nipples."

"That's the idea. Come here querida, and let the fiesta begin."

"It can only be a quickie because I haven't got much time."

"I don't particularly like quickies, not with you anyway, but so be it."

She came into his arms, and his kisses were not unlike the first time they had kissed. She was aroused by his warm breath on her neck. They were like unbridled animals. His hands were all over her body.

"Do me a striptease," he said, "and take off your bra and panties very slowly."

She did just that, and then they lay on the daybed, grasping at each other feverishly. Her nipples were hard, and he sucked them with growing excitement. A tingling sensation went through her body as he caressed her.

"Your skin is so silky and smooth," he said. He was intoxicated by her scent and could feel her trembling in his arms. His tongue and fingers caressed her sex languorously as he watched the pleasure in her eyes. He could not wait any longer and, cupping her buttocks, he raised them to receive his penis. He took her with swift thrusts that sent them both reeling and spent with pleasure on the narrow couch. *I am in love with this woman*, Luis thought. *This is not mere sexual attraction.* He realized he was consumed by Julia and wanted to possess her totally. He had never been this mesmerized by a woman before in his life. But how will he ever convince her to leave Jean Claude?

"I am going to be with Jean Claude this weekend," she said, looking at him with a feeling of guilt. She felt guilty with Luis; she felt guilty with Jean Claude. The guilt seesaw was always there; she had no peace of mind.

"Great, so I can do what I want."

"And, what is that?"

"Whatever comes to my fancy."

Julia was very curious to know what he would be doing but she could not ask him. He would not tell her anyway. She had no right to say anything. They got up eventually, got dressed, and had some coffee. He then went on his way, blowing her a kiss. "Call me when you're free, and it better be soon."

Reveil de l'Innocente (Awakening of the innocent)

CHAPTER 10

Julia, Claire, and Luis

A week after the yacht party, Julia went shopping to the open-air food market in Ferney-Voltaire, a small French town on the outskirts of Geneva. They had a great farmers' market there, selling all kinds of food and bric-a-brac, much cheaper than in Geneva. She had to get a few things for a picnic Jean Claude had planned on his boat. They were going to go around the lake and visit the small towns on the French side.

While she was going from stall to stall picking up the necessary items, she saw Luis with his arm around a woman doing some shopping. They were laughing and talking, and she was gazing at him amorously. Julia felt faint. It was the same woman who was at the pool the day he came to say hello. Her heart skipped a beat. *So that must be Claire,* she thought. *He is still seeing her. Well, of course, he is still seeing her since I'm not really available. The relationship is not dwindling as he told me. He lied to me.*

She felt very jealous. She hated the thought that he would still be sleeping with Claire. She kept her distance but followed them to see where they were going. She saw Luis accompany Claire to his car and, after putting the parcels in the car, they drove off. *Hm,* she thought. What could she do about this? She would have liked that Luis break off with Claire completely. But that was unreasonable. He would certainly not stay in the sidelines while she was having the time of her life with Jean Claude.

She suddenly thought of a bright idea. She was going to create some mischief. Luis had told her that Claire ran an antique shop in the Vieille Ville (old town) and had given her the name. It was something like L'Insolite (the Unusual). She looked it up in the phone book and found it.

117

The Monday after seeing them, she was on a mission; she dolled herself up and went to Claire's boutique. She had a plan. Luis' birthday was coming up in a couple of weeks and she decided to buy him a gift from Claire's shop. While Claire was busy dealing with a customer, Julia checked her out from head to toe. Claire was a rather attractive young woman with an hour-glass figure and big boobs. That already made Julia feel complexed, and it annoyed her as she could picture Luis fondling those knockers. She did not like that vision at all. There would be comparisons made. She could tell that she was a phony blonde because her eyebrows were dark. She was very well dressed. Of course, she was well dressed. Would Luis go out with anyone who did not look good?

Julia started looking around the shop, touching various objects. After the client left, Claire came to her side and asked whether she needed any help.

"Actually, yes. I am looking for something out of the ordinary to offer my fiancé for his birthday," she said with her heart beating a mile a minute. "His birthday is on the sixth of August." She was sure that Claire knew Luis' birth date.

Claire raised an eyebrow. "What kind of object would he like? Asian, European, African?"

"I think I would like to get him an erotic statue from the Far East, if you have any."

"Yes, I do have some. If you'd like to step this way, I'll show you what I have."

Julia followed Claire to the back of the store. There on a table lay three small erotic statuettes made of ivory; one of a copulating couple, another of rather a large phallus on a diminutive man, and yet another of a woman fondling herself.

"This is exactly the kind of object I'm looking for," said Julia, picking up the objects and scrutinizing them. "I'm so glad I found something he would appreciate. He is Argentinian, you see, travels a lot and scours antique shops during his travels, so it is difficult to find him original ideas for gifts." She watched Claire's expression as she said this, and she saw the color drain from her face.

"Which one would you like?" asked Claire with a tremor in her voice that did not go unnoticed by Julia.

"I think I'll take the couple copulating. It would be very apropos. I'm sure he'd love it. How much is it?"

Claire turned the statue over and said, "495 francs."

"That's perfect. Would you wrap it up for me please?"

Claire was livid, but she did not lose her composure. How dare Luis get engaged to another woman? He had just had sex with her on the weekend. The bastard. She wrapped up Julia's gift with unsteady fingers and thanked her.

Julia was very satisfied with herself. She had been very unscrupulous and bitchy. She was sure Claire was very disturbed. There would be a row between Luis and Claire, and she wondered what Claire would do. Maybe she would leave him, but then he would find another girlfriend or girlfriends. She was sure Luis would be angry with her, but she knew she had him in her claws and she did not think she would lose him. She walked out of the store confidently with a mischievous smile on her face unseen by Claire. She had fixed Claire. She knew Claire would be cursing her under her breath. But *all is fair in love and war*, she told herself.

After Julia left the shop, Claire was beside herself. How dare Luis lead a double life? How dare he betray her this way? Where did this woman who said she was engaged to him come from? She then remembered their lunch at the InterContinental Hotel swimming pool, when Luis had gotten up and gone and talked to a woman sitting in a cabana. He had come back to the table, saying that she was a very old friend who was engaged to the guy who was swimming. What did this charade mean? This Julia was engaged to a guy a couple of months ago, and now she was engaged to Luis?

Claire had given a dinner party the Saturday before and had invited a few friends and also Luis, of course. He had been her boyfriend for over a year now, but Claire was never absolutely sure of Luis' feelings toward her. He had never told her "I love you." She had a little doubt in her mind that maybe he was seeing other women because, lately, he seemed to be busier than usual. She knew he cared for her, for he was always very attentive and they had good times together and the sex was wonderful.

Luis had a good time during the dinner but, once or twice, his mind drifted toward Julia. He would look at Claire and think of Julia. He wanted to have Julia for himself alone, but he knew it was going to be an uphill battle. The way things were going, it looked highly unlikely with a formidable opponent like Jean Claude to deal with. Luis felt frustrated. He had never had any trouble getting a woman he desired up until now.

After the dinner, when all the guests had left, Luis went out on the terrace, contemplating the full moon in the pitch-dark sky. Claire came and joined him.

"You're in a very pensive mood," she said.

"Yeah."

"A penny for your thoughts," she said and stood next to him, nestling against his shoulder. She held on to his arm and waited for Luis to embrace her. She had no doubt that he would make love to her that night otherwise he would have left with the other guests. Actually, they had not had sex since the week before, and he had acted rather detached whenever she saw him. He had not been the same playful Luis. Luis did not make a move, so Claire shifted her position and put her arms around his neck and kissed him on the lips. She got a mild response. What was the matter with Luis? He had always been so hot and eager to have sex. Why was he standing there like a stone statue? *Am I not attractive to him anymore? Does he have another girlfriend?* she asked herself.

Luis eventually came alive and kissed her back. The kisses became more ardent but suddenly the image of Jean Claude making love to Julia came in front of his vision. *What the hell*, thought Luis. *Julia is getting screwed by Jean Claude this weekend, so I might as well have some fun too.* Claire was wearing a strapless dress, and she was rubbing herself against him. He yanked down her dress revealing her ample bosom. Balloon-sized breasts with huge nipples came into his vision.

"They're gigantic," he said. He was hallucinating.

"Do you like them?" asked Claire, not knowing what had come over him. Luis got himself together and fondled her breasts wildly, pinching them, squeezing them together, and sucking both nipples at the same time, which made Claire whimper in ecstasy. He was disappointed that they were not as firm as Julia's. Suddenly Luis stopped because Julia's face came into his vision again. He pushed it away mentally and pulled Claire in a fierce embrace. He raised her skirt and caressed her buttocks. They were soft, not hard like Julia's. *I'm always thinking of Julia*, he told himself. *Why am I always comparing the two women?* He lowered her panties and took them off. He then took her by the hand and led her inside, and they lay on the bed. Claire was excited. It was the same Luis now, eager to have sex. Claire took off her dress, and Luis took off his shirt. Claire unzipped his trousers; Luis had an erection already. She took his penis in her hand, brought it to her lips, and licked the tip. Luis groaned and lay back, letting Claire take him in her mouth. He liked having sex with Claire. It was so effortless and uncomplicated. He did not desire her with the same wild intensity that he desired Julia but, what the heck, Julia was with Jean Claude this weekend. What bothered him was the image of Julia always interfering.

After having sex they lay back on the bed, glancing at the full moon through the open window.

"I love you," said Claire, caressing his chest.

"*Je t'aime bien aussi*," said Luis.

"*Je t'aime* and *Je t'aime bien* are not the same thing," said Claire.

"Claire, Claire, I can't commit myself to you, not yet." *Not ever,* he thought. "I like you a lot. I enjoy your company, you're great fun, but I can't offer you anything else at this time. I can't promise you anything."

"Luis, I understand, I'm patient, I'll wait." She did not want to lose him. He spent the night at Claire's and the next day they visited Yvoire, a touristy small French town on the northern tip of Lake Geneva. They had lunch there and went in and out of the quaint, trendy boutiques. They had a wonderful time.

Claire thought of the weekend and then of Julia's visit to her shop on the Monday. It did not make sense. She had to find out what was actually going on. She called up Luis at the office on Tuesday morning and told him she had to see him that evening as she had something important to discuss with him.

"What is it?" asked Luis.

"It's too long to discuss over the phone. I'll tell you when I see you."

Luis suggested that they have dinner together. She agreed. She took great care with her appearance, put on a little makeup because Luis did not like overly made-up women, and put on a provocative dress with a low neckline, revealing her ample bosom.

He came and picked her up, and they went to a restaurant in Chambésy, on the outskirts of Geneva. Quite a cozy place. There were not too many people. She acted quite normally with him until after they had ordered their dinner.

"So, what did you want to see me about?" asked Luis.

"I didn't know you were engaged to a certain Julia Chamoun," Claire blurted out.

"What did you say?"

"You heard me. What's the story there?"

"I am not engaged to anyone. What are you talking about?"

"Oh, come off it, Luis. Are you playing dumb?"

So then Claire told him about Julia's visit, and Luis laughed like hell.

"Oh, that Julia," he said, "she is up to her usual pranks."

"Usual pranks? Is that what you call it? A woman comes in my shop and tells me she is engaged to a certain Argentinian and buys him an erotic birthday gift. You call that a prank? Do you take me for a fool?"

"I'm not taking you for a fool Claire, but I assure you I'm not engaged to Julia or to anyone else. I know Julia very well, she is a good kid, she was just trying to pull a prank. There is nothing between us."

Claire wanted to believe Luis. "Are you sleeping with her?"

"Claire, I will not be put to the third degree here. You know I like my freedom and that I can't be tied down to anyone, you know that."

Claire then started crying.

"Claire don't do this."

"It's just that I don't know why you are with me," she said, still sobbing.

"We do not have an exclusive relationship. I have always made that clear to you. I have never promised anything to you and you have accepted it up to now."

Claire stopped sobbing. "Can you imagine what I felt when this woman told me you're engaged to her? You think it's a joke but I was devastated."

"I told you it's just a joke, forget about it," said Luis, thinking of how he was going to deal with Julia.

"So, what now, we continue seeing each other while another woman pretends she is your fiancée?"

"If you want to. And, she is not my fiancée."

"I don't believe there is nothing between the two of you."

"Let's eat our food while it's hot."

Claire nodded but was not entirely satisfied with Luis' explanation. She was in love with Luis and knew the feeling was not reciprocated but she did not want to lose him. They had their dinner but the conversation was somewhat strained. Luis then took her home and kissed her good-night.

"Take care," he said.

"Do you want to come in?"

"No, not tonight, I'll call you."

Claire's suspicions were confirmed. Luis was having an affair with the Chamoun woman otherwise he would have come in and they would have ended up in bed. She wanted some time to think through this new situation. Should she leave Luis?

I am my Beloved's

CHAPTER 11

Luis' Birthday

Luis was quite angry with Julia for doing what she did. He did not know how to deal with her. He did not call her for a few days and waited until she called him a couple of days before his birthday.

"I am free this weekend. Jean Claude will be out of town, so I am inviting you to dinner tomorrow, Saturday, in the same restaurant where you took me the first time, and we'll celebrate your birthday. How does that sound to you?"

"Did you ask me whether I was free this weekend?"

Julia was taken aback by his curt tone. This was a new Luis. "No, um . . . well, are you free?"

"Yes, I am free. I'd like to see you before then though, so I'll come to the gallery this afternoon."

Julia felt by the tone of his voice that there had been some trouble with Claire over her prank. She braced herself for his visit.

Luis walked into the gallery at 4:00 p.m., put the Closed sign on, and took her by the hand to the back of the gallery without saying a word. Julia was very apprehensive and did not like the way Luis was looking at her.

"What's up?" she asked.

"You know what's up."

Julia could see that he was really very annoyed. "I suppose Claire spoke with you."

"She certainly did."

"And so you're angry with me."

"I certainly am. Why did you do that, Julia? Are you that insecure?"

"I saw you in Ferney-Voltaire with your arm around Claire, all chummy-chummy, buying groceries, and it made me extremely jealous."

"You felt annoyed and very jealous, and what about the way I feel when you are with Jean Claude and sleeping with him?"

"That's different, that's—"

"It's not different, and you know it. If you want me to be with you only, you only have to say the word. Leave Jean Claude and be with me, then there won't be any other women."

"But I can't leave Jean Claude, he is my solid rock. He loves me unconditionally, and I love him and I am going to get married to him. The relationship with you is volatile. I can sense it. The minute you'll have me all for yourself, you'll be looking around, and I will be left aside to fend for myself, pining over you."

"Why do you have this idea about me? It is so unwarranted."

"Because you're young and very attractive and there will be lots of women swarming around, and you'll be tempted."

Luis then got hold of Julia's shoulders and pulled her toward him.

"You're so very wrong. You're such a silly woman, Julia. Deep down, I'm a one-woman man and I want you desperately. I have never felt like this about any other woman before. It is torture for me to think of you in Jean Claude's arms." He brought his lips down hard on hers, and his kisses were demanding. "It does not matter how many women I see or sleep with, it's all mindless. Just looking in your eyes and seeing the passion in them drives me insane."

"So what are you going to do with Claire?"

"I'm not going to leave her, if that's what you'd want me to do, unless she leaves me after this incident. I like her company. She is not complicated, unlike you."

"And you compare us while you're in bed, I guess," said Julia, walking away from his embrace.

"Julia, come here, don't walk away. Let's get one thing straight. You and I do not have an exclusive relationship because of your involvement with Jean Claude and, somehow, you and I have to accept this until things change with you and Jean Claude. Can you live with that?"

Julia came back and faced Luis. She put her hands in his shirt and scratched him with her fingernails.

"There, I'm branding you," she said.

"I should spank you for what you did," and he got hold of her and bit her neck lightly. "Would you like me to brand you by giving you a hickey? How would you explain that to Jean Claude? But I care for you too much to cause any trouble between you. I don't want Jean Claude to find out about us and leave you. I want you to leave him of your own free will. Do you understand that?"

Julia looked in Luis' eyes and saw his candor. She nodded. She realized that he did care for her. "Sorry," she said and hugged him.

They then kissed and said they would not talk about this incident anymore. They agreed that he would pick her up on Saturday and go to dinner to celebrate his birthday.

Claire called him up on Saturday morning to wish him Happy Birthday and wanted to know if she was going to see him that day. He declined with some excuse but Claire knew that he was going to be with Julia.

"You know what Luis, I think I will give you some space and will not see you for some time. I think it would be best for both of us."

"If that's what you wish." Luis had not expected that Claire would continue seeing him after what had happened and accept his elusive behavior. She was not a dope and guessed that he was carrying on with Julia. They hung up.

Luis came to pick Julia up the next day and told her, "Don't wear any underwear tonight."

"What do you mean? Why shouldn't I wear any underwear?"

"You'll see," he replied with a sheepish grin on his face. "Also, wear something with buttons in front."

"But I am already dressed up."

"Then go and undress yourself."

"But I'll be cold with no underwear."

"No, you won't, you'll be sitting next to me and I'll warm you up."

"I don't know what you're up to, Luis, but you're crazy, you know that?"

"Perhaps I am. *You* make me crazy."

Julia went in her bedroom, took off her underwear, and changed clothes and put on a silk print blouse with buttons in front. She felt sexy with her nipples brushing against the silky fabric and wondered what Luis had up his sleeve.

They went to the same restaurant where he had taken her on their first date. They sat in the same corner booth side by side. Julia then gave him the gift wrapped up in silvery paper tied with a black ribbon. "Happy Birthday" she said reaching out to him and planting a kiss on his lips. Luis opened the gift and laughed out loud.

"You're priceless," he said kissing her back, "I love it."

When it was time for dessert, he ordered *profiteroles au chocolat*, their favorite dessert.

"Julia, I want you to unbutton your blouse discreetly—cover yourself with your shawl."

"What? Am I going to do striptease in public now?"

"No one will see you, it's so dark in here."

"So that's why you didn't want me to wear any underwear. What are you up to, Mr. Luis Ortega?"

He then took some chocolate sauce from the dessert and rubbed it on her right nipple and, bending down, he licked it off. "Delicious," he said and rubbed some chocolate on her left nipple and licked it off also. Julia was tingling all over and, at the same time, trying hard to cover herself up with her shawl and looking around to see whether anyone was looking at them. Nobody was.

"Are we going to have sex in public now?" she asked.

"Sort of" he said. "Open your legs."

Julia couldn't believe her ears. What was he going to do next? He glided his hand up her skirt and stroked her sex while kissing her on the lips. She got wet immediately. He then took his hand away and licked his fingers. "Even more delicious," he said.

"You can't do this, Luis, people will see. I'm going to the restroom to wipe myself off." She buttoned up her blouse and marched away resolutely.

Luis was always doing these outrageous, reckless things in public. She liked it and found it very exciting and unusual. Something Jean Claude would never do. Well, Jean Claude was more mature.

One time, Luis was standing behind her in a crowded elevator and he raised her skirt and pinched her bottom. She gasped and leaned against him so that the other people would not be aware of what was happening.

Another day they had an early date to go to the movies and dinner. He knocked on her door. She was ready with her coat on. She opened the door and the first thing he said was "Are you wearing a bra?" She looked at him in exasperation and opened her coat and showed herself. "Good you're not wearing one. I can detect your nipples through the fabric of your dress, and they are erect and inviting. Did you rub them with ice, or are you horny in anticipation of seeing me? Also, are you wearing any panties?"

She rolled her eyes. "What are you? The bra and panty police now?"

"Would you like a little rumble before going out or would you prefer a longer one when we get back?" His eyes were already undressing her. She loved the thrill of being desired.

"There won't be any rumbles before or after. Change of plans. Jean Claude is arriving from London and he'll be coming here straight from the airport at about 11:00 p.m., so we don't have any time for sexual activities."

Luis's face closed up. "So you're ripe and horny with that thought?"

She did not respond. They went to the movies, and he was very pensive throughout the film. He held her hand but they did not fondle each other as they usually did. Then they had a quick bite to eat in one of the fast-food cafés next to the theatre.

"I really don't like playing second fiddle to Jean Claude," he said. She did not respond. There was really nothing to say. It was the truth. He was second fiddle. He drove her home in silence and stopped the car in front of her building. Luis was quite angry and he had a strong urge to possess her.

"I don't know why I'm torturing myself panting after you. Your first priority is Jean Claude, and I come second, being squeezed in between his schedule."

Julia did not make a move to get out of the car.

"Kiss me," she said.

Luis wanted to resist, but his desire was stronger and he grabbed her face between his hands and kissed her hungrily, biting her lower lip.

"Ouch," she said. "Be careful, don't leave any marks."

He kept on kissing her and slid his hand under her blouse, cupped one breast, and fondled the nipple, which was immediately erect. He heard a faint moan, and he kissed the other nipple. He then put his hand under her skirt and caressed her sex, which was already moist and twitching. He loved it when he aroused a reaction in her. It was so erotic. Her legs weakened, and she felt totally dominated by him. He was consumed with passion as he watched her lying with her head back against the car seat, quivering. Her body was vibrating under his touch as usual. She brought her arms around his neck and kissed him back. He continued his caresses, and she started having spasms. He brought her to orgasm with his fingers.

"So now you'll be dry for Jean Claude," he said with satisfaction.

"You're such a cunning bastard, you took advantage of me."

"Don't blame it on me, you could have gotten out of the car and not succumbed, querida."

"I'm a very confused person and am in a quandary with this situation. I don't like it one bit. I do love being with you but I also love being with Jean Claude. He is my future. I know where I'm going with him, to a safe place. He is like a rock and I do need a solid man at this juncture in my life. With you, I don't know where I'll end up. It's all so nebulous. You make me fly and Jean Claude brings me down to earth. I've played around quite a bit, you know, and I have finally found what I was looking for. I'm planning on marrying Jean Claude and have his children. Admit it, you're too young for me and, in any case, you have not even proposed marriage, so what the hell am I thinking of? You're not ready to be tied down, you're too young for a stable relationship. You still have a lot of time ahead of you. I do like your charisma, your craziness, and your sexuality, and you make me laugh like hell, and we do have a lot of fun together but that's not enough. I'm sorry, Luis, if you want to go away I won't restrain you although I don't want you to. I want my cake and eat it too. I don't know what to do. I'm in a fucking dilemma here."

"I can't make up your mind for you, Julia," he said, kissing her chastely on the lips. He accompanied her to her door, then got in the car and drove off. She could tell he was hurt but she could do nothing about it.

Amants (Lovers)

CHAPTER 12

Elena and Luis

A week later, Luis met a young woman at the post office in his neighborhood. She was mailing some parcels and Luis was standing behind her, appraising the tall blond woman, when some papers dropped from her hands to the floor. Luis bent down to pick them up and gave them to her. She smiled and thanked him.

After his business at the post office, Luis went to get a cup of coffee at the café in the mall upstairs of the post office and saw that the tall blond girl was there sitting by herself having a coffee. She beckoned to him to come and sit with her. Luis acknowledged her sign and went over to her table and sat down. They introduced themselves. Her name was Elena, and it turned out that she lived in the building next to Luis'. It was a quadrangle of apartments around a common park. She was half Swedish and half Venezuelan. They chatted and Elena told him that she was studying at the Interpreters' School in Geneva. Luis briefly described his work. They got to talking about movies and it turned out that they were both movie buffs.

Subsequently, she said she was going to the movies that evening to see a much acclaimed French film and asked whether he would like to come along. He had nothing better to do, as Julia was seeing Jean Claude that evening, so he agreed. He picked her up at the designated hour. She was provocatively dressed in a tight-fitting pale blue dress with a low neckline, accentuating her big boobs. Luis could immediately tell that this girl was available. The signals were there.

After the movies, they had a bite to eat at a fast-food joint next to the theater and the conversation flowed very easily. He drove her home and, at her door, she invited him in for a nightcap. Luis realized that this was going to be an interesting end of an evening. He did not doubt that he would end up in bed with Elena. She was putting out all the signs and he was curious to see where they would lead to. Julia had been unavailable for over a week now; her mom had fallen and broken her hip and had gone in the hospital, so Julia had been quite busy with that problem every day for the past week and, the rest of the time she had been seeing Jean Claude, of course. So there had been no time for him. He agreed and followed her into the apartment. It was a one-bedroom apartment, very sparsely furnished but quite cozy, with books strewn all over the floor and on all available surfaces.

"Make yourself at home," said Elena. "Help yourself to a drink, the bottles are next to the fridge. I'll go and change into something comfy." *Oh, oh*, thought Luis, *here we go, the fun starts*. Luis mixed himself a drink and was looking at the art and photos on the wall when Elena came back after a few minutes wearing a semi-transparent white lace negligee, which left nothing to the imagination.

"Wow, that was fast," said Luis, sizing her up and down.

Elena came and stood next to him, and he got a whiff of her perfume as she mixed herself a drink. She turned around and said, "Chin."

"Chin to you too."

Elena then put her drink down on the counter and, brushing against Luis, kissed him on the lips.

"Well, did you like the movie?" she asked.

"Are we here to talk about the movie?"

"Absolutely not" was her reply, and she took him by the hand and guided him toward the sofa.

Oh, oh, she is a fast one, thought Luis. Here was a beautiful girl offering herself to him. He was certainly not going to refuse her advances. *Julia has Jean Claude*, he kept reminding himself, and he had no compunction of having some fun on the side also, not that Jean Claude was Julia's fun on the side. *He* was the fun on Julia's side.

He embraced her and they kissed. Luis was aroused. He opened her negligee, and out spilled her large breasts. Elena was looking at him provocatively, offering them to him. He grabbed her by her ass—much to his dismay it was soft. He then fondled her breasts, but she did not make any moaning sounds. She stayed rather cool. Her face was expressionless. He saw no reaction. So unlike Julia. *Julia again. When will this comparison stop?* He asked himself. She took him by the hand, and they went into the bedroom. She lay on the bed and, in so doing, her negligee opened up, completely exposing her sex. Luis saw that she had a full Brazilian. He did not particularly care for bare, shaved pussies. He preferred Julia's fuzz. Nevertheless, Luis stroked it and Elena unzipped Luis' trousers and expertly massaged his private parts. *This girl knows what she is doing,* he thought, *and it is going rather fast.* He then took his clothes off and things happened very quickly. They had sex. There was no tenderness in it. It was very mechanical, with no sensuality. Elena was quite experienced and aggressive. She did not seem to have any inhibitions. Luis did not particularly like sexually aggressive women. He preferred Julia's languorous, sensual lovemaking.

"Let's take a shower together," she said after they had climaxed in a frenzy.

Elena walked ahead of Luis. *She does not have a good ass,* he thought. *In fact, she has no ass, not like Julia's. Is this what I'm going to do? Compare every woman I sleep with, with Julia?* He followed her into the shower stall, and Elena took hold of his penis and said, "You have a very good-looking one, you know that," and she knelt in the stall and took him in her mouth. All this was done in a very mechanical fashion with no emotion. Luis was nevertheless aroused and he pulled her up. They embraced and kissed while the water was running down their bodies. Luis turned her around against the shower wall and had sex with her from behind this time. It was over very quickly but was quite satisfactory.

After the shower Elena asked Luis to stay the night, but he refused. He could not visualize a whole night with Elena. Two times sex was enough. He did not want to feel obligated and give her false hopes. She was just another casual lay and he never spent nights with casual lays. He told her he would call her. They exchanged phone numbers.

So now he had been unfaithful to Julia again. Claire was out of the picture and he had Elena as a consolation prize. He did not feel guilty at all.

He saw Elena on and off after that incident. They went out for dinner, to the movies, swimming, and short day trips. He did not go away for a whole weekend with her. Julia did not know of his relationship with Elena, and he was not going to tell her. Luis was aware of the fact that Julia wanted him all for herself. She was very possessive and did not realize the ridiculousness of her demands.

Elena was very frank about their relationship.

"I like sex and I like you," she said, "but I'm not in favor of exclusive relationships and I don't think you are either. So let's say we are friends with benefits, as Americans like to call it." The arrangement suited Luis like a glove. Elena was fun and a free spirit with no complications and had no ulterior motives so Luis continued seeing her on and off.

Baignade (The Swim)

CHAPTER 13

Julia, Jean Claude, Elena, and Luis

A few weeks after Luis' birthday dinner, Julia was having lunch with Jean Claude at the poolside restaurant of the InterContinental Hotel. It was a perfect summer day, and he was making plans for a three-day weekend trip to celebrate her birthday. Julia was going to be thirty-seven years old.

"Where do you want to go, Paris or Rome?" he asked her.

Before Julia could answer, she saw Luis come in to the terrace and sit at the bar. He glanced her way and winked at her. She froze, and the color drained from her face.

"What's the matter? You're acting as though you've seen a ghost," said Jean Claude.

"No, I just thought of something. What did you say?"

"I asked you where would you prefer to go for your birthday, Paris or Rome?"

Just as Julia was going to reply, she saw a quite attractive tall, young, blond girl walk in and take a seat next to Luis. She kissed him on the cheeks three times as was customary in Europe. Julia hated that ritual and she hated it even more that a girl was kissing Luis. Who was she? It was not Claire. She had taken care of that. Did Luis invite her over to join him so as to make her jealous because she had told him that she could not see him the coming week? She had told him that she was very busy with Jean Claude, going to various functions followed by her birthday weekend. But then Luis did not know she was going to be at the hotel restaurant with Jean Claude. Nevertheless she was very upset. She would fix his ass.

"I think I prefer Paris," she said in a matter-of-fact manner.

"You don't seem happy at the prospect."

"No, I am very happy, why do you say that?"

"Well, you're not smiling, for one."

"Sorry, Jean Claude, it's not that. I just thought of something that I forgot to do—some paperwork, and I am preoccupied with it."

Their lunch came and they resumed their plans for the weekend, but Julia kept looking in Luis' direction. The pair seemed to be engaged in a very friendly and intimate conversation, the girl leaning toward Luis all the time and touching him. Luis was not glancing at Julia at all. *What the hell were they talking about?* She asked herself.

At one moment, Jean Claude turned around to call the waiter and he noticed Luis. "Hey, isn't that the person you were talking with some time ago at the pool?"

Julia pretended ignorance then looked at Luis' direction. "Yes, it is, that's Luis," she said, clearing her throat.

Luis saw them looking at him and waved at Julia. Julia barely raised her hand in return. Luis got off his chair and started to walk over to their table. *Oh my God, he's coming this way. Why is he doing that? What am I going to do?* Julia asked herself. Luis stopped at their table.

"Hello, Julia, long time no see."

"Jean Claude, this is Luis; Luis, this is Jean Claude."

"Pleased to meet you," said Jean Claude.

"Likewise."

Jean Claude was always very friendly and asked Luis if he wanted to join them for coffee if he had finished his lunch.

"Thanks a lot, but I am with a friend," said Luis, pointing toward the direction of the bar and the girl.

Jean Claude turned his head and suggested that he bring his friend over too.

Julia was speechless. *Now what? How can she make conversation with Luis and this girl and Jean Claude?* Luis brought the girl over and introduced her. "Elena, meet Julia and Jean Claude."

"Pleased to meet you," said Julia clearing her throat. This was a nervous tick she had whenever she was uncomfortable with a situation. *Pleased my ass.* She was not pleased at all.

"Very pleased to meet you Elena," said Jean Claude.

Julia and Jean Claude were seated opposite each other at a table meant for four, so Luis sat next to Julia and Elena next to Jean Claude. It was a very awkward situation for Julia sitting at the same table with her two lovers and she tried to keep her cool. Luis seemed completely at ease while Jean Claude and Elena were aware of nothing. Julia felt she was sitting on a pile of dynamite and that she would explode any minute. At that moment she hated all three of them.

"So, Luis, what are you up to these days?" Julia asked to break up the frozen atmosphere.

"The usual, taking care of the business in Geneva, trying to convince my father that I can run it without him and that he should concentrate his efforts in Argentina and leave the Geneva business to me and my brother Eduardo." He then went on to explain to Jean Claude the kind of business his family was involved in. Jean Claude seemed to be genuinely interested. In the meantime, Elena was fawning on Luis.

"And you, Elena, what do you do?" asked Jean Claude.

"I am a student at the Ecole des Interprètes (School for Interpreters)."

"What languages do you work in?"

"French, English and Spanish," was her reply.

Huh. Luis is going out with a student, a young chick, barely twenty-one years old, thought Julia and she was seething as she glanced down at her dessert. She did not feel like taking part in the conversation. While waiting for the coffee, they chitchatted about this and that. Elena looked like a sexed-up bimbo to Julia as she did not have much to say except lean toward Luis and touch his arm. She had a big bosom and it was spilling over on the table as she leant forward. This infuriated Julia to no end. *Don't touch my man and put away your boobs*, she wanted to scream.

"We were just planning a weekend trip to Paris for Julia's birthday," said Jean Claude.

"Oh, when is your birthday?" asked Luis, pretending that he did not know.

"Saturday," said Julia.

"Oh, I love Paris," said Elena. "We should go there sometime Luis, we never seem to go anywhere." She extended her arm toward Luis and took hold of one of his hands, looking at him with her big blue eyes, fluttering her eyelashes.

Obviously Elena thinks her eyelash fluttering is quite sexy, Julia thought. *Over my dead body will Luis take you to Paris.* She had a strong urge of yanking Elena's hand away from Luis'. She looked at Luis sideways, challenging him to reply to Elena.

"We'll see," said Luis, as cool as a cucumber.

Julia was furious and she stomped her high heel on Luis' foot under the table. Luis did not show any discomfort with the pain. He did not even wince but kept a stoic face and did not look at Julia. His left hand was on his knee under the table, and he very discreetly took hold of Julia's thigh and pinched it. Julia almost jumped up.

"I think a beastie crawled up my leg," she said, looking flustered then regained her composure. No one paid much attention to that.

Elena persisted and also took hold of Luis' other hand and looked at him imploringly. Julia felt like slapping her. *You stupid bitch,* she thought. She then felt she was choking on her dessert and started making gagging noises. Luis yanked her off her chair and gave her the Heimlich maneuver. Julia spat out whatever was blocking her windpipe. Jean Claude then jumped up from his chair and grabbed Julia away from Luis and hugged her and comforted her by stroking her hair.

"You're okay, don't worry, just take deep breaths."

Julia let herself be embraced by Jean Claude, feeling very safe in his strong arms and looking daggers at Luis. He was standing two steps away from her, not knowing what to do. He then gook a glass of water and handed it to her.

"Here, sip this very slowly."

"Thanks Luis, for reacting so quickly and doing the maneuver," said Jean Claude.

Luis felt very helpless not being able to comfort Julia himself and resented Jean Claude's role. He would have wanted to hold her in his arms and soothe her. He could see that Jean Claude was like a fortress for Julia. She clung to him for his protection as her breathing started getting normal. How could he compete with a fortress? In Julia's eyes, he, Luis, must appear like a sand dune.

"Calm down, it's all right, you are going to be fine, I'm here," said Jean Claude, continuing on stroking Julia's hair. "What happened sweetie? Did the dessert go the wrong way?"

"I think so." Julia clutched at Jean Claude and stayed in his arms, still looking at Luis. She felt so safe and taken care of.

Luis sat down and, out of frustration for not being able to hold Julia, he involuntarily smashed his coffee cup with his fist. His hand started bleeding, and Elena screamed and was all attention and wanted to take care of it, but Luis brushed her off and wrapped a napkin around his hand. Everyone was seated again, and conversation resumed with Jean Claude and Luis doing most of the talking. It was all a blur to Julia, and she could not wait to get away.

"I am afraid I'll have to go now," said Jean Claude after some time. "Unfortunately I have some urgent business to take care of." He called the waiter and settled the bill and told Julia to call him if she needed him.

"I'll be over tonight," and "It was really very nice meeting you both," he said to Luis and Elena.

"Actually, I have to go also, my grandmother is waiting for me to visit her in the retirement home," Elena said, getting up from her chair. "Luis, are you going to accompany me? I am sure she would love to meet you."

"No, not today, I would like to go over to Julia's studio to choose some art to give as gift to one of my colleagues for his second wedding anniversary."

"Are you coming over tonight, then?" asked Elena.

"I'll call you," said Luis.

"Okay then," said Elena and kissed Luis on the lips and said good-bye to Julia, sauntering away, wiggling her nonexistent ass.

After they were out of earshot, "Are you trying to make me jealous?" hissed Julia.

"She is of no importance. I ran into her this morning and asked her to have lunch with me."

"You ruined my lunch by bringing that empty-headed bimbo over to our table."

"How would I have known you were having lunch here? Don't forget, I live across the street, and this is my hangout. Actually, Elena lives next door also, and she is not an empty-headed bimbo."

"How very cozy and convenient."

"I do have a life and friends, Julia. You don't expect me to pass my days waiting for you to call me, do you? I am not going to live the life of a hermit. Be reasonable."

"Bastard. There was Claire and now there is Elena, both of them blond, both of them with big boobs. How many more are there around?"

"Julia, believe me, whatever is going on with these women is of no importance. Remember, we do not have an exclusive relationship you and I, which, may I remind you, is of your choice. Just say the word, leave Jean Claude—he does seem like a very nice guy though, and from what I see, very caring toward you—and be with me. Our relationship would then be out in the open, and there would be no reason for me to see anyone else. You are a handful, and I am the faithful type you know, although you doubt it. You're the one being unfaithful to your fiancé."

"Oh stop it. The minute you'll have me all to yourself you'll want to screw around. I know your type. And you know I can't leave Jean Claude and will not leave him. I need time to think, to digest everything that is happening. It is too quick and sudden, I am overwhelmed and am in a quandary. I don't trust you that much. I don't know you that well, and I will be the stupidest girl to put myself in a vulnerable position."

"Let's talk about this, come over to my apartment now, unless you have something more important to do," he said.

"No, I can't, I'm exhausted, I'm going home. What happened during lunch has terribly upset me."

"Give me your keys, I'll drive you. You're in no condition to drive."

"No, I don't want you to come over," said Julia rather loudly and looking very annoyed.

"Don't create a scandal, give me your keys, people are looking at us."

Julia gave in and handed Luis her car keys and they drove to her place in silence. When they were in front of her apartment building, Julia got out of the car and went toward the door of the building.

"Okay, I'm home now, safe and sound, so you can go away."

"I'm coming inside with you."

"I don't want you to."

"I'm coming anyway," said Luis and followed her inside.

Once the door was closed, Julia turned around facing Luis with her arms akimbo and said, "Now what?"

Luis walked over to Julia and he took her in his arms. She started pounding on his chest.

"You bastard, I hate you, you upset me too much. I don't want to see you again, go away." Julia tried to fight him off, but Luis held her still.

"For heaven's sake Julia, calm down, will you?"

He had a way of holding her face in his hands and looking at her with his bottomless dark eyes that melted away her resolve.

"You don't really want me to go away, do you?"

Julia then started crying against his chest. "I don't know what I want," she uttered softly.

"You have nothing to worry about," Luis reassured her, planting kisses all over her face before devouring her lips. His warm breath on her neck was intoxicating. The chemistry between them was almost palpable, and the magnetism they had for each other was way off the charts. She gave in.

After a few minutes of kissing, Julia drew away, took his hands into her own, and said, "I cannot stand the thought of these hands touching another woman," and then she took one hand, brought his fingers to her lips, and gave a slight lick to one of his fingers while looking in his eyes in a provocative manner.

"You know what you're doing to me, don't you?" asked Luis.

"No, I don't."

"Yes, you do. You're a big tease, you set out to entice me with your finger game, looking at me with those sultry eyes, but you don't go any further."

"I see that your other women are all very endowed in the mammary department. Is that what you like, big boobs?"

"Anything bigger than my cupped hand is wasted," he said, and he crushed her to him and started to unbutton her blouse. She was wearing no bra. Her breasts were exposed, and Luis groaned and started fondling them lovingly. "This is the size I like," he said while shivers ran up and down her body. "You are a witch," he kept saying over and over, licking and biting one nipple, then the other. The feel of his stubble on her nipples made her delirious. She unbuttoned his shirt and nuzzled against his chest. She loved his scent. It was like an aphrodisiac. She was instantly aroused.

For the first time in her life Julia was experiencing what it was to lust after a man. She was in the middle of a current that was carrying her away from any sensible position. She had lost all control of her actions. She then put her hand in his pants. He had a hard-on, of course. He groaned again. He was also in high arousal mode. He thought he would explode. He took her hand away and carried her over to her bed, and they undressed each other.

"Give me that pussy," he said, burying his head between her thighs. She was wet and ready. They rolled off the bed and landed on the floor. She abandoned her body to him and it responded to his caresses. He lifted up her pelvis to meet his thrusts, and he took complete possession of her.

"You say you don't want me to touch another woman and yet you are touched by Jean Claude all the time."

"It's not the same," she said.

"Explain the difference."

"Well . . .," she stuttered.

"You see, you cannot explain yourself." He got hold of her shoulders and asked, "What do you want, Julia? Tell me what you want."

"I don't know what I want. I am so confused. I want to marry Jean Claude, but I also want you," was her feeble reply.

"Well, that can't happen, and you know it. You may have some imaginary solution to your problem, but it is not what real life is about."

"I just don't know what to do. I know I can't have both of you ad infinitum."

Luis wanted to give her an ultimatum but was afraid of the ensuing result. He was sure she would choose Jean Claude, and he did not want that final solution. He could not bear the thought of losing her. So he went along with her indecision, and it was killing him. His life was being disrupted by playing this hide-and-seek game. She was so irresistible, and he was obsessed by her femininity and sensuality. He could never get enough of her eyes, her face, her hair and her exquisite, lithe body. The whole package was so unbearably sexy, so seductive; it drove him nuts. No other woman had had that effect on him. No other woman had had so much power over him. He had always had the upper hand. He had never before wanted to feel attached to any woman and, here he was, enslaved by Julia. They lay on the floor, panting in each other's arms.

"Every time we meet, we have sex," said Julia.

"What's wrong with that?"

"We'll get bored with each other."

"Maybe you will, but I certainly won't—you are so much under my skin. I want to devour every bit of your body until there is nothing left. I wish I had an effigy of you in my pocket, then I could play with your boobs and lick your pussy whenever I wanted to and do some other naughty things as well."

"What other naughty things?"

"You don't want to know."

"You mean have kinky sex with me?"

"Whatever. Coming back to today, you did not say one word to Elena."

"Why should I talk to her? I had nothing to tell her except ordering her to get off you." She leaned over and kissed him and put her hand on his sex, which immediately got hard. His youthful virility set her on fire again. She lightly caressed him. He grabbed her and, with one swift motion, flipped her over and smacked her on the butt.

"This is for you being such a bitch," he said and bit her buttocks.

"Ouch" she said, "that hurt."

And then he spooned her and took her from behind. They lay on the carpet, satisfied and exhausted.

"I want to suck all your wetness so that when Jean Claude tries to make love to you this evening, you'll be completely dry, and he will be extremely disappointed."

She then remembered that Jean Claude was coming over that evening but, dry or wet, she could not possibly have sex with him, not after two sessions with Luis. She was physically and mentally drained of all energy. Luis had always that effect on her. She had to think of an excuse. Life was getting too complicated. Why couldn't she keep both men? She did not want to choose. She loved them both. They were so different, and they were both endearing and sexy. With Jean Claude, she felt like being on firm ground with her life planned out for her. There were no surprises. With Luis, she felt in limbo, not knowing where the current would lead her. It was impossible to choose. She wanted them both.

"You're fucking her, aren't you?" she asked out of the blue. He did not reply.

"Well, answer me."

"Does it make any difference?"

"It does to me. You are comparing us, aren't you?"

"I cannot compare you to anyone, my dear," said Luis with a mischievous grin. "You're unique," he added and kissed her again and again.

"Yes, but . . ."

"Oh, just shut up and relax."

They got up then, showered and got dressed, and he went away promising to call her.

Jean Claude came over that night, and they stayed home and watched a movie. He had his arm around Julia on the couch but could sense that Julia was not in the mood for lovemaking and, therefore, he did not initiate any moves. He could read Julia like a book. If she wanted sex, she would act like a kitten and brush herself against him. But she did not do that this time. Jean Claude never insisted. He always let her make the first move. He never wanted to impose and be rejected or get a charity fuck. After the movie, he stayed over and they went to bed, cuddled in each other's arms.

Luis was supposed to call Elena that evening and take her out to dinner. He knew that she would expect the evening to end up with sex. Well, he could not do that tonight. He had his limits. He was not a machine. What excuse could he come up with? *My dick is limp—I had two sessions this afternoon, so sorry, babe, I can't perform tonight.* Sex with Elena and Claire was always comfortable but mechanical and certainly not mind-blowing like it was with Julia. It was just ordinary, mindless sex. Once over, he forgot about it. With Julia, it was always like new each time and very intimate and sensual. His desire was constant and they had long, drawn-out orgasms. He wanted more and more. Was it because she was unavailable? He kept asking himself that question over and over again. If she ever left Jean Claude and took up with him, would he still feel the same toward her and would he be tempted by other women? He was sure he would not be. She was all he wanted.

Luis called Elena and arranged to pick her up to go to the movies. In the movies, she put her hand on his thigh, but Luis did not react. Elena was disappointed. She was expecting some petting. After the movie, they had a quick bite in the vicinity of the theater, and he accompanied her home and left her at her doorstep.

"Aren't you coming in?" asked Elena.

"No, I am very tired today and will go home and straight to bed."

"Don't you want company?" she asked flirtatiously, putting her arms around his neck and rubbing herself against him at the door.

"No babe, sorry, I'm really very, very tired."

He kissed her chastely on the lips and started to walk away. Elena grabbed hold of his arm and pulled him back.

"You're fucking her," she said.

"What? Who am I fucking?"

"Julia, of course, it's so obvious."

Luis let out a big laugh. "You're ridiculous," he said.

"My dear Luis, you're in love with Julia and she is lusting for you. It was so apparent at that lunch. The air between you two was charged with so much electricity that I thought sparks would fly out any minute and then the shit would hit the fan. The only person unaware was Jean Claude, who happens to be very much in love with Julia. First of all, it was so obvious she hated me and was glaring at my hand on your arm and was almost ready to pounce on me like a feral cat. I don't know what game that woman is playing, but it is quite dangerous."

"Yes, you're right. I am involved with her." Luis had no need to lie to her.

Elena then shrugged her shoulders. "It does not make one bit of difference to me. As I told you before, I am not in favor of exclusive sexual relationships, so we can continue as is, if that's what you want. For me, sex is fun. I don't want to be attached to anyone or hook him into marriage."

Luis liked her attitude and felt relieved. He was freed from the burden of pretense and guilt. "It's fine with me," he replied and walked away to his car.

Couple

CHAPTER 14

Julia's Birthday in Paris

Julia and Jean Claude arrived in Paris on Friday evening and checked in at the Hôtel Plaza Athénée on Avenue Montaigne, which was just opposite Bernard's apartment in Paris. For a fraction of a second, Julia wondered whether Bernard still had the apartment and whether they would run into him.

"My ex-fiancé has an apartment or had an apartment across the street," she told Jean Claude.

"Are you still in touch with him?"

"Yes, we remained friends, and he calls me from time to time. Once or twice, I went to lunch with him when he was visiting Geneva. He works in Brussels now."

As it was already late, they went out to eat in a restaurant around the corner from the hotel and went straight to bed after having sex.

On Saturday morning, Jean Claude announced that they were going to go and look for her birthday gift.

"I'd like to buy you some jewelry. Do you have any idea of what you'd like?" he asked.

"Oh, Jean Claude, how sweet of you. Um ... I like Lalaounis jewelry, he has a boutique in Paris. Actually, I already have a few pieces by him." She did not tell him that it was Bernard who had given them to her.

"Lalaounis it is, then."

They took a cab to the boutique, and Julia stood in front of the window, admiring the jewelry. They were exquisite gold pieces, replicas of ancient Greek and Byzantine jewelry studded with precious stones.

"Do you see anything you like?"

"Well, I don't know Jean Claude, they are all so beautiful. Well, actually, I'm rather embarrassed. I don't know your price range. They must be rather expensive."

"Do I look poor to you?"

"No, but still, I'll let you choose something for me. You have excellent taste."

"Okay, how about a bracelet? Do you like bracelets?"

"I adore the bracelets." They went in the store and Julia tried on several bracelets and finally decided on an eighteen-karat yellow gold bracelet with two lion heads studded with emeralds and rubies. Jean Claude bought it for her. When they left the store, Julia hugged him, kissed him and jumped up and down the street with joy. Jean Claude liked this childish manifestation of joy, and he so much enjoyed giving her pleasure.

They went out to dinner and had a candlelit birthday celebration at an exclusive restaurant, then came back to the hotel and, upon opening the door of their room, Jean Claude said, "Close your eyes."

They entered the room and Jean Claude told her to open her eyes. There were candles everywhere, and the bed was strewn with petals of red and pink roses, some of them floating onto the floor.

Julia gasped. "Oh, it's so beautiful," she said. "How did you arrange all this?"

"Everything can be arranged."

She turned around and hugged him. "Oh, I love it," she said. "You certainly know how to make a woman feel special."

Jean Claude loved Julia passionately. She was the best thing that had ever happened to him. Sometimes he was even afraid of his unbridled emotions because he loved her unconditionally. He loved her face, her vivacious smile, her expressive eyes, her lithe, youthful body, her femininity, her liveliness, her sensuality and specially the scent of her silky skin. He could not get enough of her. He wanted to spend his days and nights with her, but she had refused to move in with him before getting married. She had told him that she was superstitious.

Right now, he was looking forward to spending an entire romantic evening with her on this bed strewn with rose petals. He opened the bottle of champagne that was chilling on the night table and offered her a drink. She sipped the champagne slowly, looking at him with her doe-like eyes, and then she hugged him again, putting her cheek against his chest, and said, "I love you." She noticed a bowl of strawberries on the table. "Um . . . strawberries," she said.

"That's for later," he said.

Jean Claude had the need to possess Julia fully but he knew he could not possess her mind, and he did not want that. He appreciated that she was a free spirit. He wanted to possess her body. He knew that she liked to be dominated sexually, and he loved it. His arousal was mounting as usual, and he drew her to him and kissed her hungrily. "Ma biche," he said and looked into her eyes. Every time he was with her, he desired her more and more. He could feel a sensual heat radiating from her, and he ran his hands up and down her soft, yielding body. She had aroused in him a sensuality that he did not think he possessed.

He carried her to the bed and lay her down among the petals with her hair fanned around her face. Her eyes were languid, her lips slightly parted, and the whole scene put him on fire. He first took off her shoes, then her stockings, and licked her toes. It tickled her, and she gasped. He then removed her skirt. He stroked and kissed her legs and her inner thighs that were burning under his touch. He pushed her panties aside and touched her sex gently and then groaned. He yanked down her panties and put his face against her mound and kissed her and took her delicate petals gently between his teeth. She gasped again and clutched at his shoulders. He removed her sweater and her bra and sucked her nipples while stroking her sex, which made Julia delirious. She was now stark-naked on the bed with the rose petals and the candlelight casting wild shadows on her body. Jean Claude was in a world full of passion and was so aroused that he had a hard time containing himself. He continued stroking her body, and Julia nuzzled against his chest, moaning and groaning. *Jean Claude is such an expert in foreplay, but so is Luis,* she told herself. *How can I choose between them?* And it was not only the sex; it was their personalities.

While Julia was pondering between her two lovers in between her pleasurable purrs, Jean Claude slipped his penis inside her, and she gave herself to him in a frenzy. They climaxed together. They were both breathless and lay on the bed in a tangle of arms and legs surrounded by rose petals. They covered themselves with the sheet and lay there for a quite a long time, saying nothing, just holding hands.

"Let's eat some strawberries with the rest of the champagne," said Jean Claude after a while. He put on his boxer shorts and went and sat on the couch.

"Come sit on my lap," he said. She started covering herself with a sheet but he told her to come as she was. She pranced over to him and sat on his lap, looking at him expectantly. After eating a couple of strawberries and feeding her a couple and fondling her nipples, Jean Claude asked Julia to slightly open her legs.

"Whatever for?"

"You'll see." And he took a strawberry and rubbed it on her sex, then ate it. "Even more delicious this way," he said.

Julia laughed. "You're getting kinky," she said.

"Do you mind? I'd like another one," and they both giggled like kids while Jean Claude was eating "strawberry à la pussy," as he called it.

Julia realized that she was in love with two very adorable sexed-up guys. They were both sexually inventive and unpredictable. They fulfilled different needs in her. She knew the situation could not go on indefinitely. A choice had to be made—soon.

Julia could not be happier with her birthday celebration in Paris and only thought of Luis twice during the entire weekend. She wondered what he was up to, probably out with Elena, she guessed. She wondered if he was as intimate with Elena as he was with her. He probably was, she thought, and had sudden pangs of jealousy. She was in no position to complain, though.

They had a grand time in Paris, a very memorable one for Julia. They spent their days strolling on the left bank, going in and out of galleries. Julia even found a gallery that wanted to represent her etchings. She was so happy about it. They sat at outside cafés and watched the people go by. The weekend was too short though, and they had to take the flight back on Sunday evening as Jean Claude had to go to work the next day.

Thou art all fair my love

CHAPTER 15

Sotogrande, Spain

While Julia was away in Paris, Luis spent most of the weekend with Elena, but he did not really enjoy himself fully because visions of Julia, screwing her brains out with Jean Claude, kept interfering in his actions. He called Julia on the Monday morning,

"So how was your weekend? All lovey-dovey? Perfectly satisfied and satiated?"

"Don't start now, Luis."

"Am I going to see you this week?"

"Um, let's see, come over to the studio on Wednesday afternoon, if you can get away."

Luis anxiously waited for Wednesday and went over to her studio. They put the Closed sign on the door, and after the usual rumble on the threadbare couch, he said "I'd like to take you away for a few days somewhere you have never been. It will be a surprise to celebrate your birthday with me this time."

"Wow, it sounds so exciting, where are you taking me?"

"Just tell me when you can arrange to be free."

"Well, let's see, Jean Claude will go away to New York some time next week. I'll let you know when exactly."

"That's my girl."

After a few days she called up Luis and gave him the dates of Jean Claude's absence.

"Okay, pack your bathing suit."

"But it's almost November, it will be cold, why should I pack my bathing suit?"

"Where I'm taking you is not cold."

"Where is it?"

"We're flying to Malaga, renting a car and driving south to a place called Sotogrande. It is a very exclusive, gorgeous resort town on the beach in Andalusia, and my father has a house there. You'll love it. It is a stretch of land between the Mediterranean Sea and Gibraltar. You can even see Morocco from there."

"He's not going to be there, is he?"

"Of course not, we'll be all by ourselves."

Julia was delighted at the prospect of spending a few days at the beach with Luis at the start of the winter.

So off they flew to Malaga. They rented a car and drove down along the southern Spanish coast to Sotogrande. The weather was sunny and balmy and the scenery out of this world.

"Have you told your father about our relationship?"

"I don't discuss my love life, oh sorry, my sex life with my father."

"You know what your father did in Morocco. He offered me a whole bunch of jewelry so that I leave Bernard and go off with him. History is repeating itself I am afraid, but without the jewelry."

"You should have taken it and walked away. Ha-ha. It would have served him right."

The authentic Spanish-style villa was set off among the cliffs at quite a distance from neighboring villas. It had a huge terrace overlooking the Mediterranean Sea. The view was breathtaking.

They arrived in the middle of the afternoon and Luis showed her around. They were in the living room, and he embraced her and asked, "How do you like this place?"

"It is so peaceful here," she said and cuddled. *He is so handsome,* she thought. *I can't keep my libido under control when I'm with him.*

He drew her toward him and raised her skirt, kissing her and fondling her buttocks when they heard someone clearing his throat on the patio off the living room.

They drew apart and turned around to see who it was. It was Carlos.

"Papa, what are you doing here? I thought you would be gone by the time I arrived. I specifically insisted on that."

"Don't worry. I am going very soon. I was just curious to find out who has captured your heart or rather your manhood. You have never brought a woman here before. And what do I see, it is our Julia, who had a fiancé and who was supposed to be married by now. How long has it been? Seven or eight years?"

"Papa, stop it and please go."

"Are you still engaged to be married, Julia? Or are you married? Where did you meet my son again after that fiery kiss you exchanged on the dance floor in Casablanca? That was some show you guys put on. I am very curious to know your story."

"Not now, papa, please go."

"I see she has cast a spell on you," said Carlos with a hint of a smile or rather a smirk. "She is a seductive witch, a beautiful one, but beware of her, she is a cougar," he said and made a growling sound. "You'll have to tame her. Other women cloy the appetites they feed, but she makes hungry where she most satisfies."

With that last sentence, he got off the lounging chair and strode off, blowing Julia a kiss.

"What was that all about? I am a witch and a cougar? You'll have to tame me? Are you going to follow your papa's advice? How do you propose doing that, Mr. Luis Ortega? Are you going to put a leash around my neck and give me orders, sit, stand up, open your legs? And what was that last sentence?"

"A quote from Shakespeare's *Anthony and Cleopatra*. He is comparing you with Cleopatra, the seductress of all men. He used to say the same thing about my mother."

After Carlos left, Luis drew Julia toward him, took out a little box from his pants pocket, opened it and presented it to her. It was a gold chain with a heart pendant studded with diamonds.

"Happy birthday, belatedly," he said.

"Oh, Luis, it's lovely. I love it. Put it on for me please."

Luis turned her around and clasped the chain around her neck.

"I will never take it off," she said.

"What will you tell Jean Claude if he asks you about it?"

"Um, I'll say my mother gave it to me, that it was hers."

The house had its own private beach, and they spent their days swimming in the cool sea without any clothes on, and the evenings in front of the fireplace listening to music. They lay on the rug in front of the fire with its amber reflections playing upon their naked bodies.

"I can never get enough of you," he said, caressing her. "Your scent is so intoxicating. A French author once said that the French woman smells like a lion (he was a misogynist), but you, my dear, smell like a kitten when you're in heat."

"And who says I'm in heat?"

He just grinned and resumed caressing her. She could not get enough of him either. She adored his eyes, his lips and his stubble and specially his magic groping hands that played her like a violin. She loved touching his skin and burying her face on his chest and kissing him. He had not told her that he loved her and perhaps he did not love her, thought Julia, perhaps he was merely as obsessed with her as she was with him. That was okay too. She lusted for him. When she was with him, Jean Claude was a distant memory but kept popping up at inopportune moments, reminding her of the choice she would have to make pretty soon.

On the last day, as Julia was lying naked on a lounging chair around the swimming pool just gazing at the cloudless blue sky, Luis walked up from the exercise room, bare chested, wearing a pair of denim shorts slung low on his waist with just a few pubic hair showing on top of his shorts. He lay down next to her exhausted.

God, he is so beautiful and desirable, she thought.

"Why don't you take off your shorts and bask naked in the sun like I am doing?"

"I'll get a hard on if I do that and a bird may come and perch on top of it."

She pulled herself up from her lying position and lay on top of him, sliding her hand inside his shorts.

"Do not wake up the beast if you don't want it to pounce on you," he said.

"The beast is already awake," she said and straddled him. "And I do want it to pounce on me."

"You want to be on top?"

"Not really."

"I didn't think so," and he flipped her over on her back and pinned her arms above her head. "I know you too well, Miss Julia," he said. "You like to lie down in total abandon and be dominated by your man in sex, but only in sex. In all other instances, you like to be in control."

"Uh-huh, maybe."

"There is no maybe, it is a fact. I love it, mind you. I am not complaining."

They rolled together on the grass, and he lay on top of her. She liked feeling his weight on her. The wind caressed her nipples, and they were erect. He rubbed his stubble against them, then kissed one, then the other, and slowly he penetrated her. She grabbed his buttocks. She adored their tautness. His thrusts became more fierce, and they climaxed together.

There was so much chemistry between them. There was a lot of chemistry between her and Jean Claude also. There was nothing she did not like about Jean Claude. He exuded strength and masculinity, and she felt protected. So she asked herself the same question over and over again, *Why am I being unfaithful to him? Am I a nymphomaniac?* While pondering that question, she was inhaling the smell of Luis' underarms and she got aroused again.

"There you go again," said Luis "I love it when you're in heat," and with that said, he licked her nipples in a slow deliberate manner, pulling them gently with his teeth, and she uttered slight moans of pleasure. His tongue slid the length of her body and found her mound. "You are always so wet and ready," he said.

"I was a Girl Guide once, and Be Prepared was our motto." They both laughed, and he caressed her languorously and erotically. She writhed under his touch. He then entered her and they had another roaring orgasm.

They spent the last evening having dinner in town and strolling along the boutiques, buying small quaint objects.

They arrived in Geneva and, as Jean Claude was still away on his business trip, he spent the night with her. He had to leave early the next morning to attend a board meeting.

"I hope I will be able to concentrate this time. I'm having a hard time concentrating on business since I have taken up with you. You are really messing with my head, babe."

"Which one?"

"Very funny."

Plaisirs d'amour (Pleasures of love)

CHAPTER 16

Luis, Carlos, and Eduardo

After getting back from Sotogrande, Luis attended the weekly breakfast meeting with his father, his uncle, his brother Eduardo, their lawyer, and their accountant, discussing the latest bid from a shipping company. They were having coffee, and in the middle of the table was a bowl of Kisses chocolates that his father had brought over from the States on his last trip over there. He loved these chocolates and had them everywhere in the office and in his home. Luis was looking at those chocolates, and they reminded him of Julia's nipples. He started daydreaming.

"And so, Luis," asked his uncle, "what do you think of this proposal?"

Luis looked up. "What?" he asked.

"Aren't you with us, Luis? Hey, come down to earth, will you. This is very important."

"He is under the spell of that sexy, sultry-eyed witch," said Carlos.

"Papa," said Luis, exasperated.

"It's the truth. You are bewitched by her. Admit it. I must say, she is lovely, very intriguing and exotic, but she is not for you. She has you by the cojones. You know, of course, that she is engaged to that banker, what's his name, du Barry. I really don't know what she is doing with you. I guess you're her boy toy. Can't you find an unattached girl? Or are you after her because she belongs to someone else and you want to exercise your power of seduction and ensnare her? I suppose she is a challenge for you."

"This is not something that I will discuss with you," said Luis. "So where were we on the bid?"

They continued the discussion until they reached an agreement, and the meeting was soon over. They all went back to their offices.

"Son of a bitch," Luis muttered to himself. *I have to stop this daydreaming about Julia.*

Eduardo came into his office and suggested lunch. They went to the Café du Palais in the museum district.

"You seem to be really infatuated with Julia, aren't you?" asked Eduardo.

"Yup, but it isn't infatuation, I really love her."

"Are you sure it is love and not lust? Maybe you are frustrated that, for once in your life, you cannot have a woman completely for yourself because she is engaged to someone else?"

"I have asked myself that question several times, but that is not so. There is something about her that fascinates me and appeals to me. She is like a young mischievous girl. She says she needs a father/lover, which, I must admit, Jean Claude is. It seems that her father never took care of her when she was a child. He was very irresponsible and she always craved for male protection. She needs the safety net, protection, security and unconditional love that a man will give her, she says. And she is adamant that this Jean Claude fulfills her needs. He is a formidable opponent."

"Then what is she doing with you?"

"I am her secret lover, she says. We have a lot of fun together, and I know that she very much enjoys being with me. Our sex is terrific, man. We are so very much in sync, and I enjoy immensely giving her pleasure. I am consumed big-time by her. I can never get bored of looking at her or touching her. I want to possess her completely, and I *do* want to take care of her. She is convinced, however, that I cannot do so because of the age difference. She thinks I'm too young to act responsibly. I would say that was me before I met her, but now I'm different, I have changed."

"You've really changed, man—you're not the playboy I know. Don't other more available girls appeal to you? What about Claire? I thought you had something there. You have been with her for rather a long time."

"Nah, Claire is tepid compared to her. She never aroused my innermost emotions. She left me, you know. She found out I was seeing Julia, and she did not want to share me. I don't blame her. I'm not really interested in seeing other girls. I just met this girl, Elena. Yeah, she is young and sexy, but she doesn't send me. There are plenty hovering around me, but compared to Julia, they are just nothing. None of them have her charisma and sensuality. I am totally enslaved by her."

"So now, you are at the mercy of Julia and you like this? I guess you can only see her when she manages to liberate herself from Jean Claude. Do you like being in the sidelines?"

"Of course not, but I have no other choice. I am trapped. I can give her an ultimatum, of course, but it would serve to no purpose. She will choose Jean Claude and then what? She is not convinced that I can love her unconditionally like he does and that I would be faithful to her. I want her badly, and this is the only way I can have her, on her terms. I hope someday she will realize that I can also give her the emotional stability that Jean Claude is providing. Sex with Jean Claude must be good also because I don't think she would stay with a guy if she was not getting it the way she likes it. I'm so frustrated and jealous."

"How can she keep up with both of you giving her sex. Is she a nympho?"

"No, not at all. She just likes it a lot. She likes the sensual part of it more than the sexual."

"And what about you, what do you like?"

"I like giving her the sensual part, and the sexual just follows. Enough of Julia and my sex life. What about you? Who are you seeing?"

"Oh, a couple of girls, but I am not serious with either of them. They are just *passagères*."

"Do they know each other's existence or are you vowing fidelity to each of them?"

"I am not vowing anything. They must know that they are not the one and only. I never say 'I love you' to get what I want. Both of them are kind of liberated girls, and I am sure they are seeing other fellows too. The only thing I have to be careful about is protection. I am too young to be attached to any one person. My eyes wander all the time. You were like that, you should understand."

"Yeah, I was like that until I met Julia. Actually, when I first met her in Casablanca, she intrigued me, and I had lustful feelings toward her after we kissed. Remember that night, when I had a hard-on after dancing with her and I could not stand up? Well, she was in my thoughts for a few days, but then I was with other girls, and I kinda forgot about her, until a couple of months ago, when I ran into her at the InterContinental Hotel. All the fascination I held for her initially came gushing back, and I had the urge to seduce her. The way she looked at me flirtatiously, giving me signals which, I am sure, she was not even aware of, were very provocative. And once I touched her, I wanted more. Her aura is unique, and I am telling you she is unique."

"What about the age difference?"

"I don't give a damn. She does not look older than me, and she does not act older either. I'm telling you, she is like a teenager. She is easy to talk to, we joke a lot, we laugh a lot, what more do I want? And oh yes, we have sex a lot. She does not call it lovemaking, it is sexmaking, she says, and love has nothing to do with sex, she insists, which is actually true. I don't care what she calls it. I love her and want to smother her with sex or love or whatever she calls it."

"You're crazy. I was not aware of the extent of your infatuation. It is frightening. You must hold on to your sanity, man."

"I repeat, it's not infatuation. It is just pure love and passion, of course. She is under my skin, and I want her there all the time. I don't know how long it will last, but I don't want it ever to end. I know I possess her body, but I want to get in her mind."

"So you are waiting for her to decide whether she will ever leave Jean Claude and be with you?"

"Yeah, I hope it will be soon, because I can't go on like this being so lovesick. It's killing me."

"Good luck, that's all I can say."

The two brothers finished their lunch and went on their separate ways.

Nu (Nude)

CHAPTER 17

Luis Again

Julia and Luis really had fun going out when Jean Claude was not around or when they could sneak out to have lunch in his apartment and then have sex. She refused to call it making love. It was sex and lust. Whatever it was, she enjoyed it immensely but always with a feeling of guilt.

"I don't care what you call it," said Luis. "Having sex or making love, whatever it is, I'll accept your definition. You are an enchantress, and I'm your slave."

Their meetings, being clandestine, were always passionate. He transported her to a level of erotic ecstasy that she had never experienced before. Actually no, that was not true; she did experience ecstasy with Jean Claude also with the added element of being enveloped with love and comfort, which was a plus. With Luis it was reckless fun. What harm was there if she was not hurting anyone? She thought that as long as Jean Claude was not aware of her infidelity, she was not hurting him. Why should she deprive herself of added passion in her life? That was an excuse, however; she should be a one-man woman. She was extremely careful in setting up these secret rendez-vous. She had to make absolutely sure that they went to places where she would not be seen by any of her friends or those of Jean Claude.

There was one time when her nosy old-maid neighbor, who disliked her, saw Luis with his arm around her, going toward his car. It was late at night, and what on earth was this woman doing in the garage anyway? They came face to face with her, and she introduced him as her cousin visiting from Zurich. Did the woman believe it? Would she tell Jean Claude "I met your fiancée's cousin the other day." And then the cat would be out of the bag. She could always tell Jean Claude that she did indeed have a distant cousin in Zurich.

It was one hectic summer for Julia. Her sex life was exciting but exhausting. Both men were ardent lovers. After coming back from Sotogrande, one evening after a dinner date, Luis took her back to his apartment, and he could not wait for her to take off her clothes. He ripped her blouse open and tore at her skirt. He then took off his clothes, and he carried her to the bedroom, lay her facedown on her stomach, raised her buttocks, and caressed and bit her globes. She squirmed and screamed.

He then turned her around. "Just lie there spread-eagled in abandonment, and I will play you like a guitar," he said. "You don't have to do anything. Just be submissive. It is more exciting to me than having an overactive woman. I don't need you to excite me. I am excited just by looking at your perky nipples and ginger-haired throbbing pussy. You are my unique and exquisite toy. I wish I could have a photo of you lying on the bed, with your thighs spread open, completely defenseless and submissive like the woman in one of your etchings called Nu."

"Would you like a copy of that etching?"

"Of course, I would. I will put it in my bedroom, and it will remind me of you every night, which is not such a good idea after all, if you come to think of it, when I have other women visiting," he said, teasing her.

"Bastard."

The whole summer went by with her juggling the days and nights between Jean Claude and Luis. It seemed to her that she was living life at a hundred miles a minute. *This cannot not go on forever,* she thought. *Why am I living this double life?* She asked herself over and over. *Jean Claude is more than satisfactory in all ways. I have finally fallen in love with a man who has everything I have dreamed of.*

She was extremely happy with Jean Claude. She was sure he would make a good husband. He was a passionate lover and he enveloped her with love and tenderness. She felt protected by him, and she was finally at peace with herself, and all that searching seemed to be over, or so she thought. She was planning their future life, having a beautiful house, kids, and travels. Her lifelong dream was finally coming true.

And now, *bam*, Luis had come along. *There is no earthly reason to hook up with Luis,* she told herself. It was as though she was being guided by someone else to mess up her comfortable existence. No, it wasn't someone else; it was herself. She was really fucked up with her emotions. Luis attracted her like a powerful magnet. At first she had thought she would be strong enough to resist him, but she had not been able to. *Nothing good will come out of this mixed up situation,* she kept repeating to herself but to no avail. All she did was keep reaching out to Luis. One thing was sure though, her relationship with Luis did not make her love Jean Claude any less. She just wanted both men.

Luis had a sailboat, and they sometimes went sailing on Lake Geneva. He was an expert at the sails, and so was Jean Claude for that matter. She enjoyed watching his muscular body, abs to die for, in short cut bathing trunks, not the floppy American kind that comes down to the knees.

"Why don't you take off your bikini," he said as he was maneuvering the sails.

"Take off my bikini?"

"I want to look at your wanton, naked body while I'm sailing."

"Look at my naked body?"

"Are you a parrot? No one can see you if you lie on the floor of the boat."

"I certainly will not take off my bikini. You will be distracted and cause an accident and I will end up naked in the lake. And the next day, the papers will say, 'Naked Artist and her Man Friend Died during a Boating Accident on Lake Geneva.' I do have a reputation *quand même.*" *Yeah, some reputation she had, juggling two lovers.* She held her position and did not take off her bathing suit.

Julia had been delighted to learn that Luis played the guitar. While Jean Claude was away on one of his business trips, she invited him over one night for dinner and asked him to bring his guitar. Since that first night with Luis in her apartment, she was careful never to have Luis over while Jean Claude was in town. She had to remind herself that Jean Claude had the key. After dinner, they sat down on the floor in front of the fireplace while he played popular Spanish songs. She loved it. It was so romantic, especially when he sang "Historia de un amor," her favorite Spanish song. And, of course, after the "recital," they went to bed. She repeated these evenings a few times whenever the occasion arose.

One day, Julia asked Luis where he had learnt his sexual expertise.

"That's a funny story," said Luis. "When I was seventeen years old, my father calls me into his study and tells me he has some important things he would like to talk to me about. I was all ears. 'Look, son,' he said, 'you need sexual orientation.' I looked at him dumbfounded. 'You're at an age when you're going to do some stupid, dumb things, maybe even get a girl pregnant. I think you should learn some essential stuff from a pro. So what I suggest is that I put you in touch with a call girl who will teach you all there is to know about sex and women. You'll be well-armed after a few *séances*, I assure you.' And with that, he made some arrangements, and I had my first sexual experience with a beautiful call girl. In fact, I had three sessions. Oh, by the way, he also told me that if a woman is sexually satisfied by a man, she'll never leave him. Well, I guess he did not practice this on my mom. So, Julia, are you sexually satisfied by me?"

Julia just looked at him and smiled quizzically.

"What do you think?" she asked him.

One day, Jean Claude was waiting for the elevator in front of Julia's door, when her nosy old neighbor, who lived just across the vestibule, came out of her apartment and waited for the elevator as well.

"Bonjour monsieur," she said. "I did not know that you sing and play the guitar. It is a pleasure listening to it, beautiful music."

"Bonjour madame," said Jean Claude with a questioning look on his face. "I am glad you like it," and wondered what she was talking about. He was puzzled. He knew that Julia did not play the guitar. There was no guitar in the apartment.

When he saw Julia the next day, he asked her, "Your neighbor, the old woman, said that she has been hearing guitar music and singing coming from your apartment."

Julia felt a cold sweat coming on but she did not flinch.

"Yes, Suzie (a friend of hers) has been here a few evenings, and she brought over new Latin tapes of some Spanish singers playing the guitar. We love listening to it." She reminded herself to tell Suzie to corroborate with her in case the conversation would ever come up with Jean Claude.

The next time she saw Luis, she told him that unfortunately he could no longer bring his guitar over and play in her apartment. She then recounted the conversation Jean Claude had had with the nosy neighbor. It had been a very close call, but the catastrophe that could have ensued had been avoided by bringing Suzie into the picture. From then on, it was decided that she would go over to his place for their musical sessions.

Sundance

CHAPTER 18

Tango Contest

Julia loved going dancing with Luis. She had finally found a partner with whom she could really dance. Her husband had been a very good dancer, but she had not found a good partner since. Luis had the grace of a panther; he glided on the floor and guided her along painlessly. They usually went to a place in France called Macumba, where Fridays was Latin night. They were very much in sync on the floor, gyrating to the sensual beat of the Latin rhythms. One day, Luis asked her whether she would like to participate in an Argentine tango contest to be held at that same nightclub.

"Of course, I would love it, but I am not that good."

"I'll teach you, and we'll practice."

The contest was in a couple of weeks, and she went to Luis' apartment several nights to practice, giving excuses to Jean Claude, some of which sounded very lame. All of a sudden, a lot of girl friends had materialized out of the blue with whom she spent some time in the evenings. Luis was a very good teacher, and she caught up on the different dance moves quite easily. She was so excited to be doing this. It had always been her dream to dance the tango again after that one night in Casablanca, but she had not had the opportunity. *What a pity that Jean Claude is not a dancer*, she thought. *Well, I suppose he cannot be everything after all.*

Julia could not sleep properly the night before the contest. She was too excited and frightened at the same time. There were ten contestants. Julia was dressed in a tight red sheath open on the right side and had donned a pair of murderous red high-heeled shoes to match. Luis was dressed in black pants and a black shirt with no tie. He looked so dashing and sexy, the real Latino macho type. Julia felt light headed and her heart was beating a mile a minute.

"I'm very nervous Luis, I don't know if I can go through with it. I'm scared. I'll miss the steps."

"Relax, babe, it will be fine. I am leading you, remember? Just follow me."

They watched the other dancers perform and commented on their styles. Some were indeed very good. The competition was going to be fierce.

There were butterflies in her stomach, but she tried to remain calm and confident. When their turn came, Luis led her on the dance floor and they performed fluidly and elegantly, with no visible mistakes. They looked stunning together, he, the dark-haired Latino and she, the redheaded nymph. Their performance got a lot of applause, and she could hear some people shouting, "magnifique," and "encore." They went back to their table, waiting for the results. They came out with the highest score and went on the podium to get their prize. They had given their names as Ramon and Margarita, in case the event would be written up in the papers, and they certainly did not want that any of their friends or acquaintances from Geneva to recognize their names. It was a very thrilling evening for Julia and she kept hugging Luis.

"I can't believe we did it," she said. "You are such a great dancer and a wonderful teacher." She felt so young and daring with Luis. They had an effervescent relationship, where everything seemed possible. He ignited her innermost fantasies, and she felt a recklessness that had been absent from her life in recent years.

They sat down at their table and she could not keep her eyes off Luis. His mere presence tingled her whole being and sent voluptuous sensations through her body. She felt she was on fire. They held hands, and their eyes locked.

"I want you," he said.

"You have me."

"No, I really want you, all of you, you know what I mean."

She did not say anything. She thought of Jean Claude and felt despondent. She wanted both men. She was trapped between her desire for two men, and the situation tormented her. Conflicting thoughts went through her overcrowded mind.

"Luis, I'm sorry, I can't leave Jean Claude. I'm not sure you will still want me as much if I am unattached. I think perhaps your desire stems from the fact that I belong to another man. Shucks, *belong* is the wrong word. I don't belong to anyone, but you know what I mean. I can't make myself vulnerable to you. I'm trying to protect myself from a lot of heartache. I can't picture a future with you. It is such a blur. I can, on the other hand, picture my future with Jean Claude. It's there and it's solid." She did not want to hurt Luis by saying this, but she had to. She could see the hurt in his eyes. She felt awful.

"That's not true. Whether you are attached or not, I still want you. My passion for you will never subside, and I love you, Julia." It was the first time Luis had ever told a woman he loved her. He was surprised at his outburst, but he meant it.

"You love me?" She looked at him and was very astonished that he actually said he loved her. She never saw that coming, ever.

"Yes, I do, more than you can imagine. Estoy muriendo. You know what it means." He looked so forlorn when he said it that Julia had a sudden pang of sympathy for him. She felt so tender toward him and felt tears welling up in her eyes.

"I'm so sorry, Luis, but love is such a big word. It's a lifelong commitment and I don't think I can have it with you for a long period, or rather, that you can have it for me."

"You underestimate me."

They were then very quiet. They kept looking at the dancing couples. They did not get up to dance again and after a couple of drinks, they left the club and drove home in silence.

"Would you like to sleep at my place tonight?" he asked. She nodded.

He put the car in the garage. They got out of the car and went into the apartment. He closed the door and put on the light next to the door and put his keys on the credenza. Julia watched all these banal movements very attentively. He then took her in his arms, inhaling her delicate scent, running his hands up and down her body.

"You're a magnificent animal," he said, holding her face in his hands and kissing her hungrily. She responded with equal ardor and tore at his shirt, taking in his male odor while resting her cheek against his chest.

"You're quite an animal yourself," she said lightheartedly, but she could tell that he was not in the mood for jokes. He unzipped her dress, which fell onto the floor. She was only wearing black lace panties. He cupped one breast and brought the nipple to his mouth, making circular motions with his tongue, while caressing the other. She gasped with pleasure. He then carried her off to the sofa, tore off her skimpy panties and knelt down between her legs. She put her legs around his shoulders, and he started licking her sex with a frenzy that drove her insane. She dug her nails in his shoulders and whimpered and groaned.

"I'd like to devour you," he said, his sinewy hands working magic on her body. He loved seeing her squirming with pleasure and letting out little cries of ecstasy.

"Go ahead, I'm all yours tonight," she said. They made passionate love as usual. Every time it was like the first time. Julia could never resist Luis. She could never get enough of his mouth and his hands, which did wonders to her suppliant body. And she never had enough of caressing his muscular, taut body. Suddenly, Jean Claude's image intervened. She managed to banish it aside with great difficulty and fell asleep in Luis' arms.

Julia woke up in the middle of the night with an excruciating pain in her abdomen. She felt nauseous and faint. She woke Luis up, then rushed to the bathroom, holding on to her side and vomited. Luis came to her rescue and, while holding her, he realized that she was running a fever. He got very concerned and suggested that he take her to the hospital immediately. She agreed. They went to La Tour Hospital, close to his home. She lay in the emergency room with Luis sitting by her side, trying to comfort her and waiting for the doctor. She was diagnosed with acute appendicitis and had to be operated on immediately, for fear of peritonitis.

Luis got very worried, especially as this happened while Julia was spending the night with him in his apartment. Julia had told him that Jean Claude was away on a business trip and was due to be back in the morning. He had to be informed that Julia was in the hospital. Julia was delirious and could not take any decisions, so Luis thought of calling Caroline, her sister.

"Allo Caroline, it's Luis, don't be alarmed but Julia is in La Tour Hospital. She had an appendicitis attack and has to be operated on immediately."

Caroline rushed to the hospital with her husband, and Luis explained the situation to them. He suggested that Caroline call Jean Claude when he got in from his trip.

"Tell him that her attack happened in your house and that you had to take her to the hospital. If Jean Claude ever finds out that this happened in my house, he will certainly be extremely upset and would probably leave her."

Caroline and her husband looked at Luis incredulously.

"Why are you doing this?" asked Caroline. "I thought you wanted Julia to leave Jean Claude. Well, here is the perfect opportunity."

"No, you're wrong," said Luis. "I don't want her this way. I don't want Jean Claude to leave her knowing that she has been unfaithful to him. I want Julia to leave him of her own free will. I love her too much to cause her any distress by creating a scandal. I don't want Jean Claude to think badly of her."

"I understand. I will call Jean Claude and explain the situation without involving you in it. Thanks so much, you're a good person, Luis, I have been wrong about you."

"No problem, just take good care of her and call me, giving me news of her condition. I'll have to leave now before Jean Claude gets here." Luis then left and went home knowing that Julia was in good hands.

Caroline was stunned at Luis' explanation and realized that he really loved Julia. She told her husband so, who agreed. After Julia was operated on and back in her hospital room, Caroline explained the situation to her. She then called up Jean Claude, who had just come back from his trip to Zurich.

"I was wrong about Luis. He is a good man," she told Julia. He cares a lot about you and, in fact, does love you. He told me so, but you have to take a decision about these two guys. It's not fair to Luis to dangle him in the sidelines. You'll have to let him go if you want to marry Jean Claude, and I think deep down that's what you have decided. Let him go, it's too cruel for him, and he is hurting, I can tell. Don't make him suffer any longer."

"You're absolutely right, but I don't know how to handle the situation, it's difficult for me, I don't want to let him go. I yearn for him."

"Anyhow, coming back to your hospitalization, now you know what to tell Jean Claude when he comes around. You were with me when you had the attack and we brought you to the hospital." Caroline had just finished that sentence when Jean Claude entered her room with twelve white roses and a bottle of her favorite perfume Joy of Patou. He came and sat by her bedside and kissed her tenderly.

"I'm so glad everything turned out all right. I was so worried when your sister called me."

"I'm so happy I'm alive."

He stayed with her for a while then told her he would come back after work.

The next day, Julia called Luis and asked him to come over at a time that she was sure Jean Claude was at work. Luis rushed over with a pot of white orchids, sat by her bedside, took her hands in his and kissed the fingertips.

"You frightened me, querida. I was so worried, thank God you're okay. You'll be out of here soon." How was she going to explain the orchids when Jean Claude came to see her again? Well, she could invent a friend's visit.

"My sister told me everything, thanks so much, Luis. I'm so grateful to you for not jeopardizing my relationship with Jean Claude."

"I do want you, but not that way, Julia. You know that I would never hurt you. I care too much about you."

"Jean Claude has suggested that I go and stay at his place to recuperate, as he has the maid and she can cater for me."

Luis agreed that it would be a good idea. He knew he could not see her during that time, but he was resigned to it. There was nothing he could do. Jean Claude was always at the rescue.

After three days Julia was discharged from the hospital, and Jean Claude picked her up and installed her in his house. He brought some of her clothes over and gave strict instructions to the maid to take good care of her and to call him in case of any problems. He also told Julia to take it easy and relax, and he would take care of her in the evenings. Julia soon recuperated.

She did call Luis a few times, giving him a compte rendu of her life but obviously she could not see him. In fact, she did not see him for quite some time because as soon as she had completely recovered, Jean Claude suggested that she go to Munich with him on a business trip. Luis felt very much left behind. Julia kept apologizing, but there was nothing else she could do. This was her life or, their life rather.

"Things have to change, babe," Luis said. "I can't be deprived of you for such a long time. The situation is killing me."

Amour, amour....(Love, love....)

CHAPTER 19

Jean Claude Again

All through the summer, Jean Claude had been worried about Julia. She acted erratically and was sometimes distracted. He sensed that something was wrong and, on several occasions he asked her, "Is there anything wrong? What's bothering you? Talk to me."

"No, Jean Claude, there is nothing wrong."

"You don't seem to be there sometimes, when I'm talking to you."

"No, really, I'm fine, nothing to worry about."

But Jean Claude was not convinced. Once or twice, he suspected that maybe she was seeing someone else, but he did not wish to dwell on such a probability. He could hire a detective and find out but he did not want to do that. He preferred not knowing if that was the case, as long as they were good together. He was sure she loved him and enjoyed his company and his lovemaking. He was rather an expert and could tell whether a woman was pretending to have orgasms or not. And Julia definitely was having them. He could not bear the thought of ever losing her and he dismissed all negative thoughts from his mind. After all, she was always available for him and never found excuses for not being with him and was almost always eager to have sex. *No, she could not possibly be seeing someone else,* he reassured himself.

Julia had become very amorous and agitated and she clung to him at every occasion, hugging him tightly, pressing her body against his, telling him, "You can't imagine how much I love you, don't ever let me go. Am I first in your life? Am I? Am I?" Jean Claude did not know where this insecurity was coming from. He tried to assuage her doubts and fears by proclaiming his undying love for her.

"Julia, of course, you're first, and you always will be. What's the matter? You seem to be frightened of something."

"Yes, I'm scared. I'm scared that something will happen to destroy our happiness."

"Nothing will happen Julia, we're going to get married as soon as your father joins us, and we'll have a great life together. We are having a great life now, married or not, so why all these doubts?"

No matter what he told her, it seemed to him that he could not pacify her state of anxiety.

Julia was indeed suffering from extreme anxiety disorder. She was preoccupied with Luis. She was not at peace. Her life was in turmoil. She felt like a chicken running around without a head. She had no one to blame but herself. It was her choice to have chosen two men to mess around with. Yes, the word was *mess. It sounds just right,* she thought.

Jean Claude had to go on a business trip to London for a few days and decided to take Julia along with him.

Julia loved London; she had been there several times on art business. Her etchings were in several galleries and they were selling well. While Jean Claude was busy with bank business, she was busy conducting her own business with the galleries. The trip was rather short, but Julia managed to do everything she needed to do with the galleries. They got together in the evenings, had dinner and took in a couple of theater shows. It was all very exciting to be away. Jean Claude had such a calming and steady influence on her that she almost forgot about Luis while in London. He was a man who took charge. He was so protective of her and thought of her well-being at all times, and she always had his undivided attention, whether it be about her work or her family. He was such an ardent lover too. He enveloped her with his passion. She felt a deep contentment as though nothing would ever shatter her life with him. *No, that was not true,* she told herself. *There was Luis in the picture. Luis could shatter her life.*

After coming back from London, Julia saw Luis one afternoon for a very short period, and he was not too happy about it. He felt discarded but did not show it and Julia was unaware of his distress. She was too busy planning her next show and getting ready to go skiing with Jean Claude.

There had been premature snowfall in the mountains and Jean Claude had decided to take Julia skiing in early November. They went to Verbier, a trendy ski resort in the Swiss Alps, and stayed a couple of nights. Julia's skiing improved with Jean Claude's coaching and she enjoyed her stay, skiing in the mornings, having lunch on top of the ski slopes, and taking lengthy naps in the afternoons before going out to dinner. And then there was lovemaking in front of the fireplace in their room. She had a wonderful time and thought of Luis once or twice and wondered what he was doing. When she came back from Verbier, she saw Luis for a quick lunch and a roll in the hay.

"I have to go to Argentina, so I guess we'll not see each other for a while. Jean Claude will be able to have you all for himself," he said dejectedly. "Maybe you'll even be married when I get back. I don't know what he's waiting for to whisk you off."

Julia did not say anything. In fact, they had planned to get married in early winter as soon as her dad would arrive from Egypt, but she did not divulge the plan to Luis. She did not want to cause any more heartache right at that time. And yet there was bound to be a hell of a heartache, and she dreaded the moment when she would have to announce her wedding date to Luis. It was supposed to be a great moment in her life, getting married to the man she had been looking for, and yet it was also the worst moment because she would be leaving Luis behind.

Luis left for Argentina, and Jean Claude had her undivided attention. It was a relief for Julia to lead a normal life for a while although she did miss Luis very much.

I sleep but my heart waketh

CHAPTER 20

Phone Sex

Luis called her every day from Argentina. He missed her. On the fifth day, just as she was preparing to go out to lunch with Jean Claude, the phone rang and it was Luis.

"How are you, pussy cat?"

"Your pussy cat misses you."

"It looks like I will be here a little longer than anticipated."

"Oh damn, how much longer?" Julia was in a hurry to get dressed because Jean Claude would be there in a few minutes, and she could not spend a lot of time on the phone although she loved to hear Luis' voice.

"Do you really miss me? Can you live without me for another ten days or so?"

"I can't promise you, but I'll try." She giggled.

"What a stupid question I asked. You have the other one to fill in for me. Why should you try? Is he working the double shift to keep you satisfied?"

"Don't go there, Luis."

"I can't help it. I'm so damn horny now. I'd like to munch on your gorgeous body. Too bad I don't have a nude photo of you."

"What would you do with the photo?"

"Don't you know what teenage boys do when they look at photos in *Playboy* or *Penthouse* magazines?"

"Nonsense. I don't think you would revert to that. You must have oodles of ex-girlfriends all lined up to take care of your sexual needs."

"I do have ex-girlfriends, but they are not lined up, and I'm not interested in them. I hunger only after you and your perky little breasts and your wet pussy, and I am extremely jealous that the other one can play with them and I can't."

"I said don't go there."

"What are you wearing?"

"A bathrobe."

"Are you naked underneath?"

"No, I have a bra and panties on."

"What color? I hope you don't wear my Valentine's Day gift when you go out with JC."

"No, I don't. I'm wearing black lace. Are you excited?"

"Of course, I am. Take them off so that I can visualize nibbling on your nipples and tasting your petals."

"What's in it for me?"

"You can play with them also and get yourself excited thinking of me." "Jerk."

"Why don't you go and lie on your bed in abandon and imagine that my mouth and hands are all over you, making you deliriously happy. This is what I'd like you to do right now. Wet the fingers of both hands and rub them on your nipples and fondle them while you make some moaning noises like you usually do."

"You're crazy."

"I'd like to continue my lovemaking, so hush. Come on, humor me, go lie on the bed and spread your legs wide so that I can munch the hell out of you, suck your pussy dry while you whimper and squirm and tell me how much you yearn for me."

"Wow, that's a biggie. I am getting excited. How is this going to help me? And what are you doing over there?"

"What am I doing? You really want to know? Well, I have a girl here who is doing things to me for a change." Luis said, teasing her.

"Bastard."

"Why should you have all the fun? Don't I deserve to have some fun too? I hope you think of me when you are doing it with JC."

"Oh, stop that. I've got to go now, Luis, I have a luncheon appointment." She did not tell him it was with Jean Claude, though.

"Come back soon, my Latin lover, I miss you."

"Ciao, bella."

Julia became very sexually aroused after this phone conversation and wished Luis was present to consummate their verbal foreplay.

Jean Claude came to pick her up to go to lunch. "You're not yet dressed."

She was still in her bra and panties and went and rubbed herself against Jean Claude.

"What's this all about?" he asked.

Julia could not get the phone sex out of her mind. She was horny as hell and wanted Jean Claude to make love to her right there and then. She nuzzled against his chest and flung her arms around him.

"Make love to me," she said. She had to have sex; she could not wait for the evening.

"Now?"

"Yes, now, I feel like it right now." And she got on tiptoes and bit Jean Claude's lower lip.

"I have a three o'clock appointment, I cannot be late, and we have to have lunch before that."

"It's only 12:30. We have plenty of time for sex, lunch and your appointment."

"Don't you want to wait until tonight? We'll have more time then."

"Tonight is too late, I feel like it right now." And she rubbed herself against him again.

Just like a cat, he thought.

"Am I being too demanding?"

"You're never too demanding with me. You're my *femme-enfant*. Okay, let's go, but I'm afraid it will have to be a quickie, and I hate quickies."

"I don't care."

Jean Claude was quite surprised at the way Julia was acting. It was so out of character and so unlike her to initiate sex so obviously but hey, she wanted it, and he was always eager. He took off his jacket, and Julia started to unbutton his shirt, then put her hand inside his trousers.

"I'm ready as always," said Jean Claude with a twinkle in his eyes. He picked her up and lay her down on the couch. He tore away at her underwear and got her naked in a jiffy. He then started to remove his clothes, but she stopped him.

"I'd like you to keep your clothes on. I have always fancied the idea of a naked woman with a fully clothed man, just like in Delvaux's paintings. It's kinda sexy. I've always been fascinated by his paintings. Sometime, when we have more time, I would like to dance with you, me naked with only high heels on and you with your suit and tie on."

Jean Claude liked that idea also and thought it was very sexy and original. He lay on top of her, kissing her passionately and running his hands all over her body, caressing her. The gentleness of his fingers explored her core, and Julia pulled his face toward her and kissed him hungrily.

For Jean Claude, every time with Julia was like the first time, exhilarating. She was so sensual and sometimes insatiable, and he loved it.

"I love it, Jean Claude," she said as he straddled her. He then brought his head down between her legs, his mouth suckling her throbbing sex and his teeth grazing her petals while his fingers tweaked her nipples. Her heart was racing like mad.

"Don't stop," she cried out.

She lost herself in his embraces and, at some moment, she forgot who was on top of her, whether it was Luis or Jean Claude. She almost felt as if two mouths and four hands were working at the same time on her body, stroking her, biting her, licking her. She did not know whose lips was doing the kissing. She felt herself intertwined with two pairs of powerful masculine legs and arms, and she was almost delirious. She uttered a few very loud moans and was in an intensely euphoric state and, at one point, cried out, "Luis."

"What did you say?"

Oops, she had to correct that. "'I wish,' I said."

"You wish what?"

"I wish we had more time."

"We can have more time tonight after my dinner engagement, if you wish."

"Yes, I'd like that."

Julia actually loved both men. She could not choose between them. They were both adorable and she enjoyed them in different ways. With Jean Claude, she was coy and loving while with Luis she was more teasing and flirtatious. They were also both very good in bed. Her sex life had never been better. Jean Claude enveloped her with eternal love while Luis exuded an aura of forbidden pleasures. With Jean Claude, she felt on steady ground. He was like a rock. The future looked solid and safe. With Luis, she felt as though she was floating on a fast-flowing river with excitement at every turn, never knowing where it would take her.

She always wondered how one can choose a lifetime partner. Things were bound to change. It was inevitable. People would change. They would not feel the same way toward each after a while. She had seen this happen often with married couples. One thing she was sure of though; she was never bored with either of them. Why should life be so conventional? She needed spice, and she had it. Maybe she should make a list of the pros and cons of each man and see who had the most pros, and maybe then it would be easier to choose and she could then take a final decision.

Her sister always told her that she was playing with fire. That she should settle down with Jean Claude and forget about Luis. That she would grow old someday and would lose her attractiveness and she would not find another guy as good as Jean Claude. Her sister was right. She knew this situation could not last forever. It would come to an end one day, and she did not know what the future held for her.

There were days when she thought she had come to a final decision—her choice was Jean Claude. Then she would see Luis, and she would be indecisive. This pendulum state of affairs went on for days and weeks. It was very nerve-racking. Deep down, she knew that the sensible course of action was to leave Luis and marry Jean Claude. She had to be reasonable and logical.

Jean Claude came over quite late after his dinner, and Julia was asleep. He took off his clothes and slipped in next to her.

"Um, my teddy bear," she said.

Jean Claude madly loved this woman, her enthusiasm, her liveliness, her smell, her skin, and he felt so contented and fulfilled whenever he was with her. He had found the love of his life. He caressed her arm, kissed her gently, and he fell asleep spooning her.

They woke up in the same position. Julia turned around and faced him and looked in his eyes. Those tender and trusting eyes bothered her. She felt so guilty. It was obvious that Jean Claude adored her, and here she was being unfaithful to him. She felt horrible. She hated herself. She stroked his face and kissed him tenderly.

"*Mon amour*," he said and squeezed her against him. His body felt so good against hers, the feeling of flesh touching flesh. She nuzzled against him. She did not want to leave the bed, but he got up because he had to go to work.

"See you tonight," he said. "We'll have a quiet dinner at my place. Blanca (his housekeeper) will prepare something to eat. What would you like?" he asked.

"Paella, if it's not too much trouble."

"Paella it will be." Julia looked at Jean Claude as he was getting dressed, and she liked what she saw, a mature body yet very muscular and virile. She liked macho-looking men but not macho-minded men. Both Jean Claude and Luis were very macho-looking, and they dominated her sexually. She liked male sexual dominance. She did not like men to dominate her in other domains, though. She was a free spirit and liked independence. Who would have thought a simple, or not so simple, kiss eight years ago would lead to such complications.

Jean Claude left to go to work, and she stayed in bed, daydreaming about both men intermittently. She then got up and had breakfast. Luis called.

"Did you have sex with JC yesterday after we talked?"

"And good morning to you too, Latin lover."

"Did you?"

"I will not answer that."

"You don't have to. I know the answer. I was a fool to get you all excited and handing you over to JC, ripe for the picking."

"Stop it please, Luis."

"I am a stupid jerk. Never again. You're a floozy."

"But you like your floozy, don't you?"

"Of course, I like my floozy. I adore my floozy, all wet and panting at the sight of me."

"You'll have her as soon as you come back. But hurry."

"I miss you bella," he said and hung up.

And now she felt guilty because Luis was miserable. This seesaw situation would never end until she took a firm, definitive action, but she was not able to be decisive. She liked being wild and reckless, but until when?

Temps perdu (Lost time)

CHAPTER 21

Luis in Argentina

After the telephone conversation with Julia, Luis felt very horny. He should never have called Julia and had phone sex with her. The result was frustrating. He did not know at the time how big a mistake that was.

That same evening, he was invited to a party given by Olivia, one of his old girlfriends; they had known each other since they were kids. She had already been married once and divorced. Luis always looked her up whenever he was in Buenos Aires. She was good fun, and they sometimes had casual sex whenever he was in town. It was nothing serious and they both knew it and she accepted it. She had invited a lot of people, mostly people they both knew. The music was great, and couples were dancing around the pool at the frenetic rhythm of Latin music. The buffet was sumptuous, and there was a lot of boozing, flirting, and cavorting going on. This was modern-day Buenos Aires, where marriages or liaisons disintegrated at parties and couples drifted apart. Some were almost making out on the lawn, others in the bedrooms or bathrooms. A few of the guests even jumped in the pool after getting rid of restrictive clothing, and the party almost turned into an orgy. Luis looked at the scene around him and, somehow, he did not feel that he was part of this kind of partying any longer. He felt out of it. He was hung up on Julia. Always Julia.

Olivia came over to him "Luis, you do not seem to be enjoying yourself, what's the matter?"

Luis just grunted and reassured her that everything was fine. And then he got drunk. He just wanted to go home to bed, but he was too drunk to drive.

"Can I go and lie down on your bed for a while until I sober up to go home?" he asked her. Olivia told him to do as he pleased.

The party ended at around 5:00 a.m., and all the guests had left when Olivia wondered where Luis was. He had not bid her good-bye. She found him still asleep, sprawled on her bed with all his clothes on. She smiled to herself. *Poor Luis,* she thought. *He was not his usual self tonight.* She undressed completely and lay down naked next to him, pulling a sheet over herself. She soon fell asleep. She woke up once or twice because Luis was speaking in his sleep and uttering the words, "Julia, don't leave me, I love you, I want you, I can't live without you." She realized this must be a girl that Luis was seeing in Switzerland. She did not pay too much attention to it and continued sleeping. *There was always a girl Luis was seeing somewhere,* she told herself.

Luis woke up groggily in the morning, not knowing where he was. He extended an arm and made contact with Olivia's naked body. In his semiconscious state, he thought it was Julia and hugged her. "Come here and let me kiss you," he said. Olivia woke up and thought Luis was talking to her, so she snuggled closer to him, and they kissed. Luis did not realize at first that it was not Julia he was kissing as he had a hell of a hangover and had not opened his eyes yet. His hands found her breasts, which he started to fondle. Somehow they felt different to his touch. They continued kissing and Olivia glided her hand in his trousers and felt his erection. She unzipped his trousers, took out his penis and stroked it, then put it in her mouth.

"Oh, Julia, no, you don't have to do that," Luis uttered.

Olivia was taken aback and stopped. She realized that Luis was still in a drunken stupor, dreaming of Julia, whoever that girl was.

"I'm not Julia," she said and continued sucking him while he was caressing her. Luis jumped up then and opened his eyes. "Oh my God," he said, "I thought you were someone else."

"Did you think I was Julia?"

"How do you know about Julia?"

"You were talking in your sleep, my dear Luis."

"So sorry," and he looked down on his erect penis and covered it up. He felt embarrassed.

"Is this a new love, then? You seem to be very taken in by this woman."

"I guess I am, I can't get her out of my mind." He had no need to hide anything from Olivia, and he related to her the problems of his relationship with Julia.

"Poor you, what are you going to do about it?"

"What can I do about it? Nothing, just wait and see. And I get horny as hell whenever I am away from her and think about her all the time. I can't let go."

"No problem," said Olivia, "we can still have fun together if you wish, and I can take care of your frustration," casting a meaningful glance in the direction of his penis. Obviously, this would not be the first time that they had had casual, mindless sex together. *She is a very accommodating girl*, thought Luis.

Luis looked at her and laughed, then thought, *What the hell, why not? Julia is screwing her brains out with JC, so I will go ahead and have some fun with Olivia.* She was a good kid and seemed to be unattached at the moment. He took off his clothes in a jiffy and pulled her toward him, tossing all his misgivings aside.

After having penetrated her, she said, "Stop, here let me give you a condom. I have stopped taking the pill because of some health problems."

They had a frenzied, unbridled sex, animal-like, no emotions involved on either part. Then they lay together side by side, contented, and did not say a word. There was nothing to say. They had satisfied each other's sexual needs. Luis saw Olivia often during his stay in Buenos Aires, and their sexual liaison continued until he left. Olivia did not expect anything more. It also suited Luis just fine.

Rise up my love and come away

CHAPTER 22

Return from Argentina

"I am so angry with you. Why didn't you come by as soon as you arrived?" Julia scolded Luis when he came to see her on his return from Buenos Aires. "You did not even tell me when you were arriving. I would have picked you up from the airport. I suppose you went to see Elena yesterday."

Luis took her in his arms and embraced her. "Don't be absurd. I knew I was going to be dead tired upon arrival, and I just wanted to go home and sleep. I would not have been of any use to you, my dear Julia, had I come around yesterday. Now I am fresh and ready to play. By the way, where is JC? I hope we will not be interrupted by him this evening."

"JC has gone to Grenoble to see his mother. She is not doing too well." Julia then walked away from his embrace, still angry.

"Why are you walking away babe, come here, let me hold you and kiss you. I am dying for the feel and smell of your sexy body."

Julia turned around and walked toward him. Luis grabbed her and pulled her against his chest. He untied the belt of her bathrobe and growled.

"Magnificent" he said.

Julia looked up at him and started melting as usual whenever Luis embraced her. She tried to unbutton his shirt; the buttonholes were too small, so she tore it off him and kissed his chest, digging her nails in his back.

"Let's take it easy," Luis said and led her to the couch. "I have something important to tell you."

"You have decided to leave Elena."

"No. It's not that. Don't cover yourself. I like to gorge my eyes on your nakedness."

"So what's so important that we can't kiss before you tell me this important thing."

"My father is semi-retiring, and I'm being transferred to Argentina to take care of the business."

"What?" Julia felt panicky. She started trembling. "You're leaving Geneva? For good?"

Luis then took her in his arms again and said, "Yes, but I'm not leaving you. Marry me, Julia, and come with me. You know I love you, I'm crazy about you."

Julia looked at him and could not believe her ears. Luis loved her and wanted to marry her?

"Since when have you decided that you love me? You can't possibly want to marry me, you're too young, Luis." And suddenly she came out with "And, in any case, I'm getting married to Jean Claude, you know that. Right after the New Year."

"What? No, I didn't know that you were planning on getting married so soon. When did that come about? When were you planning on telling me?"

"Oh, Luis, I'm so sorry, but that's what I decided because I can't go on this way having two men in my life at the same time. It's driving me nuts. I don't eat properly, I don't sleep properly. I'm always in a state of exhaustion, panic and fear. I'm living on the edge. I have to lie to Jean Claude all the time. He does not deserve this. He is a very good and decent man, and I can't continue on treating him badly and cheat on him any longer and, most important of all, I love him. He is the man for me. You must understand this. You started out as a fling, and then you grew on me and I got stuck to you, but I'll have to unstick myself and lead a normal life. I love you also, Luis, very much, in fact. You're my flowing river that takes me to unimaginable places. I want to hold on to you but it is unreasonable. I have to let you go."

"Julia, what are you saying? You're going to let me go? I can't stand this." And Luis gripped her shoulders tightly and drew her toward him and started to kiss her hungrily.

"Luis, be reasonable, you're too young to get married. I am seven years older than you are, and I will want to have children almost immediately, and I can't oblige you to accept that. You don't want to be a father now, do you?"

"I want everything that comes along with you. You want children? Then I want children."

"No, you don't mean that. You can't mean that."

"How can you tell me what I mean or not?"

Julia looked at Luis and saw the hurt in his beautiful dark brown eyes.

"I have to let you go Luis," she said with tears welling up in her eyes.

With one swift movement, Luis took off her robe and carried her to bed. He then took off his clothes and crushed her to him.

"I won't let you leave me, you're everything to me," he said and kissed her face and her body hungrily, running his hands up and down. He was consumed with passion. His lips travelled down from her lips to her nipples to her sex, and he groaned, and with the flick of his tongue, he separated her labia and licked her.

"Oh Julia, you drive me insane, you can't leave me."

Julia started sobbing but she snuggled up to him and matched his ardor. She took his penis in her hand and caressed it gently and inserted it into her. They made passionate love as usual, and then they lay exhausted and consumed and fell asleep. When they woke up the next morning, they tried to talk, but they were both too emotional. Luis enveloped Julia in his arms and just looked at her. He was hurting badly. She felt devastated but could not utter a word.

"I'm going to the Middle East tomorrow on a short business trip. I'll see you when I get back and hope you'll change your mind about marrying JC. Please think seriously about my proposal."

"My mind is made up, Luis. I will not think further." And she started sobbing.

"So last night didn't mean anything to you?"

"Of course it meant something. It meant a lot. It reinforced my love toward you but I must let you go, it's the reasonable thing to do."

They kissed again, and Luis left feeling very unhappy but still hoped that she might change her mind.

"I'm not giving up on us," he said.

Julia felt shattered. She just let Luis go out of her life—her darling, impulsive Luis. She did not know how she got through with her daily activities but she was exhausted at night and flopped into bed. Her mind raced and her thoughts were getting extremely confused.

Luis called her. "Sleep tight, my love, and think of me," was all he said. She reached out to take her birth-control pill, then remembered that she had not taken one the night before. She froze. *Oh my God, and it is just the right time of the month to become pregnant* she thought. She hoped by missing one day would not make a difference and reminded herself to ask her doctor about it the next day. She did not call Luis. What could he do about it anyway?

The doctor told her that missing a pill could indeed make her pregnant and Julia started getting quite anxious about it. She tried to brush the thought out of her mind. She did not need this added complication just when she had decided on the sensible course of action, which was to marry Jean Claude and let Luis go. The only thing to do was wait for her next period.

Rêve (Dream)

CHAPTER 23

Meeting Eduardo

Luis called Julia on his return from the Middle East, but Julia would not see him. She told him that her decision was final and that there was no need to prolong the agony. He was very heartbroken but could not do a thing about it.

"If you ever change your mind, you know how to get hold of me," he said as they said good-bye. She was crying on the phone.

Her decision having been taken, Julia started concentrating on the plans Jean Claude had made for the rest of the winter. They went skiing a few times in France and Switzerland, and Julia got into a routine. She did not hear from Luis again and presumed he had left for Argentina to take on the business. She missed him terribly of course but she was determined to let go and tried very hard not to think about it.

"You did the right thing," her sister told her. "He'll get over it in time, he's young."

What about me, will I get over it? She asked herself.

A month went by, and Jean Claude made plans to take Julia on a boat trip up the Nile for New Year's. They would first meet her father in Cairo and make the final arrangements for his move to Geneva. His visa had come, and he was getting ready to leave.

Julia was doing some last-minute shopping for her trip to Egypt a couple of days before their departure and stopped at a café to grab a cup of coffee when she saw Eduardo, Luis' brother, come in. He gave her a peck on the cheek, and after *how are you's* and *what have you been doing*, he came out with, "Do you know that Luis got married?"

"What?" She felt weak in the knees, and the color drained from her face. She could hardly concentrate on what Eduardo was telling her. She thought she would faint but tried to get a grip on herself by taking deep breaths and holding on to her chair. She tried to focus on what Eduardo was telling her.

"He got married in Argentina, very soon after leaving Geneva, and they are having a baby. Actually he had to marry her because he got her pregnant on his other trip it seems, but don't ever tell him I told you this. He was very devastated. He was not ready for this turn of events. He did not want to marry this woman, but he did not want a child to grow up fatherless. He really loved you, Julia, and he was miserable when you left him, and I suppose he found consolation elsewhere. But he was not careful. It is not really like Luis not to be careful. This is really very strange. I don't really know the details of his involvement with this woman and what actually transpired between them or how she got pregnant. All I know is that her father is in business with ours and that we know the family since a long time. Luis and this woman, Olivia, already knew each other when they were young, and they had dated when he came back to Argentina during the summers when he was studying in the U.S.

"What are you talking about? His wife is pregnant?" she managed to blurt out with a broken voice, and she fell off her chair and was almost fainting, but Eduardo caught her on time before she fell on to the floor. He revived her by tapping on her cheeks.

"Are you okay, Julia, what happened? Shall I call an ambulance?"

"No, no, I'll be fine," she managed to utter. "Could you please call a cab, I don't think I should drive."

"I'm taking you to the emergency clinic," said Eduardo.

"No, no, it's not necessary, I'm okay."

"No, you're not. You're very pale. A doctor has to check you out," he insisted and took hold of her arm, walked her toward his car which was parked right outside the café. He drove her to the emergency clinic of the Cantonal Hospital.

"I'll wait for you," he said.

Julia insisted that he leave her, that she would be all right, but he did not listen to her plea. Together they waited for the doctor.

"I shouldn't have told you this news. Obviously, you still care for him and it bothers you. But you *did* leave him, Julia. He wanted to be with you, and he was so sure you wanted to be with him also. I have never seen Luis so much in love and attached to a woman before and, believe me, he has had plenty. You broke his heart, Julia. But I guess you had your reasons."

Eduardo waited outside in the reception hall while Julia was being examined by the doctor. She was very agitated and frightened. They did some blood work and a urine test. After a while the doctor came back and announced to her that there was nothing wrong with her. She had just had a drop in blood pressure and also happened to be pregnant.

"Your husband must be very happy, I'll call him in."

"He's not my husband nor the father of the child, he's just a friend," she said.

The doctor did not ask further questions and told her that all her vital signs were okay otherwise and that a gynecologist should take over from here on. Julia did not tell Eduardo that she was pregnant. She told him that the problem seemed to be only a sudden drop of blood pressure. Eduardo took her home and left when he was reassured that she was fine.

When she was settled on her sofa, sipping some herbal tea, Julia began to put two and two together and realized what had happened. Missing out on the pill one night had gotten her pregnant.

When Jean Claude came to see her after work that evening to finalize their plans for the trip, she did not tell him about the pregnancy. How could she? She needed time to think and ponder how she was going to handle this calamity. They were supposed to leave on their trip to Egypt in a couple of days, and now she had this monumental problem to deal with. How could she deal with it? What should she do? She tried to act calm, hoping that Jean Claude would not notice her anxiety. She went to bed early, reliving the events of the last night she had spent with Luis.

She had not known that she was pregnant when Luis had come back from the Middle East. It had been too soon to tell. She supposed that when he was in Argentina and had the phone sex, he had gotten this other girl pregnant. Julia realized that she was now in one big mess. She would not tell Luis she was pregnant and burden him with yet another unplanned pregnancy. Two women pregnant at the same time by the same man. What a farcical situation.

So the father of her child was definitely of no help and she refused to complicate his life even further. She could not lie to Jean Claude and pass the baby as his. It would not be fair. And also, Jean Claude knew she was on the pill. So did Luis, for that matter. She was in a dilemma. She called her sister, went over to see her and told her everything. She was very agitated and incoherent.

"Julia, I told you the shit would hit the fan one of these days. You have really messed up your life."

Julia started crying. "I don't know what to do."

"You could have an abortion. You know that in Switzerland this is very easily arranged. All you need is the consent of two doctors."

"I can't kill Luis' child or any child for that matter."

"Then you have to tell Jean Claude the truth."

"He'll definitely leave me and I can't bear the thought of losing him also."

"There's no other solution my dear, you have to come clean."

"But he has planned a dreamy trip for us—we're supposed to leave tomorrow."

"Do you know what you're saying? You're pregnant, trip or no trip."

"Maybe I'll have a miscarriage."

"Maybe this or maybe that, get a grip on yourself."

Julia then decided that she would definitely have to confront Jean Claude but did not know when to divulge her condition. Before or after the Egyptian trip? She wanted badly to go to Egypt though and, if she told him before, all plans would be cancelled. She decided to tell him after the trip. Maybe she would miraculously have a miscarriage during the trip, then the problem would automatically be solved. She wanted to brush her predicament aside for the time being. She knew she was being really stupid and illogical. *How can she brush a pregnancy aside?*

Jean Claude suspected something was very wrong with Julia; she was acting erratically, but she kept reassuring him that everything was fine.

"I'm just jittery about the trip."

"There's nothing to worry your pretty little head about, come now, Julia, relax." And with that said, she felt temporarily comforted. She went from being anxious to utter denial mode.

Her sister had been right. She had fucked up her relationship with Jean Claude, a decent, honorable man who adored her so much. And she loved him too in her own crooked way. Could his love withstand the truth, or would he think she was a slut and leave her? For the first time in her life she felt afraid and abandoned, without a man to take care of her, to dote on her, and to love her. What was she going to do? She looked up to God for help. She always did this in very difficult situations.

But then why would God come to her help when she never went to church and called for God's help only when she was in dire need of something? But wasn't God supposed to be merciful and forgiving of sinners? Did God really understand the mind of complicated women? What could God do to help her in those circumstances? He would never condone an abortion. He would not help provoke a miscarriage. That would be like willing an unprovoked abortion. All God could do is influence Jean Claude to forgive her. Would he do that? Could he do that? Why was God a *he* anyway? God was a *he* because all the images of God she had seen as a child was that of a man with flowing white hair and a white beard.

She fell asleep in Jean Claude's arms the last night before leaving on their trip and had nightmares. She needed and loved Jean Claude so much. She did not want to lose him. She dreaded the moment when she would have to talk to him about the baby. She did not want to hurt him but how could she avoid that?

"You're really not yourself," said Jean Claude, sensing that there was something really wrong with Julia.

"I'll be okay, just jittery," she reassured him, but she was trembling inside.

Julia somehow finished her packing and they flew to Cairo.

Songes d'une Nuit (Dreams of a night)

CHAPTER 24

Trip Up the Nile

Their plan was to see her father first, which they did on the very first day. Julia had not seen him for over fifteen years since she had left Egypt. All his plans were made and he was leaving Cairo to join them in Geneva after the New Year. They stayed at the Hilton Hotel overlooking the Nile. The weather was perfect and the view was stupendous. Cairo was a bustling metropolis, much too crowded, very polluted and the constant blasting of car horns ruined the atmosphere. Memories of her dancing days with her ex-husband came back to her as they went to the rooftop nightclub on the first evening. Cairo had changed so much since she had left. Unfortunately things never stayed the same. Places deteriorated, they never improved, especially big cities like Cairo, where there had been a population explosion. They went to all the touristic places, the Pyramids, the Egyptian Museum—such a disorganized place—the Khan el-Khalili bazaar, where Jean Claude bought her some jewelry from her friend, the Armenian jeweler, who was still there. Of course, they also visited Heliopolis, where she grew up and had gone to school. She showed him her school and the house where she grew up. It was a very nostalgic four days for her, seeing all her old haunts. Then they flew to Luxor, where they saw all the sites and got on the boat trip up the Nile to Assouan and Abu Simbel.

The boat was rather small but quite luxurious. It had the comforts of a five-star hotel with its wood paneled cabins and brass fixtures, which were polished every day. It was full of Italian tourists who were very boisterous, which suited Julia fine because they made her temporarily forget her predicament.

The first evening, while having dinner in the cozy dining room, she noticed a couple sitting not far from them. They were engrossed in a heated discussion. She suddenly realized that it was her ex-husband whom she had not seen for over twelve years, and his companion was a young blond woman. Probably his wife or girlfriend. They had exchanged some Christmas cards over the years but otherwise she had had no real contact with him. *Fancy seeing him again in Egypt, the place of our union. What a small world and what an unexpected coincidence,* thought Julia. He was trying to get the attention of the waiter when he noticed her and did a double take. He got up from his table and approached theirs.

"Julia, is that you? What a coincidence meeting you here after all this time."

"David, how are you? Yes, a coincidence indeed. Jean Claude, this is my ex-husband, David. David, this is my future husband Jean Claude," she said, giggling. Both men greeted each other politely and sized each other up.

"Is that woman your wife?" asked Julia.

"No, just a girlfriend. I had to come back to Egypt because my father passed away, and there is some inheritance business to take care of."

"I'm sorry to hear that. Is your mom still alive?"

"Yes, she is doing fine."

"Would you like to join us?" asked Jean Claude. He was curious and wanted to find out what kind of man Julia's ex-husband was. Julia did not care about this arrangement but could not do anything about it. Jean Claude was a very sociable person. Had he not invited Luis and that Elena chick to their table at the InterContinental Hotel in Geneva?

"Thank you, I'll bring Lilian over," David readily agreed. He was also eager to find out what Julia had been up to since they had divorced. He still had feelings for her deep down inside.

He hasn't changed much, Julia thought as David walked away. *He has the same deep set eyes and same swagger.*

Lilian, the young woman, was introduced and they sat down to have dinner together. A good Italian band was playing dance music, and she got up to dance with Jean Claude while David did the same with Lilian. The conversation flowed easily, catching up on their lives and professions. Lilian was a model. David had become a well-known photographer in New York, and his girlfriends would obviously have been models, she guessed. She had a slight pang of jealousy.

The orchestra started to play the Dean Martin song "Sway" and David asked Jean Claude if he could dance with Julia. Jean Claude agreed of course, and Julia got up to dance with David. This had been their favorite song in the old days. She felt a pang of nostalgia.

"Remember?" asked David.

"Of course, I do."

He was such a good dancer, and they swirled and twirled around the dance floor in perfect unison. She came back to the table breathless. The evening ended soon after, and they retired early as everyone seemed to be tired.

Julia and Jean Claude enjoyed the boat trip up the Nile admiring the virgin landscape that had hardly changed throughout the years. There were still some papyrus plants along the banks of the Nile. The two couples spent some time together on the boat and Julia enjoyed Lilian's company. Jean Claude did not seem to mind David's presence. After all, there was nothing to be jealous about. Julia had divorced him twelve years ago, and she would soon be marrying him.

On their way to Assouan, they stopped off and went on a side trip to visit the temples at Edfu and Kom Ombo. The boat then continued sailing up the river to Assouan and finally to Abu Simbel, their final destination. They were scheduled to go on a tour to see the colossal monuments that were cut into solid rock. The weather was extremely hot and, after five minutes of walking under the scorching sun, Julia felt faint and stopped.

"What's the matter, Julia?" asked Jean Claude.

"It's too hot for me. I don't think I can continue. You go ahead, I'll try to find a shady place and relax. Or, better still, I'll go back to the boat. I have seen the sites before so I won't miss anything."

"I'll take you back," said Jean Claude.

"No, please don't, you have not seen them, you go ahead, I'll be fine."

"I'll take her back," volunteered David. "I've seen the sites also, and I have some important paperwork to do, so I don't mind accompanying Julia."

Jean Claude was hesitant but he finally agreed, and Julia and David walked back to the boat. Julia was very silent; she was thinking of the baby and how she was going to confront Jean Claude.

"I can sense there is something wrong," said David. "This is unlike you. I know you, it is not the heat that's bothering you."

Julia felt the urge to confide in David. "Yes, David, there is something terribly wrong. I am pregnant," she blurted out.

"What's so wrong with that?"

"The baby is not Jean Claude's."

"What?"

"You heard me, the baby is not Jean Claude's, and he does not know it . . . yet."

"So whose is it?"

"It does not matter."

"So what are you going to do about this situation?"

"I don't know why I'm even confiding in you. I'm in a real mess and don't know how to get out of it. You see, I was seeing another guy while engaged to Jean Claude and something happened—too complicated to explain—and I found out I'm pregnant."

"So do you love this other guy?"

"Yes, I do, or I did, but I also love Jean Claude. It was just too complicated and I finally left the other guy and chose to be with Jean Claude, making plans to get married."

"So are you planning on telling this guy about your situation?"

"No, he got married in the meantime, and his wife is also pregnant, or rather he married her because she was pregnant—because he got her pregnant. It sounds very farcical, doesn't it? Real life is sometimes stranger than fiction."

"What's the matter with this guy, doesn't he wear a condom?"

"You would not understand, or perhaps you would if I told you the whole story, but it's too long, and I haven't got the energy nor the inclination."

"So what are your plans?"

"I'll have to come clean with Jean Claude, then he'll leave me of course, and I will be with child and no man or father to the baby." She then started sobbing. They had arrived to the boat. David put his arm around her and took her up on deck and tried to calm her down.

"Look, Julia, this may come as a surprise to you, but I still love you despite the dirty trick you played on me by divorcing me on a whim. I haven't really gotten over you. I have found out that I can't have any children, a condition I've had from birth, it seems. So I'm proposing this"—and he took her in his arms and held her tenderly, trying to comfort her—"come back to me, and we'll go back to New York and get remarried and pretend to everyone that the baby is mine, born prematurely."

"What? Are you out of your mind? I couldn't do that."

"Why not?"

"I do like you a lot and do have feelings for you too, David, don't get me wrong, but our chapter has been closed since a long time, and I could not possibly rekindle it with this solution."

"Maybe you can, if you tried. You loved me once, you could love me again. The baby will have a father at least. Stop thinking always about yourself and focusing on your navel. You have always been very self-centered, always me, me, me. Think of the baby that is in your womb craving for attention and protection."

"David, you're right, but I don't know, I'm so confused. What do I tell Jean Claude? That I realized I don't love him and that I decided to reunite with you and not mention the baby at all? It would be very cruel. I can't hurt him that way. He is the most decent man I have met."

"You'll be hurting him anyway by admitting that you had an affair and are having a baby by another guy."

"I know, I know, I'm so mixed up. I don't want to lose Jean Claude."

"Okay, then tell him the truth and see what happens. If he leaves you, I'm here to take over. Give it a thought at least."

"You're so kind, David. I appreciate your proposal, but I don't want to mislead you either. I don't love you or, let's say, I don't love you in the way you would want me to love you. It wouldn't be fair to you either."

"I'm willing to take the chance that you may resume your feelings toward me. At least you'll not be alone bringing up this baby."

"Thanks, but no. As soon as we get back to Geneva, I will talk to Jean Claude and see what happens."

"Contact me one way or the other." He led her to her stateroom and, holding her face in his hands, said, "I love you, Julia, I always have." He then embraced her and kissed her chastely on both cheeks. "Keep cool, my love, you're not alone in this world, there's always me."

"Thanks, David," Julia said and went in her room, closing the door.

Julia could not believe her ears. What a turn of events. And now David wanted her back. Jean Claude came back after his tour of the monuments and found Julia resting in bed.

"Are you feeling okay now?"

"Yup, it was only a heat problem."

They resumed their trip up the Nile, socializing with David and Lilian. David was very concerned about Julia but did not show any emotion in the presence of the others. Once or twice when he found himself alone with Julia, he asked her about her thoughts concerning her future. "I'll let you know," Julia kept repeating.

The trip ended and they all flew back to Cairo. They took their leave of David and Lilian, had dinner with her father on their last evening and then flew back to Geneva the next day.

Aphrodite

CHAPTER 25

Back from Egypt

Julia was in a way relieved that they were finally back home but did not look forward to the showdown. Jean Claude accompanied her home from the airport and she made up her mind to tell him everything as soon as they were in her apartment. She decided that she could no longer go on living a life of deception. She would not pretend that the baby was Jean Claude's. That was out of the question. She was going to come clean. She had hoped for a miraculous miscarriage while on the trip. She had taken hot baths and exerted herself physically, but the fetus stayed put. So God was not helping her there. She dreaded Jean Claude's reaction, not to mention the hurt and humiliation she would cause him. She could not visualize what her life would be like after her confession. She was worried and very scared, but she had to confront the inevitable situation.

During the flight on the way home, Julia had been very silent, nervous and brooding; she was bringing up different scenarios in her mind of how to broach the subject. None of them seemed good. Jean Claude, on the other hand, could sense her discomfort. He did not understand why she would look so unhappy after their marvelous trip. Had the presence of her ex-husband bothered her perhaps? He did not like seeing her this way.

Jean Claude put down her suitcases and Julia went and flopped down on the couch.

"Do you want me to stay with you for a while? You are very quiet. Are you feeling okay?"

Julia looked at him crestfallen. "Yes, I am . . . uh . . . no, I am not. I have something to tell you, and it's not pleasant at all."

"How can it be not pleasant? We just came back from a great trip."

"Jean Claude, I don't know how to tell you this, but I cannot marry you." There, she said it, avoiding looking into his eyes but looking at the floor, shifting her feet from one side to the other.

"What? What happened? Is this a joke?"

"No, it's not," and Julia burst into tears and was on the verge of having a panic attack.

Jean Claude took her in his arms. "There, there, calm down, everything will be fine, you're just very tired. You were not used to the heat, I guess."

"No, it's not that."

"What's the matter, then? Did I do anything wrong?"

"You did nothing wrong, and everything will not be fine after I tell you what's bothering me. I am pregnant, it is a calamity."

"What? This is not bad news. This is not a calamity. It is a blessing. Why are you so distraught and want to cancel the wedding? I am delighted at the good news," said Jean Claude, never doubting for a minute that the child was not his.

"It is bad news, Jean Claude, because the baby is not yours. There, I have said it, and I hate myself for having done this to you." She started sobbing uncontrollably.

Jean Claude's face became ashen. He could not believe his ears. He took his head in his hands and just looked straight ahead. A while back, he had sensed that something was wrong with Julia, but things had settled down the last couple of months, and Julia had been her old self again, lively and loving. He remembered that at one time during the summer months, he had had doubts that she was seeing another man and had almost wanted to hire a detective but had reneged because he did not want to know, as long as he had Julia. She was all he wanted. He loved her unconditionally and wanted to marry her and have children. After some time, Julia had bounced back from her restless days, and they had resumed their life as though nothing had happened. Now his doubts had been validated. She had been seeing another man. He could not believe his ears, but he did not want to know who the man was.

"I am not a good person, Jean Claude, I don't deserve you. I cheated on you and this is the result. I am pregnant with another man's child." Her heart was pounding like mad and she thought she would explode. She continued sobbing.

"I knew something was wrong since a few months but could not put my finger on it."

"So there, now you know. Here, I am giving you back your ring." She took it off her finger and put it on the coffee table. "You deserve better than me. So just go away and forget me. I am so sorry. I don't know what else to say. I am just so very, very sorry."

Jean Claude collected himself although he was utterly dumbfounded. How could this happen? This was certainly a dream. This could not be true. His Julia leaving him?

"Does this guy know you are pregnant?"

"No, I left him before knowing that I was pregnant. I'll tell you the whole story because you have the right to know."

"I don't want to know who it is, and I don't want to know the details."

"I met someone during the beginning of summer and I cheated on you. I never stopped loving you, though. I don't know if you believe me, but it's the truth. I was infatuated by this person and had an affair with him during the summer. At first, I thought it was a temporary crush and that I would snap out of it, but things got out of hand and it became more serious, and I continued with the deception. I realized I was in love with two men at the same time. Can you understand that? I cannot understand it myself, but it happened. I was very unhappy with the situation, and I knew I had to finally break it off. He knew of your existence. He wanted to marry me and take me away to his country, but I refused and told him that I had decided to stay with you. I broke off the liaison two months ago."

Julia looked at Jean Claude to see how he was taking all this. He had his hands on his face and was not looking at her.

"I was very happy with my decision," Julia continued with tears running down her cheeks "and relieved because I loved you so much more, and I realized that I could never leave you and go off with someone else. However, I did not know at the time that I was pregnant. You must believe me, Jean Claude, when I tell you that I did not know of my pregnancy. I only found out just two days before going on this trip, but I didn't want to spoil your plans because I knew how much you were looking forward to going to Egypt. I was hoping that I would have a miscarriage while on the trip, and then I could resume my relationship with you as though nothing had ever happened. You were wondering why I was taking so many hot baths and exerting myself so much. I wanted to provoke a miscarriage."

Jean Claude was listening without saying a word. He was devastated and kept shaking his head.

"The only time that I forgot to take the pill, this happened. I will not tell the father of this baby of my pregnancy because, in the meantime, he has gotten married in his country and his wife is also pregnant. I don't wish to complicate his life by burdening him with this added responsibility. All during our trip, I also thought of having an abortion when I got back but then realized I could not go through with it."

Jean Claude sighed a few times but still did not utter a word.

"I told the whole truth to my ex-husband the morning I could not go with you to see the monuments at Abou Simbel. Remember I stayed behind? Well, he accompanied me to the boat and sensed that I was not myself and asked me what the problem was. I told him the whole story. He seemed to be the only person I could unburden myself to. He then told me that he was still in love with me and that, if you would not marry me because of the baby, he was willing to have a second go at our marriage. This rather surprised me and I saw a flicker of hope. He also told me that he cannot have children and that he would raise the baby as his. This was a very tempting solution, but I could not go through with it. That chapter of my life with him is definitely closed, and I cannot go back. My feelings for him have changed, and I consider him a good friend, nothing more. So I decided to tell you everything. Now you know. I am with child, and our plans of having a future together have gone down the drain."

Jean Claude was deep in thought. He loved Julia unconditionally; he could not bear the thought of living without her. He would not leave her. He could not leave her. He then looked up and took Julia's hands in his. "Julia, I don't want to know the details, but did you just say that you chose to stay with me and get married before knowing you were pregnant?"

"Yes, you're the love of my life. I never fell out of love with you even though I was cheating on you. I went ahead and spoiled the one good thing that ever happened to me. My ex-husband even suggested that I pretend that the child is yours, but I could not live a life of deceit. It would haunt me for the rest of my life." She continued sobbing uncontrollably.

Jean Claude then wrapped his arms around Julia. They were strong, secure and resolute, and Julia nestled against him. "Do you really love me, Julia? I know you have strange thoughts about love, but I would like to know once and for all if you really love me since you say you did in fact choose me over the other guy. I know you will not lie to me, not now."

"Yes, I do love you, Jean Claude, more than I have ever loved anyone, but what's the use I have betrayed you, and I would not blame you if you don't ever want to see me again."

"But I do want to see you again, and I do want to marry you and bring up this child with you. I adore you more than you can possibly imagine. You made a mistake, that's all."

"A mistake, you call it," she said, still sobbing while holding on to him in desperation. "I am pregnant, Jean Claude, pregnant. This is not a simple mistake. Here are two men who want to marry me, and the baby is that of a third. This is like a French farce," and she suddenly laughed hysterically, with tears running down her cheeks.

Jean Claude shook her. "Get hold of yourself, Julia. This is not the end of the world." He embraced her tenderly and covered her face with kisses. She could feel his tears on her face. "Oh, Julia, my Julia," he said.

"You are very angry, I know that," she said.

"Yes, I am angry but not because of what you think. I am angry at myself for not having been sufficient for you. I should have understood you better and perhaps prevented what happened."

"Do you know what you are saying, Jean Claude? You have been more than sufficient. I just lost my way, voluntarily. No one obliged me to do the things I did. There was nothing lacking in our relationship that I had to go and look for it elsewhere. I am just very impulsive, and I do things without thinking. It's my fucking artistic nature. And you're telling me that you still want to get married after all the heartache that I have caused you, being with another man during a whole summer and lying to you and being dishonest with you and getting myself pregnant? I hate myself for being this person." She was hysterical.

"Julia, Julia, hush, be quiet," he said stroking her hair and trying to pacify her. "Calm down, you'll harm the baby. Everything will be okay. I repeat, I don't want to know the details, and I don't want to know who the guy is. All I know is that I still love you, and I cannot live without you, with or without child. I cannot change how I feel. Love is not something that you can turn on and off. You are under my skin. I have wanted you more than any other woman in my life. I am crazy about you, and I will take care of you if you let me."

He crushed her against him, and he was almost trembling. Julia felt so good in his warm, protective arms and wished she could stay there forever. He was so dependable.

"No, Jean Claude, it won't work. I will always see the hurt in your eyes. I do love you very much, but it would not work. Raising another man's child is not fair to you. You will resent it."

"Don't be silly, Julia. Of course, it will work. I will raise that child as my own and we will have other children. I beg you, think. My poor baby, don't cry please. It is breaking my heart seeing you like this. How you must have suffered when you found out your situation."

"How I must have suffered? What about you? Are you not suffering now?"

"No, I am not. I am a big man, and I can rationalize. There are worse things than this in life, and this is not a bad thing, it is a good thing. There is a life in you that needs our love and protection."

Julia could not believe her ears but nevertheless felt relieved hearing Jean Claude's reasoning and hugged him. "I don't know what to say. You're such a good man. I don't deserve you."

"There is nothing more to say. We now make plans. We are going to have a baby."

"Oh, Jean Claude, you have made me the happiest woman in the world, and she clung to him desperately. They both cried and embraced and slept contented in each other's arms. Julia's world had not shattered after all. She was so grateful for everything. She slept like a baby in Jean Claude's arms, something she had not done in a very long time. Life was good. Jean Claude had fixed it. He was her indestructible dependable rock.

She called her sister the next day and told her everything.

"You're so lucky," said her sister. "You've got a very good man there, try not to fuck up ever again."

"I'm deliriously happy, you can't imagine. I love Jean Claude more than ever. And it is not gratitude. It's love, and it's passion. It's what I've always wanted. I also loved Luis, though."

"I'm very happy for you, sis," and they hung up.

She contacted David and told him the good news. He was happy for her but sad that he had lost her forever.

Julia's father arrived a week later and they had a quiet wedding at the Mairie of Geneva, the guests being only her parents, her sister and her family, and a few friends. Jean Claude's mother could not come because her health did not permit any travelling. They visited her the next weekend. Her infidelity was never mentioned. They made plans for the baby and she fixed up the baby's room with great enthusiasm. She did not want to know the gender beforehand. She wanted it to be a surprise.

Seven months later, Julia gave birth to Nicolas, a beautiful baby boy with dark hair and eyes. Jean Claude was very proud and dotted on him and helped change diapers on the nurse's days off. Julia knew she had chosen the right man. She was sure God had listened to her prayers. She was so very, very grateful for everything.

She soon fell pregnant again and gave birth to a baby girl, Natalie. Jean Claude could not be happier. He was a *papa poule*, taking care of his children. They led a charmed life. She thought of Luis once or twice and wondered what he was up to but that's as far as it went. She did not try to make contact with him nor did he try to contact her. To Julia it felt that the Luis episode was a faraway, unrealistic dream.

A couple of years later, Jean Claude was given a promotion to move to New York and be president of the PBSU in New York. They moved to New York into a sprawling house on Long Island. Julia resumed her painting. Jean Claude had a studio built for her adjacent to their house, and she found a couple of galleries in the United States to represent her. They had a very happy family life with the children's various activities, exploring the United States and taking trips back to Europe every summer. They decided not to tell Nicolas that Jean Claude was not his father, and the kids grew up thinking they had the same father.

Then one day, after twelve years of marital bliss, calamity struck. Jean Claude got killed in a highway accident while going to work. Julia was beyond grief. Her perfect world had disintegrated. She was devastated and even thought of taking her own life. She did not think she could live without her Jean Claude. He was her pillar, and she missed him very much. Her rock had crumbled. She started falling to pieces and had a nervous breakdown. She saw a therapist and it helped. Bringing up the children became her priority.

Her father had died of a heart attack the year before, so she asked her mother to come and live with her and help her in bringing up the children. By then, Nicolas was twelve and Natalie, eleven. With the help of the therapist and her mother's presence, she slowly started to function again and led a relatively normal life. For the first time in her life she found herself without a man. Jean Claude had been everything to her, husband, lover, friend. He was irreplaceable. Her children gave her the strength to carry on, and she did.

Bonheur (Happiness)

CHAPTER 26

La Jolla, California

Julia's life without Jean Claude felt barren to her. If it were not for the children's activities she would have felt like a robot going on with her daily activities. Her painting also saved her from going stark raving mad. Jean Claude had been an exceptional human being and their life together had indeed been a fairy tale. She thought God punished her for her infidelity by taking Jean Claude away from her.

A friend of hers, who lived in La Jolla, suggested that she come and rent a house there for the summer to get away from the memories for a while. Julia readily agreed. Luckily she was financially very well off—Jean Claude had taken care of that—and she could afford it. She found a three bedroom house with a swimming pool overlooking the ocean in Bird Rock and moved there with her mother and the children.

The kids got busy with their activities, surfing, playing tennis and taking music lessons (her son played the guitar, and her daughter played the piano). Both children were avid tennis players, and she enrolled them at the La Jolla tennis club. Julia was still very sad inside her heart, but she did her best not to show the kids so that they could go on with their lives. They too missed their father very much because he had always been very involved in their activities. She also took up a few activities and made a couple of new friends and was quite happy in La Jolla. She wished that the summer would never end. Life was easy and laid-back in California, and she entertained the idea of moving from New York to make a clean break. Without Jean Claude, New York was not the same and did not offer her any peace.

One day, she was sitting on the bleachers at the La Jolla tennis club, watching her son play a tennis match, when she noticed a man on another court who had just finished his game and was wiping himself with his towel. He was tall, dark and had a great body. Her heart skipped a beat. He looked like Luis, more mature, heavier. *It can't be,* she thought. He started walking toward her, and when he came closer to the bleachers where she was sitting, he looked up and met her gaze. It was indeed Luis. She thought she would faint. She felt paralyzed. Signs of recognition came into his eyes at the same time. *It can't be Julia,* he thought. He took off his sunglasses and took a closer look, and he saw her, smiling. *The same irresistible, flirtatious smile,* he thought. He could not believe his eyes. This was incredible. He had found Julia again, *his* Julia, the love of his life.

"Julia?" he said, looking up at her with the same mischievous dark eyes. "Is that you?"

Julia managed to come down from the bleachers without tripping.

"My God, Luis, I can't believe my eyes. What are doing here?"

"What are *you* doing here?"

They embraced. Her heart was pounding like mad, so was his. All her pent-up emotions came to the surface, and she started crying.

Luis held her at arm's length. "Why are you crying? Let me look at you, you haven't changed one bit. 'Age cannot wither her nor custom stale,' from *Anthony and Cleopatra,* very apropos as far as you are concerned."

"You haven't changed either," and she continued sobbing. "I'm crying because I'm overwhelmed with emotion. I can't believe my eyes."

"Same here. This is incredible, fancy meeting you here after all this time. How long has it been, eleven, twelve years? Let me get changed, and then we can sit down and talk."

"I don't have time now. My son is finishing off his game, and we have to go home and have dinner. My daughter and mother are waiting for us."

"Which one is your son?"

Julia pointed him out. Luis looked at the dark, lean teenager and wondered from whom he had gotten his coloring. Neither Julia nor her husband had that coloring. Actually Nicolas was the spitting image of Luis. It was so obvious. Could she tell him Nicolas was his son?

"Where is Jean Claude?" Luis looked around the tennis club. "I still remember the name of your rock."

"I lost him, he died," and Julia continued crying. Luis held her close and patted her back trying to comfort her. How could he comfort her? It must be a terrible loss for her.

"I'm so sorry to hear that. When did that happen? It must have been awful for you. Okay, don't talk about it if it is too painful, but I have to see you. We have to talk. When can we meet? Why don't you take your son home, have your mom fix their supper, and then we can have dinner somewhere quiet and talk. We have a lot of catching up to do. I won't let you run away this time."

Julia agreed to his suggestion, and they decided to meet at Roppongi at 8:00 p.m.

Julia was overexcited with this totally unexpected encounter and felt weak in the knees. She thought it was a dream, and she almost pinched herself. She rushed home to tell her mom.

Luis was overjoyed, having met Julia again so unexpectedly after so many years. He was curious to know her story. All his love and desire for her surfaced once again.

As Julia was driving Nicolas home, "Who's that man?" he asked.

"He's a very old friend of mine whom I have not seen since before you were born." *He's your dad,* she wanted to say. When they got home, Julia took her mother aside and related her meeting Luis.

"Oh no, not again," said her mother.

"What do you mean no, not again? This is an incredible coincidence, he and I being in La Jolla at the same time. I am curious to find out his story. I am meeting him for dinner."

"Don't do anything stupid, remember you're emotionally very hungry," her mother said as though she was still a child. She was forty-nine years old, for God's sake. *Fucking old,* but luckily, she did not look it. *Here we go again,* she thought, *a dinner with Luis, just like the first time.* Where was his wife?

She took her time to decide what to wear and finally decided on a black sheath with a V neckline just like the first time. She felt like a new person going out on a date with a new man. On the other hand, she also felt very apprehensive and anxious. What would she talk about? What would he say? She looked at herself in the mirror and did not see the young woman of twelve years ago, but she still looked youngish, and she had not lost her figure. Her heart was fluttering in her stomach as she went to meet him at Roppongi. She entered the restaurant and saw him sitting on the patio with a glass of red wine in front of him. He looked as dashing as ever, and all her yearning for him came back.

But did he feel the same toward her? And where was the wife? And what about his child?

Luis got up, kissed her on both cheeks and said, "You smell the same." He felt like crushing her to him and covering her face with more than two pecks on the cheeks but restrained himself.

And I smell the male in you, thought Julia. She wanted to bury her face in his chest and stay there forever. She had not touched a man or been touched by one for over a year. And now, there was Luis standing in front of her, his male aura intoxicating her. *Same bottomless dark brown eyes boring through me,* she thought. He had a few wrinkles on his face, which made him look more mature. She desired him more than ever.

They sat down, and their eyes locked. They both felt a little embarrassed. Luis ordered a glass of red wine for her, and they ordered their food. Then they just looked at each other and they were silent, waiting for the food to arrive. *She still has that habit of licking her upper lip with her tongue,* he thought.

She spoke first. "Where do we start? You tell me your story first."

She has the same effect on me, I want to crush her against me, thought Luis as he put down his wine glass.

"My story—let's see, after you banished me from your life, I left for Argentina to run the business there. I found out that I had impregnated a girl a couple of months prior, when I had gone there at the time when you could see me very rarely and were having a great time with JC all winter, going all over Europe. Don't smirk, it's true. I was so mad at you that I started going out with this girl—a childhood friend—with whom I had had casual sex during the years, and slept with her one night when I got drunk at a party. I forgot to put on a condom on time and things just happened."

He took a sip of his wine and continued, "When I came back to Geneva to ask you to marry me, I did not know that she had gotten pregnant. But after you broke off with me and I went to Argentina to take over the business, she told me she was pregnant and thought of having an abortion. I refused. I did not want to kill my child, so I married her and we had a baby girl, Angela. She is the apple of my eye. We divorced a year after because the whole marriage was a sham. We both realized it. I have been free since then. My ex-wife got remarried to an American and lives in L.A. so I see my daughter very often. I left my father's business to Eduardo, and I am living here now and have my own software company. I don't feel like travelling for business all over the world anymore. I want to be close to my daughter, I want to see her grow up. I often thought of you but did not want to make contact. It was very painful leaving you. Eduardo gave me some news now and again. And now, what about you?"

"Me? As you may have guessed, I married Jean Claude, and we had . . . two children, Nicolas, whom you saw, and Natalie, our daughter. We lived in Geneva for a while, then he got transferred to New York and we lived there for a few years. I got used to New York and we were quite happy there. Then, about a year ago he died in a car accident while going to work. A truck hit him"—she had tears in her eyes as she was relating—"and my whole life shattered. I felt as though my heart had broken into little pieces, and it would never be whole again. They say time heals, but time will never heal Jean Claude's loss. If it weren't for the kids, I would have collapsed."

Luis wiped the tears away from her face gently with his fingers. "Don't talk about it. I see that this is very painful for you."

"Anyway, a friend suggested that I spend the summer in La Jolla, to be away from the places that would remind me of Jean Claude, and that's what I am doing. Actually, I am thinking of moving here because life seems to be easier in California, and the weather is superb."

"That would be great," and he took hold of her hands in his and looked at her. He was so excited, having her sitting across from him. She looked so forlorn and vulnerable. He wanted to jump out of his chair and take her in his arms, comfort her, and be her protector and never let her go. He did not know how she felt about him, though.

She smiled at him demurely and said, "Yes, that would be great."

Their food was served, and they talked about their lives some more and about the children. They had a lot of catching up to do. There was a certain uneasiness though. They had been passionate lovers and, after a separation of twelve years, him having had a wife and child and Julia a husband and two kids, they were sitting across from each other, talking of their past. Luis was yearning to embrace her and start all over again. Julia was looking at Luis' lips and yearning for him to kiss her. The magnetism between them was stronger than ever; it had never died. It was obvious to both that they were still attracted to each other, but they did not know how to resume where they had left off.

After the dinner was over, Luis accompanied Julia to her car and took her in his arms in a gentle embrace. She rested her face on his chest.

"What now?" he asked.

"I'll follow you," she said suddenly feeling reckless.

Luis still had the same effect on her after all these years. She melted when she looked at those intense dark eyes with the straight abundant lashes.

Luis was thrilled. There was nothing else to say. Julia wanted him and he craved for her. He lived in a beautiful house in La Jolla shores. Julia parked her car in his driveway and thought *I'm being very reckless again,* and was very quiet and self-conscious when she followed him inside his house. Her heart was beating wildly in anticipation of what was to come.

Luis, on the other hand, felt quite relaxed; he had found his Julia. The minute they were inside the door, Luis kicked it shut and took her in his arms, and they started kissing passionately and grabbing at each other.

"Julia, where have you been, my love? I missed your skin, your smell, it's been such a long time." He crushed her against him, taking her face in his hands and kissing her again and again. He was wild with desire.

She held on to him, closed her eyes, and gave herself to his caresses and felt his manhood pressing against her body.

"Are you going to tease me like you did the first time you kissed me in my apartment?" she asked.

"Not unless you want me to."

"I want you to." She looked in his eyes and wanted to relive every moment of their first encounter back in Geneva.

He then backed her up against the wall and gazed at her for a long time. He adored her almond shaped eyes and her face and the way she looked at him, quivering, her lips slightly parted. He covered her mouth with his lips, pinned her arms above her head and kissed her eyelids, earlobes, the hollow in her throat, her armpits, down to the V of her neckline. He pushed aside her neckline with his teeth, baring her breasts.

"Aha, no bra and magnificent as ever," he said, "a little fuller but just as perky. You're a phenomenon." He kissed her breasts, brushing her nipples with his stubble. Yes, he still had the stubble that drove her crazy. Shivers ran up and down her spine and she gave in to him.

"Luis, take me," she said and arched her back offering him her bosom.

"I will, babe, I will," and he let go of her arms and cupped her breasts and kissed them again languorously at first, sucking her nipples while she was whimpering.

Julia was ecstatic. The usual sparks were flying between them as he ran his hands up and down her body. She held on to him gasping for breath. He lowered her dress to her waist and crawled one of his hands up to her sex, which was wet.

"Wet as usual. Can't you ever be different?" he asked jokingly.

She couldn't help laughing at that remark. "I'm like putty in your hands. You can do whatever you want with me."

"I love hearing you laugh."

"I haven't really laughed for a long time."

She looked up at him, gazed at his bedroom eyes, draped her arms around his neck and caressed him. His hair was the same, long at the nape. She loved it. She was so hungry for his caresses; she bit him on the side of the neck and kept repeating, "Take me, Luis. It's been so long."

He tried to take off her dress. "Zipper in the back," she said. He worked the zipper and her dress fell down to her ankles. She was left with only a thong on.

"Dental floss, as usual," he said which made her laugh again. He swooped her up in his arms and carried her to his bed and lay her down, with her long red hair fanned out around her head. She looked the same as she had the first time he had laid her on her bed, lying in abandon, waiting for his caresses. He yanked off her panties.

"The same reddish pubic hair," he said. "You are so enticing. I can't wait to devour you. I wish I had two lips and four hands, then I could be all over your body at the same time." He fondled her breasts, kissing her hard nipples; then his lips travelled down to her navel and finally to her sex. "You're still crossing your ankles," and he spread her legs apart, put a pillow under her butt, and nibbled on her inner thighs, his lips travelling slowly up to her sex. She was in an ecstatic frenzy as his stubble rubbed against her labia. She whimpered and moaned and dug her fingers in his shoulders. His body was so hot and hard and desirable as it had always been. He licked her relentlessly, thrusting his tongue in and at the same time playing with her nipples. He made her squirm with ecstasy. He loved seeing her in full abandon as always. Then she climaxed with one big moan.

Luis realized that his desire for Julia had never gone away. He entered her gently, moving around slowly at first then after a few frenzied thrusts, he climaxed also. They lay back panting, all arms and legs intertwined.

"You kill me as usual," he said. "Julia, marry me."

"What?"

"You heard me, marry me."

"But we just met."

"You mean we met again. I'm not letting you go this time. I'll kidnap you and keep you chained in my house."

"And, what about my children?"

"They can come and visit you."

"You'll get bored with me, having the same woman all day long."

"You're joking, me get bored with you, never in this lifetime."

She caressed his back and his chest; then her hand held his limp penis, which sprang to life immediately, and they had another go at it with the same unbridled passion as before.

Julia was then silent and wondered whether now it would be a good time to tell Luis about his son.

"You're very quiet all of a sudden. What's the matter?" asked Luis.

"Luis, I've got something serious to tell you, which I never thought I would ever do because I did not think you would reappear in my life again."

"What is it? That you're mad about me and can't live without me?"

"That too. However, this is more serious than that."

"What can be more serious than wanting to be with me?"

"Luis, Nicolas is your son, there, that is more serious, don't you think?"

"Nicolas is my son? When did that happen? How? Why didn't you tell me? How can you keep such a secret from me?"

"Luis, I found out I was pregnant two months after you left. You were already married, and your wife was expecting. I found out the day before I left to go to Egypt with Jean Claude. It's a very long story."

Julia then related all the circumstances—her forgetting to take the pill the last night they were together, her meeting Eduardo, the trip up the Nile, her ex-husband's proposition and finally her confession to Jean Claude. Luis was flabbergasted. He cursed under his breath.

"*Chapeau* to Jean Claude," he said. "He was a very decent man. He must have loved you as much as I love you."

He took her in his arms and asked again, "Julia, you have to marry me, you have no excuse not to."

"You're asking me because Nicolas is your son?"

"Stupid woman, I have always wanted to marry you but you refused, thinking I could not take care of you. Julia, you're the only woman I have ever wanted. You don't know the power you have over me. I cannot be with anyone else. I tried, but I could never forget you. I've always wanted you and only you. Everyone else was a distraction. Please say yes."

"No, Luis, I won't marry you. I am seven years older than you. You will regret it. You are still young."

"Julia, will you stop pointing the difference of age between us? It's the most asinine thing I always hear from you. *I'm older, you are young, and you will want other women.* Shut up and listen to me. Age is just a number. You are a very young woman as far as I am concerned. Hell, you don't look over thirty. Stop this nonsense." He took her in his arms again and kissed her with unrestrained ardor.

"Please say yes. I can't live without you."

"First, let's decide how we're going to tell Nicolas that you're his father."

"We'll have to think about the best way to broach the subject. It won't be easy."

"Luis, no, I won't marry you. I'll live with you with the children of course, after we tell Nicolas that you are his father."

And with that, Julia curled up against him on the bed.

"I will have to get up and go home soon," she said, "and remember the French proverb 'Le marriage est le tombeau de l'amour' which, in my opinion, should go like this: 'Le marriage est le tombeau de la passion,' and I don't want ever to lose the passion we have for each other."

Of Armenian origin, Peggy Hinaekian was born and raised in Egypt. She immigrated to New York with her first husband, where she pursued a career in fashion designing and fine arts.

Having grown up in a cosmopolitan environment, Peggy read books in English, French, and Armenian at a very early age. She kept a diary since age twelve until she married an American whom she met in Rome during the summer of 1963. They had two boys and lived in Geneva, Switzerland. After their children went to college in the United States, they also moved there.

Peggy Hinaekian is an internationally recognized, well-established artist living and working in California, Florida, and Switzerland (website: *www.peggyhinaekian.artspan.com*).

This is her first novel, which is entirely fictional, except for the settings. The illustrations on the cover and inside the book are her own etchings. She has also written short stories and vignettes.

website for artwork:
www.peggyhinaekian.artspan.com

website for novel:
www.OfJuliaAndMen.com

Cover illustration and 26 images of the etchings in front of each chapter are the author's artwork.

CPSIA information can be obtained
at www.ICGtesting.com
Printed in the USA
FSOW02n0738150816
23788FS